The Shroud

By

Dale Fowler

Dedication

Two long-time friends played a role in getting *The Shroud* to a published book. Jim Hamric read a screenplay of mine (CRISSCROSS) a couple of years ago and pushed me to write a book version. I have to admit without Jim's prodding I would have never moved to the book format and as a result, *Crisscross* was published in August of 2013. Jim helped proof read drafts of both books and I have come to depend on his judgement when the proper communication values are present.

Another dear friend, Ron McConnell, not only has proofed the books but made some directional changes that added a great deal of continuity to *The Shroud*. His input elevated the finished product and gave *The Shroud* a very real sense of adventure and buttoned down loose ends that I didn't anticipate. His thinking parallels mine which is spooky and great at the same time.

For their ongoing friendship and interest in my writing, I dedicate *The Shroud* to them. Thanks again for all you do in helping me iron out my twisted mind and keeping me on the rails for *Crisscross* and *The Shroud.* These two friends have been an intricate part of my writing process, but please don't tell them... I'll never hear the end of it.

TABLE OF CONTENTS

CHAPTER ONE

Man of the Cloth

THE RED FLOWING robe moves side-to-side around the feet and calculated steps of the old priest in front of Dr. Royce Benders. The Doctor focuses on those footsteps unable to admire the long, stained glass lined hallways they walk. The excitement has narrowed his concentration. He did notice the deeply rooted scent of old things trying not to show their age. Of countless hands and ancient sweat that cleaned the wooden archways and glass for hundreds of years, some because of unwavering beliefs and others forced through the bonds of slavery.

It's April of 1984, years of science and theology are about to collide for the resurrection of heaven and hell.

The three priests leading the party make little sound, their feet hit the marble tiles on rubber soled shoes. Dr. Benders' leather shoes and those of his colleagues strike the floor, a defined tap bouncing off the walls and racing down the hallway letting The Shroud of Turin know of their impending arrival.

The lead priest stops suddenly. The Doctor almost runs into the frail looking man bearing the red cloth. Dr. Benders glances at Doctors Sanders and King to see if they notice. Both men are eyeing the vaulted ceilings paying little attention to his clumsiness. A young priest off to Dr. Benders' right gives him a nervous look, slightly smiles and returns his gaze to the stone floor.

For the first time he can ever remember, Dr. Benders has nervous moisture surfacing on his palms. He is close to the ultimate human relic, the Shroud embracing Jesus in the tomb and what Dr. Benders believes is a gateway to the heavens.

A number of large keys slide around a metal circle held tightly by the old priest standing inches from the Doctor's face. The priest selects a key with eyes seemingly familiar on the order, but he hesitates to insert it and let these medical minds brush up against the holiest of Christian artifacts. Maybe the old priest knew or sensed something Dr. Benders is thinking? Would they later bow at his feet or nail him on a cross for those thoughts?

Doctor Benders' hands are rubbed on the white smock, but the sweat quickly returns. The locking mechanism is ancient. The key rolls around inside the bowels of the lock, seeking recognition and finally gets it. A large wooden door is pushed open, not happy it creaks and moans at the brazen strangers' greed and intent.

The group enters a small room becoming claustrophobic with all six men putting on gloves, masks, and booties on their shoes. The old priest is first to finish; he looks at Dr. Benders and their eyes lock momentarily but his weathered face is covered, little expression escaping. The Doctor needs to focus and let these outside distractions remain outside. He looks inside the medical bag and retrieves a large microscope and a scalpel. Time to be a scientist he asserts to himself. The others in the medical team ready their tool chests to rub, trim, and extract their pound of ancient flesh from the bleeding and tortured body once lying on the linen weave in the throes of death.

A second key teases the door of the last barrier and the treasure is finally in view. The three priests fall to their knees surrendering to its appearance and Dr. Benders bows down on his. The other scientists watch with a sense of trepidation, more embarrassment than envy. Latin words fill the room from the kneeling priests, not a strange language to any in this inner sanctum.

The three priests rise and take the glass top from the metal coffin that houses The Shroud's fully extended fourteen feet of linen cloth and set it against the wall. Everyone can smell the linen's bad times from the centuries of adulation and ignorant abuse. Primeval smoke from burning buildings and whale oil candles permeate the air. The Shroud is crying out for help, most certainly like the man who was laid on its texture the day of his crucifixion.

All the priests return to their kneeling position for the next five hours of scientific examination. Notes are written, blood removed, and analysis performed quietly. Dr. Benders rapidly moves past his nervous energy and gets down to business. It is easy to take a small piece of the cloth containing a clot of blood for his DNA work, work he knows will lead to the Second Coming of Christ. On the return flight to Los Angeles he prays for God's endorsement.

CHAPTER TWO

The Ugly Truth

JIM CIRMAH LOST all interest in playing the pickup soccer or basketball games that seem to occupy most of the seventh grade boys at Mitchell Middle School in Dallas, Texas in 1998. He didn't want anything to do with the Mitchell Wildcats football team. He had started at linebacker during the sixth grade, a rare accomplishment competing with kids two years older than him.

His life fell into a grinding existence ever since his mother's death eight long months before. In spite of the understanding and extra leeway from the football coach and other teachers, he didn't want to participate in anything requiring one ounce of concentration or focus. The drugs to help make him acclimate back into a young human being only made him angry and short tempered. He's been in two fights already, looking for a third to brush up against him when the next corner is rounded.

The accident that killed his mother was not your run-of-the-mill fender bender involving someone drunk or running a red light. Jim heard the term freakish mentioned numerous times when friends and relatives swarmed the house for the few days sandwiched between the accident and funeral. His stepfather, Odis Staymen, used the term "God's Will" to describe a bird flying from one tree to the next, so it's no surprise he used it to convey the last moments of his mother's life.

Jim didn't care too much about God's willingness to direct anything since Odis married his mother four years ago. Only ugliness has any fun in the Cirmah family since his arrival. Jim is ready to give God credit if Odis suddenly dies from a massive heart attack, and until then he didn't care to be one of the flock.

A cattle truck blew a tire and jumped two lanes crashing into a concrete guardrail. A seventy-pound chunk of guardrail fell forty feet below onto another section of interstate smashing the windshield of his mother's SUV killing her instantly. God's Will notwithstanding, she was dead, and Jim's life is about to free fall faster than that block of concrete hurling down to the freeway below.

The only man in Jim's life that meant anything to him up to this point is his Grandfather, Denzel. A wealthy rice farmer in Arkansas stern but fair, Denzel took Jim to his farm during summer and winter breaks teaching him how to fish and hunt. Jim was driving a combine at twelve-years old earning money used to buy a sixteen-gauge shotgun and the endless boxes of shells he'd shoot trying to hit ducks flying into rice country by the thousands from Canada.

The farm and his Grandfather represented good times and tempered the realities of dark things happening at his house in Dallas.

Jim is quickly hardening to life's unfairness. When his stepfather quoted the Bible hitting him with a two inch leather belt, his anger toward God and Odis built like a lava field boiling under the surface ready to explode.

He long ago stopped the incessant complaints about the quick-tempered, alcohol fueled Odis to his mother; there's only excuses because she's terrified of being alone. Jim's real father left the family three years into Jim's life right after the birth of his younger sister, Brenda. It's never clear to Jim why he abandoned the family; his mother always drifted off into "life's not fair" routine when asked. Soon it mattered little to Jim; he didn't have curiosity or emotion about a man walking away from him and his sister as babies.

Brenda was an outgoing little girl for the first few years of her life but at age six she became withdrawn and distant when Odis moved into the house. It confused Jim at first; Brenda spent much of the time in her room writing in a diary or deep into school books. Jim is just the opposite, hating the inside of the house and staying outside to play street sports. He'd do anything to get away from the biblical glare of Odis and the Christian shrine covering the house on every wall. Soon he would get the chance to leave it all behind.

Jim made up his mind to make a stand. That stand came in the form of refusing to go to church with Odis and Brenda three Sundays ago. It's bravely executed, but Jim knew Odis might beat him half to death for making such a statement without his mother being around.

Strangely, Odis only yelled obscenities Jim guessed didn't come from the Bible but calmed down rather quickly. He grabbed Brenda's hand and went to church without him. The house long ago ceased being a home to Jim, so the last few weeks he looked forward to his Sunday morning freedom defying yet one more position of authority in his life.

Jim and the Dennis' twins built a treehouse in a black oak stand of trees only a block away from the house. This Saturday he's surprised to see Brenda perched in the treehouse when he opens the trapdoor crawling up through the floor.

She smiles at him and Jim sees a spark of life missing for a while. Jim smiles back but issues a warning. "You know we don't allow girls in our treehouse."

Although this thought had been discussed by the guys, it had never been challenged with the actual appearance of a girl sitting on a milk carton case in their treehouse next to him.

Brenda has a backpack setting next to her and several books lying around her corner of the treehouse. She starts to gather the belongings to leave.

Jim looks out the window at the lot below hoping the Dennis' twins wouldn't climb the tree and find his sister in the sacred temple they spent many weekends constructing. Her anxiety to obey her brother slid a sliver of guilt down Jim's back and he immediately gave her a moment of reprieve.

"You can stay for a while... but if David or Darren show up, you've got to go." He knew he had to draw the line, sister status notwithstanding.

All Brenda could muster is a second smile and tentative voice. "Thanks, I'll sure leave shortly," she concedes. "Nice treehouse." She tries to regain favor.

Jim listens to her faint sentence and realizes this is the most he's heard fall off her lips in several weeks. He didn't understand the answer to his sister's withdrawal, and certainly has no idea the tool defining her troubles changing both of their lives forever lies innocently next to her backpack.

Jim takes the treehouse compliment in stride as if expected, after all it did come from his sister.

"Yeah," he brags.

"We've already had two dirt clog battles in the fort with the Wilcox brothers...won both."

Brenda looks out the window on her side of the treehouse suddenly turned fort imagining the clay dirt clogs raining down on the local bullies.

"Don't doubt it....you could really chunk a dirt clog from up here." She summarizes displacing a slight smile.

Jim is impressed with Brenda's war strategy recognition.

"You can come up any time the twins aren't around." A large concession is made.

Brenda and Jim enjoy another thirty minutes of solitude twenty feet off the ground before the Dennis' twins pull up on bikes, and Jim quickly ushered Brenda down the tree to return home and a make believe world. In her rapid haste to leave, Brenda inadvertently pushes an opening to her soul and darkest secrets under the edge of the milk carton case used as a chair. The diary is a habit she penned daily and didn't have a clue it fell from her backpack.

After the twins join Jim in the treehouse, the boys get bored shooting rocks using a sling-shot at birds flying into the wrong tree. A decision is made to go to the Dennis' house for a football throw around. Several more neighborhood boys join the toss around and soon a game of tackle football breaks out and lasts till dark.

Jim avoids going home whenever possible and when Mrs. Dennis asks him to have dinner, he jumps at the chance. He returns home around 10:00 Saturday night and easily gets by Odis passed out on the living room couch and goes to bed.

Sunday morning starts down the usual path, Odis put on the same jeans and blazer he wears to church every outing with the exception of a new golf shirt he bought at Target. He wakes Brenda up and together they are at the church thirty minutes early for the first of three services Odis ushers for.

Jim gets up around 9:30 and goes over to the treehouse knowing the twins would show sooner or later and plans how the day will be set. When he gets there the twins are passing a book back and forth not one of the three *Playboys* they managed to sneak away from Odis. It is Brenda's diary. The twins look up at Jim, a mixture of wonderment and fear in their eyes.

Jim realizes who owns the small book having seen it in Brenda's tow many times, but the thought of reading its contents never entered his mind. In his eyes, Brenda is the little sister writing about butterflies and unicorns. Darren Dennis hands Jim the diary and the brothers immediately scamper down the tree and head home. Jim senses something is terribly wrong in the diary from their reaction, and sits in the treehouse unwillingly exploring the antics of the child predator he lives with.

Brenda's writing isn't filled with great detail, but leaves little doubt about the ongoing horror her life's been during the previous four years. The power Odis wields over Brenda is absolute and heightened since their mother's death. Jim could only read a small portion of the diary before his stomach demands he stop. He knows enough to make a decision altering many lives for years to come. He heads home, a heavy grip on the diary and his heart.

Odis Staymen is a vile person no matter what angle you assess his personality. The day Brenda lost her diary in the treehouse, he loaded a shopping cart with Grey Goose Vodka and Budweiser. His love for vodka started as a teenager and the affair so intense, he's in the advance stages of liver disease. He ignores his liver because it remains silent in its distress, but the ulcers in his stomach demand immediate attention screaming pain.

Placating the strong message in his stomach, he starts out drinking vodka but finishes on beer to maintain a high and insure a little less Pepto-Bismol consumption. On a good weekend he'll empty two fifths and a case of Budweiser.

Staymen, beyond being an alcoholic, is a pathetic human being. He was abused as a child and witnessed two older sisters sexually molested by his father. A family tradition he carries on beating Jim and the sexual abuse of Brenda since she was six. His mild-mannered response to Jim's refusal for church has its roots firmly planted in the fact he's planning on leaving the family after collecting the $25,000 insurance policy his deceased wife carried at her job in a small credit union. That check is coming in the mail in two weeks, but Staymen will never cash it.

The sixteen-gauge shotgun is pulled from the corner of his closet and loaded with five shells. Jim's mind is swirling with activity pacing back and forth in his bedroom. The thoughts are not questioning the intent to kill Odis, but what is the best plan to execute it.

He decides to watch Odis pull in the driveway through the living room window, then hide in a small bathroom next to the kitchen only a few steps from the front door. When Odis walks into the front door, he'll come out to do the world and his sister a favor.

A long forty minutes later the plan is put into action. Brenda opens the front door and starts up the stairwell to her bedroom on the second floor. Jim watches posed on a small crack in the bathroom door, but for some reason Odis isn't right behind her. Odis is talking to a neighbor about a strange dog running around in the neighborhood and depositing unwanted things on their lawns. The next door neighbor is a drunk too, and likes the way Odis thinks. Far more will be deposited on the front yard than dog feces for the neighborhood to talk about shortly.

Jim opens the door slightly as his sister closes her bedroom door at the top of the steps. He eases out into the kitchen, the shotgun pressed against his shaking shoulder firmly like his Grandfather taught him. Odis disengages the next door drunk and heads up the three steps to the front door intent on visiting Brenda in her room.

When he opens the front door Jim is no more than ten feet in front of him, the shotgun pointed at his chest. Odis stops. He is shocked at first taking in the threat, but it quickly wears off replaced by anger.

"What the hell are you doing pointing that shotgun at me, boy?" The man wearing the clean Target shirt demands.

Jim didn't contemplate conversation; in fact, he intended to blow him away the moment he came into the room but now the devil's tongue is wagging at him.

"Staymen, you ain't ever going to hurt Brenda or me again." A determined voice predicts the immediate future.

Brenda hears the exchange and comes out on the small landing on the second floor.

Odis Staymen did what he always did when angry at Jim; he unbuckles his Texas Longhorn belt, pulls the belt from the loops in his jeans and starts toward the barrel of the sixteen-gauge he foolishly believes will never be used.

Brenda screams watching Staymen advance and Jim turns his head at her voice. Odis grabs the barrel of the gun in the distraction and tries to yank it away from Jim's grip. The first blast knocks Odis back to the open front door. Before he gets through the doorway, Jim fires a reflex second shot ripping the once-new Target golf shirt leaving no doubt just how dead Odis Staymen has suddenly become.

Jim doesn't remember much about the events following the shooting. He and Brenda sit on the couch holding onto one another when the cops came through the front door and kicks the shotgun away from the coffee table in front of them.

Jim is cuffed and put in the backseat of a squad car. The last time he sees Brenda alive, Mrs. Dennis' arm is around Brenda's shoulder. Both are crying as the police car pulls away from the dog shit still lying on the ground covered up by a blanket.

The criminal process in Texas is hard on anybody that jumps across the bold line of the law. Jim has a number of things in his favor when going to court, not-the-least he's only thirteen-years old and killed a child molester. But murder is taken seriously even in the so-called "gun capitol of the free and brave" and there's a price to pay.

He spends the next eight years in a boy's reform school run by a number of tough Catholic priests wielding a strong hand when it came to discipline. Jim left one child beater bleeding on the ground only to be introduced to a dozen others carrying the same leather Bibles and belts. Jim finds his repentance in many strip clubs but no churches when released shortly after his twenty-first birthday and moves to Southern California.

Nothing is left in Dallas to keep Jim Cirmah. Sadly, Brenda committed suicide three days after her seventeenth birthday when her boyfriend tried to touch her breast and she panicked in the process. Odis Staymen's last gift to the Cirmah family is an everlasting one.

CHAPTER THREE

Not Private I

JIM CIRMAH STUDIES the length of the pool table eyeing the eight-ball setting temptingly close to the right rear pocket. All he has to do is drop the nine-ball lying half-a-foot from the side pocket; aiding the task, he gets to set the white ball at the correct angle due to his opponent's scratch. The Q-ball kisses off the nine dropping in the side pocket and continues down the green surface stopping a convenient ten inches from the eight-ball. Jim stretches his six-three frame over the end of the table and knocks the eight-ball home.

A smile erupts on Wayne Davis' face, Jim's best friend since Jim moved to L.A. nine years ago. They connected by a chance meeting at the pool table being played on now. Wayne walks to the other side of the table and collects twenty dollars from two new bar faces not having a clue Jim Cirmah is a pool hustler, honing his game over many beers and bets.

Jim and Wayne are polar opposites physically and mentally. Jim towers over Wayne's five-eight height and is two-hundred and fifteen pounds of muscle he works on daily. Wayne might be the north side of one sixty after a few beers, but hasn't exercised since wearing black socks in a middle school gym class. Jim has a mean streak honed by a love for boxing he gravitated to serving his time in the juvi-home. The priests encouraged it, so Jim trained and boxed many sanctioned Gold Glove events and even more fights outside the ring. He seldom lost at either. Jim didn't live in a depressed world many would fall into considering his family history, but if someone enters Jim's circle and crosses the thinnest of lines they better be prepared to defend themselves.

Wayne likes the fact that Jim is tough. Wayne manages a couple dozen young computer junkies that repair commercial and residential computers with the Geek Squad by day and hack their way through all kinds of mischief by night. His only touch into rugged comes through his card and pool playing around Jim and a relief from the boring 'other life' making him a living. Jim's reason for liking Wayne may be no more complicated than opposites attract. Jim has always been a protector of the oppressed; and when Wayne is in the tough bar scene Jim likes to frequent, he definitely falls into that category.

Jim made his living by photo chasing wayward husbands and wives at night, and bringing back not-so-nice guys that jump bail to avoid facing whatever justice the law attaches to their resumes. It made him enough money to get through next month's bills, but more importantly places him on the edge between insanity and mayhem. It also gave him a legitimate reason to carry a .40 caliber pistol, supporting the addiction to weapons developed on his Grandfather's farm years ago.

Because of his youth, Jim's shooting of Odis was sealed by the court in Texas and he slid under the radar when the State of California ran their background check to get a weapons permit for his private investigator line-of-work. The job connected him to the law and lawless. Many of the people he knows are cops that came to him because he ran the streets and has a feel for which way the wind is blowing when standard police procedure didn't work. Several on the force hang out with Jim, all cut from the same cloth constantly on the prowl seeking energy coming from trouble. Jim rarely disappoints.

Wayne walks around the table and hands Jim a twenty earned as eight-ball partners. Two bikers, displaying more ink than the U.S. Constitution, lay eight quarters on the table to pay for the next game and challenge Jim/Wayne to a round of eight-ball. Wayne drops the coins in the slot, pushes the lever in with the quarters and the pool balls hit the end of the table ready to be racked. As Wayne racks the balls, Jim finishes his beer and glances at his watch. He walks over to Wayne.

"Got to go…can't play anymore tonight," Jim relays.

Wayne looks at the bikers and back to Jim. "These guys can't stay with us, easy money."

Jim walks over and puts the pool stick back into a rack on the wall.

"Have no doubt you're right, but got an early day tomorrow," Jim asserts. "Henry's at the bar, he can partner with you."

Jim is torn about leaving at this point even though it is close to 1:00 a.m. Something about the two bikers looks familiar and that usually means trouble. He shrugs off his instinct and heads out into the night getting home hours earlier than usual. Jim doesn't live in the best of neighborhoods; partly a reflection of his finances, partly a kinship with the unwashed masses and equally wayward souls fighting through life against the odds. He pulls into the driveway, positive of movement in the second floor bedroom window. Someone is in his house. In Jim's usual style, he meets trouble head on pulling his weapon and easing into the backdoor.

Winston, a worthless English Bulldog, glances over at Jim's entrance exhibiting little interest. The fact someone is on the second floor and his dog sits in the kitchen lying on blanket does not surprise Jim. The dog is damn lazy, only barking and farting when inconvenient for Jim.

Jim looks into the small living room and adjoining dining room turned Man Cave not seeing anything out of order. He approaches the stairwell cautiously, moving up slowly avoiding the third step that makes a loud noise under the slightest of pressure. At the top of the landing area he checks out the second bedroom and small bathroom with similar results. His bedroom door is shut at the end of the hall. He's sure it was open when leaving earlier in the day.

Having someone in the house didn't come as a total shock. Jim has a long list of people having numerous reasons to want him hurt or worse. Ex-husbands paying large child support and alimony abound in his profession, not to mention dozens of felons going to jail because he's good at what he does. He once found a crack addict in his kitchen rummaging for food next to a resting Winston. He fed the man and gave him a ride downtown after a warning the next time a break-in wouldn't end so nice. All of this added to a naturally suspicious mind bordering on paranoia.

An ear placed on the bedroom door confirms something is happening behind it. Jim leans into the door and pushes through. Somebody is taking a shower in his bathroom pretty much eliminating any crack head's visit and most of the crooks he dealt with in the past. Still cautious, he goes through the door and sees the outline of a well-endowed woman washing out a thick mane of black hair behind the foggy shower door glass. Jim is not sure exactly which lady friend is in the shower. Numerous options abound; but he's not exactly unhappy this one decided to join him.

A tap on the glass with his pistol makes the showering body jump. A "damn" interrupts the silence from the mystery woman.

"Give me one reason not to shoot the shower full of holes," Jim threatens in less than a menacing voice.

"Blow job," the confident voice of Janey Shaw announces as she goes back to rinsing her hair.

Jim's expression shows a quick approval. He walks back into the bedroom and undresses, soon returning to the shower stepping in.

"So," he asks calmly. "How did you get in?"

Janey smiles looking at his cut-body lathering up next to her.

"A ladder is leaning against your bedroom window…. climbed in." She answers rather simply.

"Really," not hiding his surprise. "That's a little scary."

Janey looks pleased. "It wasn't hard, got a lot of Tom Boy in me," she relates proud of the climbing skills and taking what she thinks is a concern on his part.

"Not talking about you," he states dealing out little grace. "The ladder doesn't belong to me…shouldn't be leaning against my house," he laments as a threat Janey doesn't understand.

"Bastard," she retorts with great aim. "I could fall to my death…that should be first on your mind."

Jim focuses on a stream of water flowing down her bare ass and slaps it.

"Nice ass, but you don't carry a gun intent on shooting me. Whoever put it there probably does. That's just the way my mind thinks." He underscores his last few words trying to regain favor on the previous blow job offer.

They soon get out of the shower and head to bed. Jim goes to the window and looks out into the night in either direction seeing nothing unusual except a twenty-foot ladder lying against the window frame. He pushes the top of the ladder toward his backyard to get rid of the threat and it falls against his house. The moment it leaves his hand, he knew it was a mistake. It slides down the house and shatters a light fixture hanging next to the back porch.

"Damn it," he shouts into the non-caring night as the glass and ladder fall to the ground.

Janey is tired of the ladder. "Get in bed," she demands.

Jim does as instructed.

CHAPTER FOUR

Bird Man

THE SUN POURS into the open window, and Jim gets up to assess the damage caused by the ladder the night before. He sees John David Glover, the next door neighbor, picking up the ladder and placing it back on his house.

"Hey J.D., how did your ladder end up on my house?" Jim yells.

John David looks up at the window. "Damn kids be my guess," he summarizes. "They took two gallons of my paint yesterday. Better not let me catch the little bastards."

Jim knows he states the brutal truth. More than one dog wandered onto John David's property over the years and suddenly disappeared.

He did like Winston, although Jim didn't have a clue why. Winston has a way of challenging anyone's patience and J.D. always seems to be fresh out.

He moves to getting his day under control. After dressing he returns to Janey, a near perfect body lying on the bed.

"Beautiful," he whispers next to her ear. "Sleep long as you want, please feed Winston on the way out...gotta' go."

Janey opens her blue eyes ever so slightly and gives him a wink.

Janey sleeps late, she's a stripper at the Booty Trap Jim has seen on and off for the last year. She's the exception to most of the girls in Jim's life, long on body and short on thoughts. Her rules are steadfast; she won't touch drugs or men that do drugs. This is polar opposite for most women playing the stripper game. When Jim needs help for business or personal life he leans on Janey, a large endorsement from a man so independent.

Jim drives to Slick Rollie's Bond and Pawnshop where he spends a lot of time. It's a source for much of his income giving him bond-jumping jobs. He earns 25% of the posted bond to retrieve the wayward soon-to-be caught criminal. It's a modern day version of the old west bounty hunter, and it does pay handsomely. Bonds typically range from $5,000 to $100,000 for retrieving a law evading soul. If he goes international, the percentage can go as high as 40% plus expenses.

Jim arrives early morning, getting a pick-up profile from Slick Rollie Silva surrounding the next bond-jumping target.

Rollie Silva is a tough man in a tough business. The Pawnshop does well, but the real money comes from the bondsman business that equates to placing money down on black or red in a Vegas casino. A person who comes to Rollie needing a bond puts up 10% to 20% of what the judge actually requires for them to get out of jail. So if a bond is $30,000, the potential criminal gives Rollie an amount between $3000 to $6000. Slick guarantees the legal system the bad guy will show up for their court date or Rollie pays the full $30,000.

Rollie got the nickname "Slick Rollie" because he finances other bondsmen that come to him when getting a risky bond staring them in the face. Slick Rollie rarely turns down any bond regardless of the flight risk having the resources to go after someone virtually anywhere in the world. None of this is by accident; Slick's business runs like a machine and he's a wealthy man in the process.

Slick Rollie has several P.I.'s going after bail jumpers but likes Jim the best. Some is performance, Jim has no fear of going after anybody regardless of who they are or where the target may be hiding. Some is their friendship derived from like-personalities, resembling a sarcastic snake coiled in the grass ready to bite with little provocation. Jim is the son Slick never had and gave him a job when he first showed up on his doorstep after getting out of the juvi-home. Rollie has poured a great deal more than money and effort into Jim's training; he's extended his feelings into the relationship. That coming from a man most say has no feelings for anything but money.

Rollie learned the hard way to hedge his bets when laying out cash on the desperate and less-than-honest crowd he deals with. He cultivated a relationship with a FBI logistics specialist having access to the deepest secrets within the Bureau computer network. Rollie can extract information around the world by making a phone call on any soul foolish enough to run on the bond deal cut with Slick. This information cost $5000 a month in 20 dollar bills delivered to a safe deposit box shared with the FBI staffer. The investment pays back tenfold and is obviously an illegal activity, but the centerpiece of his success.

After thirty plus years in the business he leaves nothing to chance and will go old school when needed. A strong network of street informants is also utilized. They come into the shop to barter their pawned items to feed drug habits and get paid to keep eyes peeled for crooks trying to hide from the law and Slick Rollie's posse.

Times have changed for many in the Private Investigator's role. P.I.'s used to do much of the footwork to track someone down. It's not that Jim couldn't do the tracking; but his time is much better utilized when Slick fills in all the blanks and he goes after the bond jumping fugitive.

Jim arrives on-time, a rare mergence of worrying about the ladder outside his bedroom wall and anxiousness concerning a bail-jumping Samoan named William Aleki. Slick's nephew, Conrad Franks, is going along to get his feet wet in the business. Conrad graduated from college two years ago but can't find a thing paying more than minimum wage. Jim calls him 'Kid' because he's been hanging around the Pawnshop most of the last three summers trying to earn a few bucks working for his uncle. Despite being only a few years older than Conrad, Jim is light years ahead in life experiences.

As Jim walks through the front door and approaches a glass case filled with weapons of all descriptions, a man's voice screams in no uncertain terms.

"Drop your weapon." The voice demands.

Jim turns rapidly and pulls his .40 cal pistol instinctively pointing it toward the voice.

A second demand meets Jim head-on. "Drop it now, mister."

Jim scans the room in a semi-circle, pistol drawn but no one meets his stare. He sensed immediate trouble walking into the Pawnshop, usually two staff members are up front at all times but not today. All the weapons and jewelry present in the store makes a large scale robbery a likely event, and Jim is convinced he's walked in on one.

He starts backing up to the front entrance when Rollie and several employees emerge from a door to the adjoining firing range laughing at Jim's misconception. Jim knows he's been had and holsters his weapon. The voice repeats but has lost its intimidation. "Drop your weapon."

Rollie walks up to Jim and slaps him on the shoulder.

"See you've heard my newest pawn." Rollie brags painting a large smile on his face.

"Who the hell is yelling at me?" Jim inquires ready to clear up the mystery and stop being the blunt of the joke although he had to admit being completely fooled.

Conrad answers the question. "Uncle Rollie picked up a parrot that's driving us nuts...you fell for it like everyone else."

"Speak for yourself," Rollie inserts. "I love my African Grey, full of character. Damn sure has brightened up this place, wouldn't you agree, Jim?"

Jim, having not seen the bird yet, has to concede. "If laughter is the judging point, I agree. Where's this African bird? I have a well placed bullet introduction to make."

Rollie points to a hip-high cage setting in the corner and the African Grey named 'Drug Lord' cocks his head to one side taking in all the attention being thrown in his direction. The bird, as if being directed, shouts out "Drug Lord" and moves around his perch expecting a reaction. They all did, laughing at the bird's ability to repeat certain words and phrases picked up at his previous home.

A customer walks in and Drug Lord loudly shouts his trademark verse. "Drop your weapon."

The man's voice being mimicked came across so acutely the customer raises his hands to surrender, looks around, and backs out the door. Even Jim, knowing the voice came from Drug Lord, flinches a reflex reaching for his weapon.

Jim gives the bird his due. "I have to admit, this is the perfect place for a bird named 'Drug Lord' to spew his police jargon on unsuspecting customers that may pull out a weapon and open fire. Where the hell did you get such a talent?"

Rollie is beside himself with his new toy. "Do you remember a small-time hood named Tim Puckett?"

"Yeah," Jim responds. "Didn't he end up in the trunk of a car in Mexico?

"That's the man," Rollie confirms. "His ex-wife brought the bird in yesterday, thought I might have an interest. Drug Lord starts shouting all kinds of cool things, had to have him.

"What else does the damn bird say?" Jim asks in amazement.

Rollie can't resist the invitation. "First of all, he mimics all kinds of noises. A siren on a police car, he can even sound like a telephone ringing."

Conrad quickly jumps in. "Yesterday I was working the front desk...twice he got me to pick up the phone without a call."

Jim walks to the bird and leans over the cage. Drug Lord looks up but doesn't say anything. Jim is starting to admire such an entertaining and smart pet, something he didn't have in Winston.

"Cool bird, you Drug Lord," Jim confirms and walks back to Rollie. "Let's talk some business."

Conrad, Jim and Rollie retreat to a private office and Slick pulls out a file on William Aleki.

Rollie puts his glasses on and starts pulling out several pages of information including a photo he passes over to Jim and Conrad.

"The Samoan jumped on a $30,000 bail," Rollie lays out. "He was arrested for cocaine possession...resisting arrest."

"Did this guy play D-tackle at USC?" Jim asks.

"Nope," Rollie informs. "That's his brother. About the same size though."

"How big is he?" Conrad is facing the reality his first job won't be an easy one.

"Really big." Slick Rollie emphasizes looking over the top of his glasses.

"Not a problem," Jim brushes off the big reference. "Where's he hiding out?"

Rollie looks back at the notes in the file. "He's staying at a complex on the East side, Hudson Apartments. I have a reliable source, says he's living with a black woman name Justine Wilcox, apartment 354."

"How reliable is the source?" Jim questions.

"Very reliable, my source lives in the same complex, knows Ill Will from a gang he used to sell drugs to." Rollie asserts.

"Ill Will, how did he earn that name?" Conrad keeps falling deeper into the pool of doubt.

Jim smiles at Conrad's timid personality. "All these gang members have street names making them look bad-ass," he contends. "We'll get the large man ….bring him in."

Rollie hands them a file on Aleki. "My informant gets his fifty inch TV back if we get the Samoan; he's invested in our success. There is one thing interesting about the building; it's a converted old hospital…has a duct system big enough for a man to crawl through above each floor. The apartment is a corner unit; he'll have to run to the middle of the building to get away." Slick leaves few stones unturned.

Jim takes the file and looks back at Slick. "Did you get the Kid a gun?"

Rollie responds like Conrad isn't present. "Conrad's been practicing with a .45, but that's too much weapon. Giving him a .40 cal like yours, but can't carry it until his permit comes in from the state. Stay between him and Ill Will."

"Damn," Jim responds. "You're taking all the fun out of this collar. Let's go, Kid, time to bust your cherry."

CHAPTER FIVE

The Collar

JIM PULLS THE GTO into a side street less than a block from the apartment building and parks. The area is devoid of foot traffic, not unusual for this rough part of town. Jim is animated, talking and moving his hands at the same time. "This job is part actor ... part bulldog." Jim relays knowing Conrad hasn't a clue what he's stepping into.

He gets out, motioning for Conrad to follow. At the back of the car, Jim reaches into the trunk retrieving a box. Conrad isn't sure what the box has to do surrounding a P.I.'s job, but a smile erupts when Jim takes out a long-haired wig and a PacBell tee shirt. He puts the shirt on and fits the wig over his ears.

"What's that for?" A puzzled Conrad asks.

"The acting part," Jim confirms. "Deception keeps anyone in the building from recognizing me."

"You got something for me?" Conrad inquires.

Jim turns his face at an angle like the African Grey 'Drug Lord.' "Who would recognize you? I've been roaming these streets for six years building a reputation."

"A bad-ass reputation." Conrad adds.

"A reputation none-the-less. You, on the other hand, have been picking up a phone dialed by a bird." Jim rubs Conrad's head making him recognize the fun in the exchange. "Let's go get the big Samoan…make some money today."

Jim pulls a utility belt from the trunk and straps it on his waist completing the phone company make-over.

Walking toward the complex, Jim lowers his voice. "All kidding aside, follow my lead… everything will be fine." Jim encourages. "I've done this many times…all these characters pretty much do the same thing when cornered… rollover…give up. It doesn't matter how big they are."

The two men find a side door gaining entrance. A climb up three flights of stairs reveals no one stirring, Jim stands for a moment on the landing before opening the door to the third floor. His weapon is pulled from a leather pocket on the tool belt and a bullet inserted into the firing chamber. An uneasy Conrad looks like he swallowed Drug Lord and Slick Rollie caught him.

"This will be over in a few minutes….it's not the Little Big Horn." Jim explains hoping to give Conrad a comfort zone.
Both go through the door and walk the hallway. An older black lady carrying groceries watches twenty feet down the hall quickly disappearing into her apartment.

Trouble is not far away. Jim walks past her closed door to the end of the hallway and leans an ear against 354 and listens. A police car siren goes off in the street outside quickly fading away. It does little for Conrad's confidence, but completely ignored by Jim. He freezes Conrad even tighter by knocking on the door. No answer comes from the apartment but a television heard in the background confirms someone is home. Jim bangs again.

After a few seconds of nervous silence, Jim yells into the door. "PacBell, need to check your phone."

Only silence finds its way to the hallway behind the door and Conrad thinks it's going to be over. After one more knock, Jim screams PacBell then pounds the door.

A deep voice finally responds from the other side. "Phone is fine, get lost asshole."

Jim steps back and kicks the door. It doesn't budge. A second kick gets the same results, he looks at Conrad. "Could use some help." Jim implores.

The two kick the door simultaneously breaking the lock and pushing the door open six inches. A chain holds it. Jim lowers his shoulder and smashes through, pistol drawn. A run into the apartment reveals an open door to the bathroom, but no Samoan. Jim cautiously enters the bedroom and notices an open window. Conrad goes to the window and looks down at a thirty foot drop to the parking lot below. Jim pulls up a bedspread finding no one under the bed. The closet is checked but the big Samoan is nowhere to be found. A look into the closet ceiling reveals a trapdoor half open and a chair below it. Jim motions to Conrad.

"Go into the crawl space...make noise so Aleki hears you coming." Jim directs.

Conrad looks at the trapdoor with trepidation.

Jim knows they must act fast. "He won't come back this way if he realizes you're there. Damn it, just make some noise."

Conrad climbs up to the trapdoor in the ceiling while Jim hurriedly leaves the apartment. After a run down the hallway, Jim spots a janitor's closet. A placed ear against the door reveals Aleki climbing down from the ceiling.

Jim stands back yelling at the door. "Aleki, I know you're there…might as well come out hands up."

A shot is fired from inside the closet flying through the door a foot from Jim's head. He ducks low to the floor glad luck stood close by.

In a calm voice to no one, Jim summarizes. "I guess that's a no?" He looks around the hallway checking the options.

A voice inside the closet interrupts. "Fuck you… ain't going back to prison."

Movement inside the closet is heard and Jim goes into a semi-panic realizing the Samoan wouldn't hesitate to kill Conrad if he retraced his steps.

"No use backing up in the crawl space, I've got Steven Segal waiting on you." Jim bluffs.

The Samoan answers the bluff. "Why don't you come get me?"

"I'm calling S.W.A.T., be here in a minute to shoot your ass." A second bluff not swallowed by Aleki.

"Bullshit, bounty hunter….you don't cash me in that way." The Samoan is a veteran of the business and figures Jim didn't have a warrant and isn't the law.

"I never get the dumb ones." Jim whispers to no one listening.

A deep breath and desperate thought helps make a risky decision. The law has probably been called, only a few minutes remain to collect his bounty. Jim pulls a can of teargas from the leather holster and fits a large plastic straw. He leans against the wall next to the door placing the straw in the middle of the keyhole.

The teargas is sprayed into the closet and the Samoan starts moving feeling the effects noted by a series of coughs. Two bullets jump out the door in rapid succession from the Samoan's gun as more teargas fills the closet.

Jim is hoping the Samoan comes this way and doesn't back up on Conrad. An electric stungun is drawn from the tool belt and he lays on the floor thinking the Samoan can't take much more. Another shot whizzes through the door and behind it the giant Samoan crashes out waving the gun and wiping the stinging gas from his eyes. He turns to Jim wildly waving the pistol squeezing off a final shot.

Jim points the stungun at Aleki's chest and fires. The Samoan falls to the floor shaking, the voltage running over his body. Jim pulls out a pair of handcuffs locking onto the hands of the unconscious Samoan. A door opens and an older man pokes his head out watching from a room down the hall.

In the P.I. trade, you need to keep witnesses to a minimum giving details to the law, so Jim intimidates anyone viewing the incident when possible. He looks at the man delivering a message. "He didn't pay his phone bill, you current?"

The man slams the door. A woman's loud scream comes from the adjoining apartment followed by a door opening. A woman rushes along the hall holding a baby. Jim hustles to the open door not exactly sure what caused the woman to go into a panic. Conrad picks himself up from the couch after falling through the ceiling tile.

Conrad looks up having little embarrassment. "Did we get him?"

"Yes we did," Jim responds. "Didn't you take the noise thing a little far?"

CHAPTER SIX

The Good Doctor

DAVID SANDERS, SR., retired early from the Denver Police Department in the late-nineties after working homicide for twenty-four years. At 46, he was too young to collect a monthly check but it didn't matter, he got away from man's inhumanity to man. David actually loved the job in many ways, but his personal life was turned upside down. A story written and lived far beyond the burned out drinking cop and a wife tired of the late nights being ignored. No, David's life certainly left a cop's negative footprint on a social and personal level, but his mental state got blasted by the loss of his son.

David Sanders, Jr., his only child, was killed just short of his 18th birthday "truck surfing" as the kids call it. David Sr. only knew about this crazy, dangerous teenage trend after reviewing a memo sent down in the department about "truck surfing" going on in California. It never dawned on David any Colorado kid would stand on the top of their truck cab and balance like a surfer riding a board off a Maui beach going 30 miles-per-hour on a dirt road. Certainly in his wildest thoughts on a double homicide day, he never envisioned his son drinking a six-pack of beer and flying off the top of his F-150 crushing his skull on a rock.

David's wife took their son's death harder than he, and she blamed the accident on his teenage girlfriend, who was drunk and driving the truck he fell from. David didn't share her feelings, no one held a gun to his son's head and made him get on top of the truck to begin with. His wife wanted to pursue criminal charges against the girlfriend, something David felt would pile one tragedy on top of another. The riff cut the last remaining string holding the marriage together.

After his divorce, David drifted around a short period of time looking for something to place his energy into. He earned a P.I.'s license and got good chasing down wayward husbands and wives. It even allowed him to stay in contact with many of his old buds still working the Denver streets at the department.

In 2004, he was introduced to Dr. Royce Benders by his previous captain on the force. Dr. Benders gave a lecture for two hundred plus medical specialists and another hundred law enforcement officials in Denver. Dr. Royce Benders crossed over from the medical profession to law enforcement because of his work with DNA. He established the medical protocol in the eighties and nineties for forensic investigation and cutting edge medical advancements in DNA science. A Nobel Peace Prize winner in genetic science, Dr. Benders set the tone for what science could do in helping redefine evidence for lawmen around the world.

David sat in the lecture sometimes in awe and sometimes in complete ignorance to the medical language coming from the brilliant mind talking on the stage. His years in homicide kept him up on most of the conversation, but he never visualized the creator of the tools used on a regular basis would be a few feet away in person. David not only appreciated Dr. Benders for his many amazing accomplishments, but the easy conversational style and humility captured his undivided attention. Attention is about to get a lot more personal for David before the evening is over.

Captain Fisher gave David a ticket to the event for more than an entertaining evening and getting caught up on forensic science. The Captain knew Dr. Benders on a personal level and the Doctor asked him to make a recommendation for someone to help manage his security. The position is far more than simply being a bodyguard, and Captain Fisher felt David is the man for the job.

After the lecture four people went to dinner including David, the Doctor, Captain Fisher, and a Catholic Bishop from Denver. David is overwhelmed not only by the Doctor but the presence of Bishop Pressey pushed him over the top. A life-long Catholic, David can't believe he's sitting among people having accomplished so much good in society for others.

The small talk continues through dinner and when dessert was served, Bishop Pressey looked over at Dr. Benders.

"What is the latest condition of the Shroud?" The Bishop asks.

Dr. Benders' face lit up instantly.

"The prognosis is good for the immediate future; I talked with the Vatican a few weeks ago...some of the measures we instigated in my first visit seem to be holding up." He responds.

David said little at the table up to this point. But he's familiar with the Shroud of Turin, the cloth wrapping Jesus in the tomb after the crucifixion, his image imprinted in blood on the surface.

"Excuse me," David inquires. "Are you talking about the Shroud of Turin?"

The Bishop turns to David. "Yes, the holiest of Christian artifacts. Dr. Benders would never brag, but the Shroud was deteriorating almost to the point of losing it until his genius and recommendations saved it."

"Please," David implores. "Tell the story."

"I have to say the Vatican was extremely bullheaded when it came to the defense of the Shroud." The Bishop relays. "Its significance so overpowering to the Church we refused to recognize its physical properties focusing mostly on the spiritual one. Listening to Dr. Benders' insistence the Shroud is a 2000 year old relic needing very specific care, we finally let the scientific community in to examine it in the mid-eighties for recommendations on how to preserve it."

Dr. Benders jumps in to the conversation.

"Thank you for those many accolades, but I wasn't the only scientist having those concerns. There was an extensive medical team I was part of; first examining the Shroud in 1984...we discovered a number of things surrounding its age, blood type, even dust particle analysis. Some amazing things surfaced including the identification of plant imprints on the Shroud indigenous only to the area where Jesus was crucified. The study helped to verify its origins... just as importantly, set up a plan to keep the Shroud from further damage that comes with the aging process." Dr. Benders summarizes.

"That's an amazing story you told, thanks for helping me understand." David responds with an even greater appreciation for the Doctor.

"Dr. Benders is really God sent. Bless you, Sir." The Bishop underscores.

With that said the dinner is over. David returns home unaware the evening was the first step in the interview process. Dr. Benders contacted him a few days later, posed a few more questions and then flew him to L.A. to see his research hospital and cutting edge in vitro fertilization (IVF) clinic. He also gave him a tour of his home to see what suggestions David would make to increase his security. David didn't hesitate to take the job offered in the coming weeks to work for Dr. Benders, the money far more than he ever made as a cop, and he believed in everything the Doctor stood for in serving his fellow man.

CHAPTER SEVEN

Death Do Us Part

DR. BENDERS LIVES in a compound overlooking the Pacific in Malibu. The main house is 8200 square feet of pure mansion, something the Doctor earned over an incredible career. A separate five car garage is topped off with a guest house David resides in. The Doctor insisted David live on the property to facilitate security needs over the last nine years, virtually ingraining him a family member. Not that David pushed back too hard, it's not exactly a terrible place to live or a view to have, but he's cognizant of the job's importance.

Dr. Benders caught the eye of several radical groups during his work on The Shroud and the IVF clinic. The hospital produces astounding results and international headlines principled in multiple births including six children born to a mother all surviving.

Several times over the years individuals have come after the Doctor. At a book signing a woman threw pig's blood on the Doctor before David could wrestle her to the floor. A second incident was even scarier, a Muslim man breached the compound walls of the home firing two shots into his bedroom window. Dr. Benders wasn't home at the time, but it illustrates how fast things can escalate. A third incident surrounds a homemade pipe bomb left under his limousine, which David found, made headlines. Constant bomb threats and hecklers are at many of his lectures and David is proficient at working local law enforcement groups in advance of any public appearances. It seems the more people try to hurt him and gain publicity in the process, the more invitations are issued for someone else to jump in the game.

When the Doctor is home, David is the sole security person. When he goes on the road, two additional security officers are under David's command. Three days a week Dr. Benders makes the trek into L.A. to work at the hospital and David has one person in the security detail beside himself. David is constantly juggling a schedule based on last minute changes affecting staff requests to outside security companies. David also manages the full-time limo driver, Rico Hernandez, who's driven for the Doctor eleven years.

Dr. Benders gets up this morning excited. His wife, Cindy, is flying back from a two week trip to London and Paris. Cindy Benders is sixteen years younger than the Doctor and a second marriage that physically could be considered a trophy wife outside looking in. At 46, she is very attractive but don't let the looks sell her intelligence short. Cindy is a shrewd business woman and runs the operational side of the clinic under an iron fist as the C.O.O. She's built a sound business platform allowing Dr. Benders a free mind to pursue his many outside projects.

Her trip to London served two purposes; secure a high-end European clientele pipeline for the clinic and find several investors for a second clinic expansion in Atlanta, Georgia. Cindy is successful on both fronts.

There's a second reason for the Doctor's excitement. He's meeting his publisher this morning to profile content of a new book he's been working on for several months. He hasn't published a book in three years and is convinced the new book represents a paradigm shift in thought, changing the way people see the world around them.

He calls David to his office on the second floor of his home.

"David, need your help this morning." The Doctor asks.

"Sure," David answers. "What can I do?"

"Need you to pick up a dozen roses and a bottle of Dom for Cindy's return this afternoon." Dr. Benders states.

"Certainly," David responds. "Can get both before going to the airport to pick Cindy up."

"Why isn't Rico picking her up?" Dr. Benders inquires.

"Rico called this morning sick with a cold…didn't want him around spreading anything." David explains. "I have a security detail coming to the compound at 11:00 but can get them here early freeing me to pick up the flowers and champagne."

Dr. Benders glances at his watch.

"Don't worry about the security detail coming early…I'll be fine. Have my publisher coming around 10:00…don't waste your time or my money."

Dr. Benders states a favorite phrase David has heard many times.

"Don't want to do either, Sir." David confirms.

David isn't completely happy about the gap in security, but he knows better arguing the point. He's lost too many of those in the past. David leaves the Doctor to order the roses and Dom, smiling at the romantic gesture rare coming from Dr. Benders.

David is usually the one covering all the flowers and cards for various birthdays and anniversaries without prodding. Something special must be happening or maybe the Doctor is just insuring he gets laid tonight? David is glad somebody will be happy before the evening is over.

David gets his errands done quickly. Then he packs two bottles of champagne on ice and leaves the compound around 9:15 a.m. Cindy's flight is due at 12:20, but the L.A. traffic is impossible to predict and can have a wide range of travel time required to park at LAX.

David has more than a hint of paranoia driving in Southern California fighting traffic congestion to pick up an important person like Cindy Benders. Early has always been a part of David's personality, a trait rarely shared by L.A. people and he fired two security agencies for staff's tardiness.

To his surprise the traffic is relatively light and he gets within a half-mile of LAX at 10:50. He stops at a small coffee shop to get caught up on his caffeine fix and down a bagel ignored this morning. A quick glance at his iPhone reveals Cindy's flight is running twenty-five minutes late, not bad for the connecting flight from New York. Plenty of time to wipe the cream cheese off his face and get to LAX. The waitress takes his order and the iPhone rings.

Kirk Fetter is on the other end of the call, a security guard David knows well and assigned to the compound this morning.

"David, we've got problems…big problems." Fetter relays excitedly.

David stands up while asking the question. "What the hell is going on, Kirk?"

"Got here a few minutes ago… started toward the house. This guy came running around the garage apartment screaming his head off… goes on and on about Dr. Benders being dead. I drew my weapon, made him show me what he found." Kirk hesitates for a few seconds.

"Kirk," David demands loudly. "What has happened to Dr. Benders?"

"Someone hammered Dr. Benders to a tree by the pool, he's dead." Kirk responds.

David is hearing but not believing. "What do you mean he's hammered to a tree?"

"I called the cops, they'll be here shortly. He's dead. Get here fast as you can." Kirk shuts the phone off.

David lays a ten on the table and rushes out to his car. He calls Rico and tells him to pick up Cindy from the airport. When he arrives at the Benders' compound, three squad cars and an ambulance is already there. More CSI is on the way. David shows his I.D., circles what has been his home for the last nine years to find Dr. Royce Benders nailed to a large palm tree by the pool.

CHAPTER EIGHT

Act of Violence

JIM'S EATING A peanut butter and jelly laden piece of toast watching Winston go through his hunger act. The dog stares at Jim licking his broad mouth containing an even larger tongue. Winston's bowl is full of dog food, but Jim is convinced Winston has no intention of living life as a dog. He neither acts nor eats like an English Bulldog, but Jim can only blame himself for indulging the dog's self-image. The toaster spits out another slice of bread and Jim spoons a pile of PBJ to the warm surface feeding it to Winston, his fourth.

The dog reminds Jim of his favorite personality in history, Winston Churchill, although he didn't think the dog earned the name in hindsight. The only trait shared is the round, ugly face even a mother pays little attention to, and of course, both English. Jim isn't too sure about the English part; Winston was a gift from Slick Rollie meaning his paperwork is probably forged. He is sure about one thing, Winston is definately never going to be much of a watch dog, throwing a kink in the original intent when Slick dropped him off.

After Winston swallows the toast ignoring any hint of chewing, Jim picks up his five pound hand weights hitting the road for a three mile run. Like everything else in Jim's life, he attacks the run with focus and drive. It's not a jog, but an all out race from beginning to end.

A mile and a half into the run he notices two motorcycle cops brandishing a radar gun at the bottom of a hill. Jim runs by smile in hand, a lot of tickets will be handed out before the morning is over. As he crests the hill, a speeding refurbished '73 Mustang approaches a block away. The Mustang is a neighborhood car Jim has admired from afar and tries to slow it down using a hand motion. The attractive blond woman driving the Mustang flies past, annoyed at the attempt to get her attention. Jim shrugs his shoulders at her petulance, she better be really attractive to talk her way out of the ticket awaiting on the other side of the hill.

Jim makes the turn around the next intersection and starts his run back to the house. In passing a convenience store he notices a picture of Dr. Benders on the front page of the *L.A. Times* revealing a headline proclaiming his death. Next to the Times is the *USA Today* profiling a similar headline and photo. Jim stops briefly to pan the story recognizing his name but not sure where it came from. A subtitle fills in some of the blanks mentioning the DNA and forensic work Dr. Benders developed for the criminal bagging industry he's a part of. After catching his breath, Jim makes the return run home even faster than the first two miles getting him to the convenience store.

Jim goes into the backdoor and Winston thinks he's in line for more PBJ toast but Jim walks by and picks up his iPad to Google the Doctor. His work on the Shroud of Turin briefly catches Jim's eye bringing him back to his grade school days filled with abuse and Christianity shoved down his throat. He loses interest quickly and jumps in the shower.

Getting out of the bathroom he hears the phone ringing and hustles over to answer. On the phone is Duke MacAfee, an acquaintance Jim knows through his pool playing friend Wayne Davis. Duke is a computer wizard that works under Wayne at the Geek Squad and sometimes runs the same bars as Jim.

Jim rubs the water out of his hair on a towel and answers. "Hello."

"This is Duke...got some bad news about Wayne." Duke tees up a negative picture.

Jim responds. "What's going on with Wayne?"

"He got the hell beat out of him two nights ago, he's in Washington General." Duke relays.

"I was with him two nights ago...left him around 1:00...he was okay then."

Jim's mind drifts back to the bikers that night.

"Not sure what time it happened, but he's in the hospital suffering broken ribs, arm, and jaw. The doctor's put him in a medically induced coma hoping to get the brain swelling down." Duke confides.

"Who did it?" Jim's tone left little doubt his intent.

"Haven't heard... the cops interviewed several at the bar, but who knows what good that'll do?" Duke confesses.

"Thanks, Duke. I'll do some checking on my own. We'll get to the bottom of it." Jim shuts his cell off and immediately dials a close friend and L.A. Detective, Ted Fox.

"Ted, hey man, I need a favor." Jim asks.

"I don't loan money for abortions." Ted deadpans.

"I'm serious, smart assed cop...got a friend assaulted at the Diamond Club two nights ago. You met Wayne Davis a couple of times; he's in bad condition at the hospital. Find out what the department knows, okay?" Jim implores.

"Isn't he that skinny geek? Can't believe he got into a fight." Ted questions.

"Yeah, that's him…loud mouth bigger than his biceps." Jim confirms.

"No problem, be back shortly." Ted hangs up.

Jim dresses and heads to the Diamond Club. There's not much doubt in his mind what probably happened. Wayne runs his mouth after a couple of beers, but no one deserves to be in a coma lying in a hospital bed. His instincts are taking over; protect those unable to fend for themselves. Jim will right the wrong, even if it gets him killed in the process. He has little choice in the matter.

The Diamond Club is a strip joint featuring a multitude of options. Food, naked bodies, and pool are on the menu. Like most of the men walking through the doors, Jim likes looking at attractive women having nothing to hide; but the food is surprising good and draws a large lunch crowd. He settles onto a seat at the bar confident he'll catch the manager in due time and orders a beer. His cell goes off.

"Talk to me, Ted." Jim answers.

"Don't have much… the club staff said two biker types left after a few games with Wayne. A little pushing and shoving but no flying fists between the three. Wayne leaves forty-five minutes later… gets pounded in the parking lot… of course no witnesses. All we have are two thirty-something biker heads displaying countless tats and leather jackets… that's got it narrowed down to 400 thousand or so in L.A." Ted lays out the limited facts to work around.

Jim sees the manager walking toward the bar. "I'll be back to you shortly… thanks for the info."

The manager walks over to a patron at the bar and shakes his hand. Jim gets up and walks to him but waits on their conversation to be over. Drake Wilcox sees Jim and leaves the customer behind.

"Come over here," Drake relays. "I knew you'd be in sooner or later."

Drake leads Jim to his small office at the end of the bar closing the door behind.

"Told the cops all I know," Drake explains. "I'm sorry for Wayne, how's he doing?"

"Drake, Wayne's in a coma. You know who these guys are... tell me now." Jim's voice did not waver.

"I like you guys, you're great patrons, but I have to protect my business. These dudes are Hells Angels...will firebomb my place." Drake pleads.

"They won't come after you on this... I'll be in the crosshairs, promise you." Jim assures.

Drake is visibly uncomfortable. "I don't know their names... the truth. They hang out at the Sims Hideaway Bar on Lawrence. Do what you have to do... keep me out of it."

"I saw them that night... all I need is their home stadium. Thanks." Jim turns, leaves the office and goes out to his car.

He hits Ted on the cell. "You know the biker club over on Lawrence, Sims Hideaway Bar?"

"No, but can find it." Ted answers. "Got the feeling it's going to be an interesting night."

Jim smiles to himself. "Depends on your point of view. Meet me there at 9:00 tonight."

"Do we need backup?" Ted questions.

"Nope," Jim says matter-of-fact. "We'll stay low-profile on this one."

"It always starts out that way." The cell goes dead.

CHAPTER NINE

Devil-In-Law

JIM PULLS HIS black '68 GTO in a parking lot a few blocks from the Sims Hideaway Bar. The car is one of the few things he's ever splurged on and didn't want it destroyed by a crazed bunch of bikers. He has a bigger concern over the car's safety than his own. Quickly he walks to the bar wearing a running suit and hiking boots.

An excitement permeates his step after he spots Ted's unmarked car parked across the street from the main entrance. No dread enters an ounce of his body, since Jim's confidence borders on a Muhammad Ali like mystique entering the ring with the crowd screaming "Ali, Ali."

Jim opens the door and slides in the backseat. Sitting next to Ted is Lance Compton, a cop that's run many late nights lock-step in the shadow of him and Ted.

"Lance, you here to back us up?" Jim questions.

Lance turns to the back seat. "Hell no, I'm here to watch you fight. Ted says you're the baddest man he's ever seen in a street fight...I usually pay $200 a ticket in Vegas to see something this cool. What's the plan anyway?"

"Yeah, what's the plan?" Ted quickly adds.

"I'll recognize the two bastards who beat down Wayne when we get in; you guys need to get them outside. I would prefer to fight them one at a time, but I'll whip both their asses if necessary." It's painfully obvious Jim didn't really have much of a plan.

"It's a good thing you're not named Eisenhower, you would have a German accent. Alright, Jim, I'll take it from here," Ted retorts in his typical sarcastic tone.

They get out of the car and head to the bar not pretending to be anything but cops, both Ted and Lance dressed in a coat and tie. Two bikers pull up and park next to fifteen bikes strewn along the sidewalk, spot the oncoming cops and suspect something isn't right. The two men turn around, get back on their bikes and race off.

"The odds just got a little better; probably no more than two dozen bikers we have to whip now." Lance laments in a somewhat joking manner.

"It's not like they'll be heavily armed... what could possibly go wrong?" Ted concludes as he opens the door.

The music screams a country song in a jukebox from the sixties when the three get inside. A thick, blue haze rolls off abundant joints filling the room in every corner.

All the lips taking a mouthful of beer/smoke stop and stare at the law walking into their lair. A Bigfoot would not demand more attention if it grabbed a beer and ate the bartender for a snack.

The three go to the bar and order a drink; it's what you do in a bar, even one like this. Jim sees the two bikers that beat on Wayne playing pool in the far end. He whispers in Ted's ear identifying them.

Ted motions to the bartender who leans down to listen. "I won't insult you with my I.D., but I do have a question. Who lives in the apartment above this bar?"

"I do... why?" The bartender responds.

"Is anybody up there now?" Ted answers with another question.

"No... live alone." The bartender answers.

"Do you own any pets?" Ted inquires.

"Where the hell is this going, cop?" The bartender demands.

"These are the simple questions; do you want me to call S.W.A.T. down to ask the complicated ones?" Ted's voice turns evil leaving little doubt he would do just that.

"Nothing upstairs but dust and dirty laundry." The bartender submits. The last question leaves a void in the bartender's mind soon to be answered. Ted pulls out his .45 and shoots a round into the ceiling. Everyone in the place hits the deck reaching for weapons. Even Jim and Lance are startled by the move. Ted steps away from the bar, gun still in his hand.

"Know this won't come as a surprise, but I'm a cop owning a bad temper. Not here to arrest any of you fine gentlemen unless I don't get what I want." Ted puts his .45 back in the holster. "I need Moe and Curley down there," He points toward the guilty two. "Come outside to fight my boy here. You know why... you put a computer geek in the hospital; he's a friend, now it's your turn. If not, I'm going to arrest you for assault and battery, take you downtown tonight."

For a long ten seconds the room is silent.

Lance turns to Jim and whispers. "Hell of a plan, Ted."

Ted starts to reach for his weapon again when a rather large man stands up at a table in the corner. His name is Buster Rand and is obviously a man of position in the crowd.

"Did you bust up a computer geek... is this cop speaking the truth?" Rand asks the two being called out.

One of the two lays his pool cue down on the table and turns to Rand. "Yeah, but this guy…"

"Shut the fuck up." The big man interrupts. "Go outside… fight this man. If you lose, I'll whip your ass again."

With that command the bar empties into the parking lot. Outside is another surprise, two black and white police cars and an unmarked cruiser is parked in the street. Seven cops are leaning against the cars waiting on the action to start.

"Thought you didn't bring backup?" Jim questions clearing the door, Ted next to him.

Lance confesses. "I did text Reynolds before we got here… didn't think he'd bring half the shift."

The cops start clapping as Jim gets close to the street and he raises a hand to acknowledge their backing. The bikers return the clap for their fighters.

Rand raises his hands to calm everyone down.

"Cop, what are the rules?"

"No weapons, no outside help from anybody… one at a time." Ted lays out the guidelines.

The two bikers take jackets off and Jim sees what he's up against. Both men are big and in their thirties. One is smoking a cigarette, a sure sign he won't last long. He's wearing short-heeled biker boots and from past experience, Jim knows they grip the street well. The other man is 6'5" and works out displaying a thick neck and even larger biceps. He wears cowboy boots and Jim is encouraged at the thought. Boots slide side-to-side in a fight and hard to maintain balance.

The crowd forms a circle and the one smoking takes the cigarette and flips it at Jim's feet.

Ignoring the slight, Jim loosens his neck and back by rolling his shoulders. He fires off a number of jabs and right hooks into the air and anyone viewing instantly knew he's an accomplished fighter.

Screaming, the first man rushes toward Jim and swings a wild overhead right Jim easily ducks. The biker gets a fist to his ear and a jab to his throat stumbling by. Jim moves closer to the big man trying to regain his balance hitting him twice on the forehead and finishes the volley on a hard right to the bridge of his nose. Blood erupts from the broken nose and the biker goes to one knee. Jim backs up, intent on letting the biker regain his upright stance. He wants the man to see what's coming his way.

The biker realizes Jim is a much better fighter, but no choice remains other than taking the beating in front of the club. And a beating he got over the next few minutes. Jim pounds his chest and kidneys, he could knock him out at any point but delays the inevitable. The biker can barely stand up and starts to spit blood. A blur of punches to his mid-section and an uppercut to the bikers' chin knocks two teeth curbside. Before he joins the teeth on the concrete, Jim swings a hard overhead right into a battered nose putting a period on the sentence. The big man hits the ground never moving. A couple buddies drag him to the side bleeding from several sources.

The crowd stands but remains silent for several seconds witnessing what a trained fighter can do to a tough amateur. Ted starts clapping and several more cops join him. Jim didn't hear anything at this juncture. His focus is intense and hopes the next guy has more fight in him. The man does.

To his surprise the man has taken the cowboy boots off and kicking the air, a trained sense of authority and bare feet. Jim has worked out with martial art guys many times and knew it could be difficult if the biker combines a good skill set and large size. He will not go headlong into those tree trunk fitted feet if he could avoid it.

The two circle the human ring sizing each other up. A fake move by a right hand fools Jim and he gets hit in the thigh by a large foot. Screams erupt from the Hells Angels. It didn't hurt Jim, but made him more determined. Two fast jabs find the mark cutting the biker's cheek, courtesy of a large ring from Slick's Pawnshop. The big man gets mad and heads straight into a heavy right hand blowing up his eye. Jim quickly follows with four shots to his chin and chest. Blind on his right side by a swelling eye, the biker gets a lucky right hand to Jim's throat in a moment of retreat. He rushes Jim, grabs his shoulder and knees Jim's kidneys. Jim hits him hard on the chin whirling around.

The fight ends when Jim hits the biker across the bridge of the nose followed closely with a hook to his remaining good eye. Five straight punches to the face falls him like a redwood tree. Jim stands over the limp body and spits on it. He heads back to the GTO satisfied.

Ted walks to a Hells Angel jacket lying on the ground and picks it up. He points to the back of the jacket and the in scripted "HELLS ANGELS" screaming, "You fuckers not only can't fight but are stupid too; there should be an apostrophe between Hell and the S."

He throws the jacket down next to the sleeping biker and walks away.

CHAPTER TEN

Midnight Hour

JIM FLOORS THE accelerator on the GTO screeching away from the parking lot. The 389 engine quickly moves the car down the curving road toward 'The Booty Trap'. His self-image parallels the muscle car; fast, tough, and not to be messed with. He looks in the rearview mirror reflecting a swelling under his left eye. Another black eye worn with pride.

How many people walk into a Hells Angel's dive and call out two of the brotherhood? He did like Ted's lack of tact and direct sense of thought. Go in, shoot a hole in the roof and challenge the bikers at their own badass game. It worked perfectly. It also meant the crowd, real or imagined, stalking him got substantially larger. All those stalking individuals made him feel alive and his direction in life weaved a little closer to the edge of the abyss.

Janey works a shift at the club ending at midnight. Jim walks into the entrance and gets recognized immediately by security. Not only is Jim a regular, he's one of their own.

The stripclub goers and staff represent a subculture of dreams and make believe. Men, and the occasional woman, look at the naked bodies sliding across the wooden stage on five inch stiletto heels and dream about the black/red lace G-strings hanging at the end of their bed. Accompanying the lace is a wild-eyed Crystal, Mercedes, or Hanna lying next to them.

The dream is perpetuated by strippers working the room giving Bill, Randy, and Sam the misdirected thought of sex for a twenty dollar bill and a fist-full of ones. The dreams are often shared but seldom fulfilled. A number of the girls will facilitate the dream for the right amount of money, make believe always has a price.

Janey is not one of them. She started in the game trying to pay for college, but her degree in physiology isn't going to earn $2000 plus a week and much of it in cash.

Jim settles at the bar, gets a beer and an ice pack for his neck. It's starting to stiffen and getting cooled down helps the healing over the next couple of days. It also gets mothering from Janey and a rubdown even Houdini's magical hands would envy.

Janey comes off the stage and sees Jim sitting at the bar. Normally she pays little attention to him other than a smile handed out at a distance. Management discourages fraternizing for the obvious effect on paying customers, the same clients Janey depends on to pay her bills. But the ice pack is too much to ignore and she comes to his side curious about the source for treatment.

"What happened to my baby?" She asks rubbing his back.

"Wayne was put in the hospital by two bikers, went to see them to exchange e-mail addresses." He answers in the typical sarcastic style.

"How bad is he hurt?" Janey inquires, a genuine interest.

"Both were lying on the ground bleeding when I left…didn't stick around to see." Jim couldn't resist the perfectly teed-up question.

"Okay smart-ass, you know I'm talking about Wayne." She states as a matter-of-fact.

"Sorry, Wayne's not doing well…in a drug-induced coma. I'm going to the hospital tomorrow to check on him." Jim relays sincerely.

"Like some company?" She asks.

"I'll get your perfect ass up in the morning, maybe do lunch afterward?" He confirms.

"You're on… that neighbor of yours is sitting on the other side of the stage…John something?"

"John David Glover is here?" He asks. "Where?"

"Over there," Janey points to a far couch. "What does he do for a living…he's throwing around a lot of cash?"

"He's a pharmacist… didn't think he'd toss any of it around, but what the hell do I know?" Jim explains.

Janey turns back to Jim and puts her hand on the side of his face. "Could you use a massage?"

"Thought you'd never ask… can't be too soon." He confirms.

"See you at my house at 12:30… got to earn a living." She walks away.

Jim takes his beer and ice pack toward JDG and sees him getting a drink from the waitress. He pays her cash and she leaves before Jim can circle the stage to talk with his neighbor.

"John David, what are you doing on this side of the tracks?" He inquires.

"You mentioned this interesting place a few weeks ago, thought I would check it out. Nice looking ladies… isn't your girlfriend in the corner?" JD summarizes.

"That's Janey… beautiful isn't she?" Jim solicits.

"That she is… buy you a beer?" JD offers.

"Sure," Jim agrees. "Did your ladder stay put since the other night?"

"Really weird at best," JD admits. "Anything missing from your house?" He motions for the waitress to bring another round.

"Nothing... probably a couple neighborhood kids trying to get into trouble." Jim states in a hopeful manner.

"What happened to your eye?" JD lowers his head to obtain a better view of Jim's expanding eyelid.

"Nothing unusual, just part of playing like a P.I. Some people don't like the investigative process." Jim has little interest in letting the neighborhood self-proclaimed "Mayor" know all the details of his life.

"Speaking of neighborhood, my friend." JD lowers his voice as if someone cares to be part of the conversation. "Did you meet that hot chick in the '73 Mustang?"

"Seen her running up and down the road, but haven't met her yet."

Jim did have an interest, he could tell she's attractive and has a muscle car taste like him.

"I got her out of a speeding ticket the other day... one of the cops comes in the pharmacy to fill a prescription for his mother every month. Asked him to let one of my neighbors off the hook. Got a date next Friday." JD is proud of his daring move.

"Good on you big guy, let me know what she's like in the rack." Jim glances at his watch and turns the newly acquired beer upside down to finish it off. "I've got a date with a pair of magical hands... thanks for the beer."

JD offers his hand and Jim shakes it. Jim leaves the bar intent on experiencing magical hands.

Janey stands at the kitchen counter eating a salad topped with a chicken breast. She takes the job and her body seriously.

What she eats and her workout routine are important. A naked profile is the quickest full disclosure anyone can offer.

Jim comes into the kitchen and grabs a bite of chicken from the plate.

"You want a salad and chicken?" She offers.

He grabs her snug fitting jeans, the jeans creating many of those dreams. "No, didn't have chicken in mind."

Janey points to a doorway down the hall. "Go take those clothes off...get on my massage table. Be there in a minute."

Jim follows direction while Janey finishes the salad. She puts a bottle of body oil in the microwave and retrieves a bathroom towel. The microwave buzzer goes off; she wraps the oil in the towel and goes to the massage room.

Jim will never admit it, but the fights have taken a toll on his body and he's heading into a deep sleep by the time Janey drops the hot oil on his back. A reflex pulls his shoulders upward, the heat settling deep into the muscle tissue. It feels really bad and really good at the same time.

Her hands push the warm liquid downward to his buttocks and the air from his lungs release. Janey is good at a lot of things, and when she places her hands on a body she controls the soul.

The bruise on his lower back is getting blacker by the minute and Janey works around the tenderness like a skilled surgeon. She pushes the long fingers into his upper back then lowers them down to the spine and rounded cheeks muscled by countless hours of exercise. She leans over, gently kisses the bruised kidneys and her naked breasts touch his buttocks. Jim feels every move of her hands and body as she repeats the moves over and over. Each time her hands gain deeper traction and get lower on his torso and thighs.

Janey extends her tall, perfectly shaped naked frame to cover his body head-to-toe executing the deep tissue massage and in the process her skin absorbs the warm oil. Their bodies slide into a rhythm; part sexual, part medicinal, part pain, and part joy. The hurt didn't go away but his mind drifts above the soreness, the warmth and curves of her body grid and release one touch point in exchange for a different one.

She finishes the extended massage running her hands and fingers deep into his scalp and hair. It's a finish pushing Jim over the top; he buries his face deep into her breasts and they make love, oiled bodies sliding in rhythm all over the padded table's surface.

CHAPTER ELEVEN

Mind Blowing

DAVID SANDERS STARES at the ocean waves pounding the beach below the Benders' mansion from the swimming pool deck. The yellow tape surrounding the crime scene breaks loose from the crucifixion tree and whips in the wind. David's seen many murders in his police career but none came packaged this way. None ever happened to a friend, and certainly none under his watch and direct responsibility. The cop instincts are clouded with personal connections and shock, but the fog is rapidly clearing like the skies over Malibu in front of him now.

A jogger runs the beach directly below the property and David recognizes the neighbor two doors down. He whistles loudly gaining a hand wave from the man; David signals back and runs down to the beach to talk.

"Peter," David says slightly out-of-breath. "You're on the beach a lot; did you see anything or anybody three days ago out of the ordinary?"

"This is shocking, can't understand how anybody could hurt such a kind man. To answer your question, didn't see anything the day of the murder, but earlier in the week I was jogging... saw this guy walking north below our properties on the beach. Strange looking guy... had jeans on, didn't look like a lost beach comber to me. I called our security guys... they didn't find anybody." He responds.

David pulls out a small notebook. "Describe strange looking person for me."

"Well," Peter looks down the beach as if expecting the man to come into view. "Late twenties ... early thirties maybe, dark headed... looked like a gang member. Had rings through his ears. Tattoo on his neck, couldn't swear to it but it appeared to be a knife blade. Long sleeves, jeans, carrying his leather shoes... nothing beach related."

"What was he built like?" David questions.

"Large guy like you, six-one maybe six-two... well built." Peter responds.

"Did the cops question you about this guy?" David asks.

"Yeah," Peter confirms. "Told them the same thing."

"Thanks for your help." David starts back up the hill.

"When's the funeral?" Peter asks.

David turns around concentrating solely on Peter. "There's a memorial service this afternoon at St. Andrews Church, probably won't be a burial service for several more days pending the investigation."

Peter continues the beach run as David heads back to shower and dress for the Doctor's service. The front courtyard is filling with limos and celebrities from every pore of politics, law, medical, and Hollywood. This is normally a time of action for David revolving around the security of the compound and all the high profile visitors, but not anymore. He was fired by Cindy Benders less than 24 hours after the murder; David offered no excuses only remorse and humble apologies on his part. She was thinking the right way; regardless of the Doctor's direction concerning the gap in the security, he should have covered it. It mattered not David performed at the highest level for nine years; he failed at the most important juncture of his career and the man he admired is lying on a slab in the morgue.

Cindy always kept the help at a distance and David was not the exception. He could stay at the compound for one week to help the new security group get up to speed. David didn't want to stay that long but felt an obligation. It also allowed him to review the crime scene at length trying to reconstruct the murder trail before having to leave. He's determined not to let this event define his life and walking away before finding out whom and why.

He dresses quickly and leaves the ocean house before the wine-sipping crowd gets into their first round of caviar. The service is scheduled for 3:00, but this is L.A. and even death is fashionably made to wait. David goes to the service out of respect and see who might show up outside the usual suspects. His detective instincts are kicking in.

To David's surprise the crowd gathering for Dr. Benders' service has already gained a sizable population two hours before 3:00. Parking is getting tight and he finds one of the few spots left two blocks from the church. The church is a beautiful old structure built in what was the heart of the city more than eighty years ago. Now it's surrounded by run-down housing and many abandoned business buildings.

He retrieves his Nikon, attaches a long lens and sits in the car observing the crowd weaving in and out in their Bentleys, Mercedes, and BMWs. The local prostitutes probably ran off in a panic thinking new pimps are coming to beat on them observing the endless high-end cars park. The camera snaps off a few pictures, more for practice and focus than importance.

David gets out of the car and heads for the church down an alleyway intent on using his security I.D. to gain admittance from the back of the church and observe the crowd. Several uniform police and detectives monitor the crowd at each entrance and David is spotted by Detective Ted Fox trying to make his way past the security. David met Fox at the compound after the murder and gave him a statement.

"David Sanders, over here." Ted shouts above the crowd and motions to him.

David sees the beckoning motion. "Detective Fox, can you get me in this place without any hassle?"

"Sure can, follow me." Fox moves to the back entrance followed by David. "You still employed by the Benders' estate?"

They get inside to a relative quite area. "Not anymore, fired a couple of days ago."

Fox looks around for someone.

"Doesn't surprise me, the filthy rich and famous have short memories. My Captain wants to speak to you, stay here... it will save you a trip to the precinct."

Fox moves off into the inner workings of the church while David makes his way to the back of the church stage. He peeks out, the pews filling fast. It endorses the love for Dr. Benders but it could hide the killer in the sea of faces below.

Fox returns with Captain Ron Cyril, a lifer in the L.A. police ranks answering only to the Chief of Police. The case has far ranging implications, finding its way to the governor's office and back down quickly.

The Captain offers his hand, and David accepts it. "You handle the security for Dr. Benders I understand?"

"Did for nine years." David responds.

"Did you like the man?" The Captain inquires.

"It went way beyond a job...he was a friend. Brilliant mind, but never pretentious. Loved him." David confesses.

"Being an ex-cop, what's your gut telling you?" The Captain seems to be interested in David's opinion.

"He stepped on many toes, mainly because of his Christian beliefs... had a Muslin get into the compound shooting at the house. He was constantly being threatened on-line. Someone crucified him for those beliefs." David maintains.

Fox jumps in. "Actually he died from a blow to the head before being hammered to the tree."

Captain Cyril turns to Fox. "Keep your fucking mouth shut... better yet, get lost."

Fox does as instructed. Cyril turns his attention back to David. "No offense, but some information can't get out."

"Sir, I understand." David smoothly reverts to his old cop working days.

"Called your Captain in Denver...he spoke highly of you." Cyril explains. "I will leave no stone unturned to get those responsible. It looked bad for you surrounding the gap in security... the timing of the murder, but everything checks out.

"Captain Fisher is a good cop, great leader of men. He recommended me for the Benders' security job. I would never let either man down on purpose." David relays.

"So, what are your plans now... you going to play cop on this murder or go back to Colorado?" Cyril inquires.

"I can't leave until this thing is solved; Dr. Benders' blood is on my hands." David is being honest, although he didn't think the Captain wanted to hear it.

Captain Cyril looks David up and down as if sizing him up for a fight. "Don't blame you...I would do the same. But, you're a civilian so stay the hell out of my crime investigation in L.A. County. Do we understand one another?"

Captain Cyril is called from a distance and he turns toward the voice and motions with his hand. Turning back to David he repeats the question. "Do we have an understanding?"

David looks him straight in the eye. "Yes, Sir."

They part company neither man happy but both determined.

David moves to the balcony and pulls out a small set of binoculars not shocked over the demand Cyril laid out, he'd do the same if reversed. He watches the church fill to the point of standing room only and continually scans the crowd looking for someone or something out of the ordinary.

The service came and went without a hitch and even the pretty Hollywood crowd is on time. Cindy Benders sits in the front as the governor and mayor talk about the brilliant and complicated man Dr. Benders had been. She openly weeps when the Bishop calls him a man of God and a man of healing. Then it's over and the crowd slowly files out.

David makes his way back to the car packing away the camera and binoculars. The radio is turned on and he listens to rock music patiently. The parking lot is slow letting cars leave its confine in the traffic.

A man in his late twenties, fitting the description given by Dr. Benders' neighbor down to the tattoo on his neck walks by the car crossing the street. David jumps out, crosses the street behind him and follows for several blocks keeping the man in sight. The crowd is thinning next to nothing when the man finally stops a mile into the chase, unlocks the door of an old building and goes inside.

The building is a closed movie theater and David tries to open the front door but it's locked. An ear is placed on the door emitting no sound. He turns around and a tall, thin man giving off less than a pleasant odor places a hand in David's face, a key firmly gripped.

"You gonna' kill him?" The man asks.

David pulls back from the close encounter. "No, but you might get shot slipping up on people like that. Do you know this guy?"

"Met him once, he beat the hell out of me…took my home." The dirty man relays.

"That key opens this door?" David inquires.

"Yeah." The man slides the key into the lock, backs up and waits on David to open it.

David glances at the door and back to the street living man. "How did you get a key?"

The man points to a lock box mounted above the door. "I used to be in real estate."

David hesitates for a moment thinking his options through. He knows the tattooed guy could be involved and dangerous, but didn't really have enough to call the cops to do his bidding and been warned to stay out of the game.

He looks over at the ex-real estate agent. "Stay here."

With gun drawn, he moves inside the dark theater. David eases the door shut behind creating even more darkness. The air is thick choking on old buttered carpet. He doesn't move for several seconds letting his eyes acclimate and listens for any sound to give him a direction of action.

The outline of a glass counter where candy was once held for ransom begins to take shape and he can see an entrance on either side leading to the auditorium not showing a movie for thirty years.

David takes the left entrance and the short hallway actually gets a little brighter moving down the passage coming out at the foot of the large screen. The source of light is a broken window above an exit door.

David concentrates on the rows of lifeless chairs neatly spaced. Nothing indicates anyone's been in or out in decades. Instinct begs him to leave, but his guilt feelings out vote his commonsense. A walk up the steps toward the projector room reveals no bad man lying in wait hidden in a row of seats to jump out at him.

He aims the gun into the projector opening standing tall to see inside. Side-to-side he points the extended weapon but reality reflects nothing except an old desk mounted with a projector, several chairs and a large filing cabinet. Surprisingly the mounted projector is film loaded.

The door is opened and the room becomes claustrophobic. Easing in, David sees a set of steps leading downward at the side of the small room and moves over to the doorway to listen. Nothing can be seen or heard from the bottom of those black steps leading to God knows what. He eases onto the first step that drops six inches. In spite of extreme caution, he almost losses balance and falls deeply into the dark hole. The limit for adventure has been mentally reached and he turns around to leave.

He holsters his weapon, goes out of the projector room and starts down the theater steps next to the rows of chairs ready to get fresh air. After making his way to the bottom of the steps, the boogie man rises from the darkness between the seat rows and hits David on the side of the head using a wooden leg previously ripped off a chair. David crumbles to the steps knocked out for more than three minutes.

When he comes around his hands are tied to an aisle seat and a blurry figure stands close by. The heavy smell of body odor tells David the homeless real estate agent is staring at him before his eyes can focus to confirm. A movie is being played across the big screen behind him that David can't get his senses around. He's tied to a seat not seeing an ass in thirty years watching a wave of light bounce off the walls exposing more than a foul stench standing next to him.

"Are you fucking crazy, untie me before you spend the next couple of years in jail?" David demands.

"You ain't no cop…looked at your I.D. A stupid P.I. fucking around in my house." The man outlines the bottom line truth.

David shakes his head. "I'm working on a big murder case with Captain Cyril of the L.A. police department. Untie me now; this is way over your head.

The man gets down in David's face. "Shut the fuck up… know who you are, but you have no idea who I am."

"Who are you?" A simple question posed by David.

The man laughs. "You walked into hell; I'm the gatekeeper." A simple answer.

David realizes this is not going to end well confronting a sick-in-the-head homeless man standing over his helpless body and his gun missing. Before another word can be spewed trying to talk his way out of the bag, the man pulls out a .38 and pops the six bullets from the cylinder into his hand. David is going to be the centerpiece of hell's entertainment guide.

The man puts one bullet back into a chamber and rolls the cylinder down his arm and flips it into the pistol. The move looks practiced.

"Ever heard of 'The Price is Right' Roulette'?" The man asks knowing the answer is no.

"Look, I've got a couple hundred bucks in my wallet… take it… leave." David senses a real piece of trouble standing in front of him.

The man's expression draws the skin around his face so tight he appears to change into something else. The voice deepens beyond the human pale, and for a moment David thinks he's watching a low budget horror film.

"Are you naïve or plain stupid…this isn't about money?" The deep voice bellows bouncing off the theater walls returning in a more frightening octave than when it left whatever strange is standing in front of David. The man's contorted face and voice decompresses into somewhat a normal look/sound and he talks like a next door neighbor borrowing a cup of sugar.

"We each pick a number...one to six. I'll start...you're the guest." The man puts his finger to his chin as if contemplating the choice of an ice cream flavor at Baskin Robbins. "Three is my number," he proclaims. "The right foot is one, the left foot two. The last number is always your temple."

The man aims the pistol at the middle of his right foot and pulls the trigger. It clicks harmlessly on an empty chamber. The gun is pointed at his left foot and explodes firing the bullet through his shoe. The sound rockets off the walls making David fall back into the seat, all his senses stunned.

The man barely grimaces over the shattered foot pointing the gun at his temple pulling the trigger on a chamber obviously empty. David is starting to see where the game is headed and his body is sweating profusely in anticipation. The higher the number taken, the less likely you get a bullet to the head but it increases the opportunity to blow a limb off. The man places a bullet in the chamber rolling it down his arm and then closed.

"Your turn," the man calmly relays. "Give me a number."

"Let's talk this out together, maybe I can deliver something you want?" David negotiates.

The stink gets close to David's ear. "One more misplaced word will get your head blown off."

David now realizes there's only one way out of this... playing the game.

"May I ask a question about the game?" He relays hopefully.

"Sure." A strangely kind voice answers instead of a bullet.

"What happens if I choose five or six?" David meekly asks.

The pistol is leaned against his shoulder to remind David who is in control. "Right foot, left foot, right knee, left knee." There's a slight hesitation in the man's speech, he leans over pointing the pistol at David's crouch. "Your balls are number five."

David's thoughts are not exactly cohesive at this point, but the strategy is obvious to buy time and pray the other guy blows his own brains out first. His eyes circle the emptiness wondering how he could die for so little. A survivor of several shootouts in his time on the force, this dark hole seems like a place for a rat to perish not a human being. The stink man brings him out of the self-pity by cocking the hammer back on the gun and placing it in his ear.

With no time left to think, he blurts out "three".

The gatekeeper points the weapon at David's right foot and pulls the trigger. David hears the click hiding behind closed eyes right before the trigger is squeezed off. The second round follows with the same result, an empty ping of the hammer. Now David is shaking, staring at a one-in-four chance he'll be dead in the next few seconds.

A large grin gets close to David's face and the pistol is placed on his temple. A gunshot blast bounces off the walls splattering brain matter on David's face. He slumps down in the chair for a few seconds, senses overpowered and blood covering his face and shirt. It takes a few more seconds to realize his head is still intact and the gatekeeper is lying against his legs, dead from a gunshot to the back of his head.

David looks up to see the neck tattooed man standing over him, a pistol in one hand and a knife in the other. He lowers the knife to David's hand and cuts him loose. Without a word spoken by either man, David's savior turns to run out the theater.

CHAPTER TWELVE

Aussie Accent

JIM TAKES THE tray full of breakfast to the sleeping Janey. For all his toughness and independence, Jim has a tenderness that endears him to the woman he focuses attention on. The breakfast is picked over and the two exchange thoughts on the parallel worlds they share, the same cast of characters good and bad. Many of the players Jim works around find their entertainment staring at the stage Janey strips on.

Both worlds have ugly. A year ago, a jealous boyfriend/cop beat one of the girls badly for flirting with a customer she is paid to flirt with. Jim's big brother instinct takes over and offers to even the score. Janey delivers the message to the girl but it's never acted on, four months later she's found dead in a dumpster. Predictably, the murder is never solved.

One of the things endearing about Janey is the ability to spend little time in front of a mirror applying make-up and still turn heads. That is Jim's thought watching her walk the hallway into the kitchen. Janey likes brand name clothes and dresses in black Michael Kors' short shorts and a red silk one-shoulder blouse. Her long legs end in a pair of Jimmy Choo stiletto heels.

Jim lets out a whistle of admiration. "Damn, you can make a gay man straight."

"Funny you should mention, several gay guys come in the club on Tuesday nights." Janey replies.

"What for?" Jim asks in a genuine questioning voice.

"Not sure, I believe it's a fashion thing. Seem to be more interested in what the girls are wearing between sets than what's happening on the stage. The food may have something to do with it." She responds.

"Do they drop any decent money on the girls?" Jim is trying to figure out the angle.

"You did say I can make a gay man straight." Janey winks.

"I'll take that as a no." Jim opens the door and walks Janey out the front door.

The GTO bellows its low throated muscle down the road toward the hospital to visit Wayne. It's a temperature perfect Sunday morning in Southern California and the ride is soaked in conversation and sunshine.

Janey turns to Jim. "So what are the plans this afternoon, cowboy?"

"Got a text from Rollie, he invited us to a late lunch and some of his sushi crowd. Thought it might be entertaining." He looks at Janey for approval.

"I could go for sushi…beautiful day to watch the waves roll in on Malibu." She confirms.

The hospital is made and they take the elevator to the third floor to see Wayne. Jim and Wayne have not conversed since the thugs brutalized him, and Jim is anxious to catch him up on the world he left during a few coma induced days.

The head nurse looks tougher than the Hells Angels Jim fought. She relays Wayne can't be seen for a couple more days. The patient is pumped up on numerous drugs to counter the induced coma and bring him back from the edge of death. Jim will come back to see him lucid and cover the Hells Angel crew revenge.

The hospital visit is disappointing, but Jim's character never dwells on negatives too long. The GTO is pointed back to the house so that Jim can feed and walk Winston before going to Rollie's. Winston cares less about Jim but rolls over instantly to let Janey rub his belly and she complies.

"You are truly all man." Janey states, fixated on knowledge escaping Jim's thoughts.

He pulls the dog food from the closet, puts it in a bowl and adds water. After setting it on the kitchen floor he confronts Janey.

"What do you mean all man?" Jim retorts. "That dog is the laziest creature I've ever been around."

"Didn't intend to insult your manhood… trying to encourage his." Janey counters. "Besides, when it comes to a rubdown… you roll over at the slightest hint it may be coming just like Winston."

"It's hard to argue with that statement I must admit." Jim's honestly flips his man card face down. "But I'm different than Winston, his manhood is challenged twice a day… he flunks every time. Someone stuck a damn ladder up to my bedroom window… probably ran throughout the house. Winston didn't move his ass off the couch, probably watching the Lakers."

"Lakers, no wonder he rolls over on his back. That's not a man's team." Janey lays down the gauntlet. "Boston… that's a man's team."

"Celtics… getting old… old as the Lakers." Jim smiles. "Don't think either team has another run any time soon."

Jim pulls Winston's large leash from a drawer and hooks it around the massive neck.

"Alright, tiger, let's hit the pavement for fifteen or twenty good yards." Jim has to tug Winston away from Janey's attention.

The trio heads out the door and parked in front of John David's house is the classic Mustang. Jim reflects on the conversation over a beer the previous night and his impending date with the blond. JDG is moving at light speed it appeared to Jim headed for the sidewalk.

Motion in JDG's backyard turns out to be the blond and John David walking across the yard in their direction. JDG waves and Jim returns the gesture.

The couple moves closer and the blond doesn't disappoint his high standards. Jim is taken back by her stunning look. Tall, shoulder length hair and a natural curl compliments a figure nothing short of stunning. A woman getting more beautiful each step closer is rare and not lost on Jim's senses.

Janey, working in the body industry, sizes her up from a different point-of-view. She admires the package from a stage perspective.

The blond heads straight to Jim and extends her hand. "I'm Deb Sweeney." The words drift off lips in a silky-sweet Aussie accent completing the sexy.

Jim takes her hand like a delicate bird pulled from the nest. He's lost in the green eyes and accent for a few seconds. "Pleasure to meet you, this is Janey Shaw... I'm Jim Cirmah."

Janey extends her hand and the two women briefly shake.

"Love your Mustang...'73?" Jim asks.

Deb quickly moves her attention back to Jim. "Yeah it's a '73, your GTO is sweet... what year is it?"

"'68, it flat hauls ass." Janey beats Jim to the answer, protecting her turf.

John David jumps in. "I once owned a '76 Pinto, does that count?"

The other three laugh at the obvious muscle car fan club only Jim and Deb belong to.

"If you owned it now, it would qualify." Jim retorts trying to include JD in the group.

"Something tells me the Pinto's gone in a blaze, the gas tank stupidly designed in the rear of the car. One bump from behind made for a really big bang. But hell, got me around for three years. Going to the movies, you guys want to join?" JD asks.

"We'll take a rain check, going to my bosses' house. Pleasure to meet you, Deb." Jim reaches out to shake Deb's hand and lays her hand in his. A flash of light shoots into Jim's head facilitated by her touch blocking his mind briefly. He stares into a black hole, reality dissipating.

Jim feels Janey's arm around his neck and finds himself twenty feet down the sidewalk Winston's leash in hand.

"Jim... Jim... you okay?" Janey's voice pierces the darkness and pulls Jim back to the light.

"That's strange... not sure what happened. Where did they go?" Jim's voice is like a child separated from his mother at the mall.

"You're scaring me." Janey looks closer in Jim's eyes. "The color left your face for a minute... we should take you to a doctor."

"I'm fine, really... no need to see anybody." Jim gathers his thoughts.

"That fight you had... maybe you got a concussion?" Janey hypothesizes.

"Be fine, just need to hydrate... ran six miles yesterday." It makes sense in theory, but he didn't believe it.

CHAPTER THIRTEEN

Art Party

JIM DRIVES THE GTO to Rollie's house slower than usual, a fact not lost on Janey. As she encourages him to get the fainting spell checked out, he drinks two bottles of water and starts to feel better. He thinks back to the contact with Deb but doesn't believe her touch has anything to do with it. It must be a timing thing. Maybe he shouldn't rid the world of two bikers at a time?

Her touch is not too bad. JD didn't walk around with any ill-effects. Slowly his mind drifts away from the mental lapses and more to her beauty and Aussie accent. He wondered what kind of bunkmate she would make by the time the GTO pulls up to Rollie's home in Malibu.

Rollie grew up in the tenants on the southside of Chicago with several generations of poverty to make up for. Like most having this kind of history, he became tough in the streets and it reflects in everything he does. What left his life is poverty. Slick's been in L.A. for thirty-one years and early in the pawn business he invested in small, single family homes to rent.

Now he owns more than sixty and the real estate values have sky rocketed over the years making his worth millions. Slick's home on the ocean took two years to complete and light years away from the struggles he endured in Chicago.

The GTO pulls inside a large courtyard surrounded by the house on two sides. The ocean is pounding the beach in the background.

Jim turns to Janey. "Time to slum it... think you can handle the inconvenience?"

"No real problem if Rollie has a bathroom." Janey answers getting out of the car.

Jim meets Janey at the front door. "Rollie only has eight or nine bathrooms, practically third world poverty."

"That's more bathrooms than most third world countries have." Janey is rarely out of a response.

Jim hits the doorbell. Soon the door opens and standing in front of them is Conrad carrying two Coronas fitted around a slice of lime.

Conrad leans forward sharing a secret. "Glad you're finally here... don't think I mingle very well in this crowd".

"Some jetsetter you'll turn out to be... bet none of them are drinking beer." Jim takes the beer from Conrad and the three walk to the pool area overlooking the Pacific.

"Over half of them own wine vineyards in Napa Valley... only Rollie has a beer." Conrad anoints Jim's blind observation.

"I guarantee Rollie has more money than any in this crowd." Jim surmises.

"None of them would be here if he didn't." Conrad's view of the pretty people isn't pretty.

"Guess we'll huddle in the corner drinking alone." Janey adds.

The walk to the open deck next to the pool quickly reveals expensive taste, and the ocean breeze blows into their faces.

Rollie sees them arrive and immediately walks over with a tall man in his fifties by his side. Jim guesses attorney as the two approach.

Slick extends his hand and introduces the man to the group. Turns out Jim is wrong. "Janey...Jim meet Walter Banes, Walter's an art dealer that keeps robbing me when I get a piece of art on occasion."

"Rollie tells me you're the best P.I. he's ever dealt with." Walter shakes Jim's hand.

"Think what Rollie means is I'm crazier than most of the P.I.'s he knows." Jim retorts.

"Takes crazy to do the kind of things we do." Rollie offers up the truth.

"May I have your card?" Walter asks. "My company needs a good P.I. from time-to-time."

Jim and Walter exchange business cards, a plate of quail and salmon is offered to the group.

"Speaking of art, why don't you show Janey your private stock?" Jim asks Rollie.

"Sure, follow me." Rollie complies.

The group moves to a hallway that goes on forever and eventually ending in a master bedroom. Rollie hits a keypad and a heavy metal door opens to a large vault-like room filled with extremely valuable art.

Everyone enters the art room, and Rollie takes pride in telling the story behind the twenty plus paintings adorning the walls. Walter fills in historical background on the negotiations taking place to obtain the paintings. It's obvious even to the uneducated eyes in the room the collection represents millions of dollars.

Rollie loves sharing his passion and smiles broadly talking about his collection and sharing floor time to Walter giving the finer details.

Their steps are retraced to the pool deck to get another beer and watch the waves roll-in when Rollie's cell phone rings. He retreats inside the kitchen taking the call and soon returns carrying a haggard expression.

"What's wrong, Rollie?" Jim reads the distress.

"Remember Raymond Dupree? You collared him last year." Rollie answers with a question.

"Yeah, the idiot hit the same Bank of America branch three times." A smile from Jim accompanies the answer. "Dupree's marble never makes the full loop in his head."

"He jumped a $55,000 bail... we need to collar him again." Rollie looks at the crowded party not wanting business to raise its ugly head today.

"Not a big problem, I'll have him back in custody long before daylight." Jim brags.

"I like a quiet confident man." Walter challenging says, "I've got a thousand dollars says you can't get this guy before noon tomorrow."

Jim retrieves five hundred from his wallet and hands it over to Rollie. "Don't have a thousand, but five hundred will do if you give me some odds? Rollie holds the cash."

"Fair enough," Walter pulls out fifteen hundred and hands it to Rollie. "Three-to-one odds."

"I like it," Jim shakes Walter's hand. "Noon tomorrow that Cajun is back in jail. Right now I want to take a walk with this beautiful woman on the beach...drink another beer. Plenty of time to bag Mr. Dupree."

Janey and Jim walk to the beach. She shows concern for his bet.

"You seem awful confident about getting this guy."

"Don't worry lover," Jim picks up a rock and throws it into the ocean. "Dupree is a complete creature of habit, I know where he'll be tonight."

Jim hits Conrad on his cell. "Conrad, do you know where Johnny's Junkyard is on Washington Street?"

"Not really." Conrad stands by the pool, phone in hand.

"It's about a mile down on Washington from the Mexican restaurant you like so much... same side of the street." Jim relays.

"Mary's Mexican?" Conrad guesses.

"That's it." Jim confirms. "Be there at 9:00 tonight... bring your new gun."

Jim and Janey walk the beach hand-in-hand, hardly a soul in sight in either direction. The sun leans toward the west ready to make the plunge into the Pacific shortly, giving Jim an opportunity to focus on Janey. Not a moment of thought is wasted on the Cajun Dupree and his capture.

CHAPTER FOURTEEN

Worthless Dog

WINSTON SITS IN the front seat of the GTO, his labored breathing not to be blamed on any form of exertion. Jim looks at the dog and back to his watch indicating five after nine. Being a time freak is tough on Jim, everybody in SoCal is accustom to late but him.

A blanket is spread over the seat to protect the car from Winston's inadvertent mess. Jim can't stand to see his GTO being abused even if the blanket is catching it. His fingers move over the phone keys texting a simple question: "Where are you?" Within a few seconds a text comes back: "Be there in two minutes."

Jim gets out of the car and retrieves a bulletproof vest wrapped it around his chest and secured it. Winston lies down on the seat, illustrating less than an attentive attitude. Jim glances at the junkyard across the road but no motion meets his vision. Conrad pulls up next to the GTO and gets out.

Jim moves quickly to Conrad handing him a vest. "Keep the talk low... put this on." Conrad does as directed. Jim pulls Winston out of the car and puts a leash on him.

"Why did you bring Winston?" Conrad questions.

"Last time I caught Dupree in the junkyard spent half the night searching car-to-car... I'm hoping Winston uses that big nose of his to hasten the process."

"I admire your optimism." Conrad deadpans.

"He's here now... not going to leave him in my GTO to slobber all over it."

Jim hands Conrad a walkie-talkie. "Here's the plan, you drive around to a vacant lot behind the junkyard... you'll see a large drainage pipe behind the property. If I don't catch Dupree in the yard, he'll head for the pipe to escape."

"How do you know Dupree is here?" Conrad challenges.

"Total creature of habit, robbed the same bank three times... last time I cuffed him was here. Listen, have your gun ready but think before firing it. I don't want to slide down the drainage pipe just to get shot in the face. That's where I'll come out even if Dupree isn't in there." Jim stares hard into Conrad's eyes to make sure the message flew home.

"I'll be careful... you can trust me." Conrad assures.

Conrad drives away to the back of the yard as Jim pulls bolt cutters from the car. He and Winston move to the side of the junkyard away from traffic and the bolt cutters work through the chain fence quickly.

Jim stays low to the ground cutting wire and turns facing Winston inches from his face. "You need to earn your keep... don't want to be here all night." Winston licks his lips as if responding. "Don't go Ren and Stempy on me... I'll hide the TV remote for a month." Jim pushes Winston into the fence hole then leans down to crawl in. Much to his surprise Winston runs off into the yard, the leash in tow.

Jim gets under the fence not believing Winston did anything involving exercise without being coerced.

"What a mistake this is, damn it." Jim talks to himself out loud knowing he couldn't depend on Winston. Now he will have to find Dupree and the dog before leaving.

He quickly calls Conrad on the walkie talkie. "Look out for that stupid Winston... he ran off on me."

"This didn't start off good... I'll watch for him." Conrad responds.

While Jim meanders from car to car using a small flashlight, a card game is going on in the junkyard office. Five men that carry the word "savory characters" on their resumes are drinking and playing poker for rather large sums of money.

Lou, owner of the yard, throws his cards down on the table disgusted. "Can't stand anymore fucking good luck... deal me out."

Doug, an occasional visitor to these card games when not beating up prostitutes, lets out a laugh. "Serves you right, last time you took all our money."

Additional drinks flow to the table, the next hand is dealt. Lou takes the card beating and goes out a side door to smoke a cigarette on a fire escape overlooking the yard. A drag from the cigarette doesn't calm his nerves; he's down four thousand in the last couple of hours. Lou stares into the night when a flash of light catches his attention; it's Jim moving in and out of the car piles flashlight in hand.

Lou rushes back inside to alert the others. "Hey, we've got company running around in the yard." Lou moves over to a stand of lockers, pulling down rifles he throws to the other men. "No one messes with my precious metals."

All five fully armed men head to the fire escape scanning the yard for movement. Doug looks deep into the dark night. "You want me to let the dog out?"

"Not yet, idiot," Lou rudely responds. "Let's have some fun first…don't think whoever is roaming around knows we're here. Besides, don't want you expert marksmen to kill my Doberman blasting away the darkness."

Dupree lays sleeping in the backseat of an old car under a jacket. Sitting in the front seat staring down on him is Winston. Dupree senses the dog's presence and sits up staring back at Winston. The dog rolls his large tongue in the air licking out a message and Dupree smiles.

"Are you hungry, big dog?" Dupree asks the question in a heavy Cajun accent, then reaches for a sack containing two, foot-long subs on the floorboard. He peels away the paper and puts half a sandwich close to Winston's mouth. Winston immediately does what he does best, eats.

"You are good dog." Dupree states picking up a beer and chewing on the other half of the sandwich.

Winston makes short work of the sub and peers intently at the beer licking the air.

"You want beer, big guy?" Dupree moves closer to Winston and leans the beer to the upturned mouth. The dog complies opening his mouth and licking the beer being poured into the endless pit. "You my kind of dog." The Cajun spouts emptying the beer can.

Jim leans on a car and takes the radio out. "Conrad, you copy?"

"I'm here." Conrad's voice pops out of the radio.

"See anything?" Jim inquires.

"All clear on the western pipe front." He confirms.

"Stay alert, Dupree is here… I can smell him."

Jim puts the radio back in his pocket and moves deeper into the car graveyard, automatic weapons open up from the fire escape spraying bullets all around. Jim dives behind a car, a hail of bullets gouge holes in the wreck next to him.

"Damn, that's an AK 47." Jim says out loud hugging the ground. The phone buzzes and he works it out of his pocket.

"You okay." A visibly shaken voice from Conrad asks.

"So far... stay put, I'm working my way to the drain." Jim relays trying to figure the best way out of this mess. He's in the property illegally and whoever is shooting can blow his head off using any weapon of choice. Most people in this situation would panic, but his juices are flowing, fully engaged to the moment.

Dupree takes a big drink of his last beer in spite of the bullets flying all around. A look to the front seat sees Winston has left. A stray bullet blasts the windshield hitting only inches from his head. The backdoor is opened and he starts crawling under vehicles avoiding the fire.

Jim takes note of where the shooting is originating and moves in a wide circle to outflank the line of fire to his left. Steady progress for the goal of the drainpipe is made between car piles.

Dupree makes it to the large drainage pipe first and picks up the grate blocking the entrance. He disappears into the hole sliding rapidly down the steep grade to the bottom of the pipe. He pokes his head out and is greeted by Conrad pointing a pistol at his face.

The five men run out of ammunition. Lou looks over at Doug. "Let Rocky out to clean this mess up."

Doug heads downstairs to open a holding pen containing a Doberman jumping up and down excited to do his job. He releases Rocky into the yard and the dog let's everyone know he's coming.

Jim hears the dog barking, getting closer rapidly. With the shooting stopped, he decides to run straight to the drainage pipe. Rocky closes in at the same time he gets to the entrance. A brief hesitation to lift the heavy grate has Rocky zeroed in on Jim's rear end. Only a few feet away and ready to pounce, Rocky doesn't notice Winston bolting out of the dark. Winston viciously attacks the Doberman.

Jim turns around stunned about Winston's actions and lays a kick to the retreating Doberman. He shoves Winston into the pipe and both slide down rapidly out of control, Jim holding Winston in his lap. At the end of the pipe they fall into a muddy pool of water drenched. Winston doesn't seem to mind but Jim stands up trying to wipe the mud off his clothes. Conrad and a handcuffed Dupree watch the futile attempts to clean the mud off. Jim looks at his soaked jeans and starts laughing at himself along with Conrad.

"Glad I could be here to give everyone a good time." Jim recognizes the humor spotlight.

"I'm not having your good time." Dupree honestly relays.

"Shut-up, if you weren't worth fifty-five hundred bucks plus my bet, I'd shoot you." Jim looks at his pistol trying to knock the mud out of the barrel walking out of the water.

"Why are you bitching, the plan worked out to perfection?" Conrad states a great deal of truth.

Jim holsters his weapon and breaks into a wide grin. "Do I know this business or not?" Jim's last attempt to save face.

CHAPTER FIFTEEN

Face of Evil

DAVID SPENT THE last couple of nights since the theater run-in featuring the foul smelling homeless man enjoying little sleep. The incident rattled him beyond the obvious close-up look at death. He's confused. Reporting the man's demise or let the body be discovered is the question. His cop instincts demand a crime report to further the investigative process, but this will certainly drag him away from the Benders' investigation. He did nothing wrong in the man's death, however, the tattooed stranger's intervention opens an Alice and Wonderland rabbit hole.

The tattooed man added to his insomnia. Where did he come from and why did he save David's life? How did the dots connect? His mind races into the morning hours figuring every angle possible.

His time at the Benders' estate is coming to a close in two days, and he wants to maximize the access. Cindy Benders pays little attention to his movements, and when she left for the clinic he slipped into the Doctor's office going into his files. Nothing held any significance except a file titled "The Shroud" that stood out because it was empty. David recalled the file held data seeing notes on the Shroud scattered around the office from time-to-time. The file's emptiness triggers curiosity.

David powers up the Doctor's Mac hoping to get lucky. Benders typically used his birthday for a password, but no access occurs entering 12-01-48. He tries again using 1948, and even put the birthday in backwards but no results.

David leaves the office and returns to his computer in the apartment. This computer is connected to the Benders' Mac, interfacing both to the clinic's system. His Mac comes on and he makes a note of the computer I.D. number. Forensic investigation can recover data from a computer even when someone destroys the hard drive trying to cover-up a crime or communication. This forensic gaze into the computer's soul can be done remotely using the I.D. number provided the right talent is looking into the system.

The best lead for David is the tattooed man and the last place to see him was the theater. He drives to L.A. staking out the theater entrance less than a block away. A temptation to break-in the rear door and perhaps flush out the man of mystery tugs at his thoughts. It could prove dangerous, a body might still be lying on the second row of seats waiting to reintroduce itself.

Two hours into the stakeout nothing but strangers scurry past the old movie vessel. David leaves to buy a burrito and Coke but soon returns to the monotony. Another hour crawls by when an idea comes to mind. Call Detective Fox and mention the tattooed man at the Doctor's service, the same guy sighted in the neighborhood before the murder.

Perhaps Detective Fox will give him something to facilitate the dot-connecting?

A look at the theater and empty sidewalk moves his hand to get Fox's card. He makes the call.

"Detective Fox." The phone echoes while using the speaker setting on the car seat.

"Sanders here," David states. "May have something for you concerning the murder."

"All ears, we could use a break," Fox answers.

"A couple days after the killing, I talked to neighbors that saw a late twenties, long knife tattooed guy walking behind the house. The guy was at the Doctor's service but I lost him in the crowd." David profiles the events.

"Think we have your guy in custody... picked him up early this morning but he ain't talking. Come on down... see if he's the same guy you saw." Fox surprises David surrounding the turn of events.

"Be there shortly." David hangs up the phone, a smile on his face and drives to police headquarters.

Fox seems to be more pliable than his boss by extending out to David. Of course he could I.D. a suspect, maybe this cooperation is short lived? David walks the police station hallway, desperately wanting to interview the man but having little chance in his mind.

Fox is sitting at a desk surrounded by several officers on phones. It seems chaotic because it is, and David gets a rush of energy falling back to his days on the force. A homicide detective spends hours marred in pursuit of the mundane and often worthless bits of information. It oozes frustration and delivers many to booze or drugs to muster the patience chasing the bottom-line truth of the case. The high/low of the hunt never leaves or arrives without a fight.

Fox sees David's arrival, soon gets off the phone and approaches. "Sanders, our guy's been here for hours, not a word spoken. Follow me."

The two men go deeper into the bowels of the jail getting to a small room. A one-way window looks into an interrogation room. The knife-bladed tattooed man sits at a barren table starring off into the distance completely detached from his surroundings.

David moves to the window and has no doubt this guy saved his life in the theater. "That's him," David pronounces. "Where did you find the man?"

Fox gets closer to the window next to David, looks at the guy and turns back to answer the question. "A random black and white patrol found him sitting in an alley next to the bodies of a hooker and man that's probably her pimp."

"Bodies, what happen to them?" David asks.

"Both stabbed to death... the knife no more than three feet away. This crazy-assed dude is a couple feet away, legs folded like fricking 'Sitting Bull'."

"Didn't run...didn't resist, anything?" David tries to figure out the sequence but nothing makes sense.

"Nope," Fox says strongly, "hasn't uttered a word since they grabbed him. Ran his prints, nothing... he doesn't come up in the California Print Bureau or the FBI's data bank. But, his prints have been distorted by some type of chemical so that's not a shock. Probably has something to do with military service, maybe special Ops. We've booked him under John Doe. This is a strange one, brother...we get freakish dudes, but he's moving to the top quickly."

The tattooed man gets up slowly from the chair directing his attention to the one-way glass mirror. Both men take note and draw closer to the glass. He moves next to the glass cocking his head to one side looking at his own reflection like a parrot seeing another bird. The man pulls his head back slamming his face into the glass making David and Fox instinctively jump back. Blood explodes on the glass, the man's nose and cheekbones broken in a flash by the violent force of bulletproof glass meeting his face flush.

Neither Fox nor Sanders has a clue just how much of an understatement the term strange applies to the man bleeding all over the holding cell floor a few feet away.

CHAPTER SIXTEEN

The Job

JIM CIRMAH ARRIVES at the Pawnshop around 10:00 a.m. having washed away the mud from the previous night's fall down the drainpipe. Winston received a couple extra peanut butter laden pieces of toast this morning for his act of aggression saving Jim's rear being shredded by the Doberman. Jim swore never to belittle Winston's manhood again.

It was a good night financially for all being capped off by the fifteen hundred dollar bet won from the art dealer, Walter Banes. The money is always needed but bragging rights are even more special.

Drug Lord does his perpetual speech when Jim enters the Pawnshop, first saying "drop your weapon, hands up." The bird runs from one side of the perch to the other, a phone ringing in the cage. Jim likes the bird's antics and watching customers' reactions.

Conrad works the register paying little attention to Drug Lord, all sounds having been heard a thousand times.

"Profitable night," Conrad confirms as Jim approaches.

"Yes indeed, my son…I'm thinking about giving you $300 of the bet from Walter helping your regular commission." Jim ups the price for Conrad's help.

Conrad smiles. "Really, thanks a lot… that will buy me a new X-box."

"Save your money, Conrad, that's how your uncle does it." Jim offers advice.

The door opens and a well dressed man walks in carrying a briefcase. Drug Lord gives directions on putting his hands up and the stranger turns to retreat out the door. Jim runs after and stops him from getting into the car.

"Sorry about that… it's only a parrot thinking he's a cop… talks every time someone comes in the door." This isn't the only customer walking away from the store since Drug Lord's introduction, but Rollie didn't seem to mind.

"Thanks, it sounded real enough." The man confirms. Both men reenter the shop.

Jim heads for the shooting range while the man walks over to Conrad.

Conrad yells to Jim. "Jim, this gentleman wants to speak to you."

Jim circles back for introductions. "I'm Steve Hopkins… my employer has an interest in working with you."

Both shake hands. "Jim Cirmah, who's your employer?"

"The Benders' Institute… we're a DNA research hospital created by Dr. Royce Benders."

"THE Dr. Benders, murdered a few weeks ago?" Jim asks.

"Yes, unfortunately Dr. Benders has been taken from us," Steve answers.

"You want me to investigate his death?" Jim likes the idea of looking into such a high profile case.

"That remains to be discussed… can we talk in private?" Steve insists.

"Follow me." Jim takes Steve to the briefing room Rollie uses to discuss bail jumpers.

Steve hands Jim a business card taking a seat in the room.

"You're an attorney?" Jim asks.

"That's my educational background; I'm in-house counsel for the Benders Institute." Steve answers.

"So, what do you guys need done?" Jim is ready to evaluate interest in the project.

"The Institute is looking for a Private Investigator, but it has nothing to do with Dr. Benders' death." Steve reaches into his briefcase and pulls out a file he opens. "There's an interview process to determine who gets the job."

Jim is not sure where this is headed so he goes in for the kill. "What does the job pay?"

Steve looks up from his papers. "As much as $39,000 plus expenses... it shouldn't take more than a couple of weeks to complete."

"That amount has peaked my curiosity. Tell me more." Jim's never done a job for that much money.

"Could you answer a few personal questions?" Steve pulls out a pen in anticipation.

"For that kind of money I'll kiss your dog." Jim's inner child can't be hidden away for long.

"Are you a religious person?" Steve asks.

"Yeah, I'm a Cub's fan... leads to a lot of prayer sessions."

Steve looks at Jim not amused. "I'll put down no. Do you drink or take drugs?"

"I answered already, I'm a Cub's fan... comes with addicting habits to cope. What the hell does this have to do with investigating...FYI: I'm a damn good P.I." Jim seems less interested as the interview progresses.

"Mr. Cirmah, I don't set the parameters for the job, perhaps you should fill out the questionnaire seriously on your own?

The interview is 2:00 p.m. Monday at the Institute if you have an interest." Steve stands up getting ready to leave.

Jim shakes his hand. "I'll be there. For $39,000 I would sell a crucifix to the devil."

Steve quickly leaves the room, and Jim starts filling out the questionnaire.

CHAPTER SEVENTEEN

The Bullet That Binds

SEPTEMBER 24, 2012 is an unusually hot and humid day in northeast Afghanistan in spite of the mountain elevation. Joe Tramazzo looks through the high resolution 8 x 32 scope at the village below searching for a specific target to remove from the war. A Taliban official has been terrorizing neighboring villages and playing havoc with U.S. politics in the region.

Sweat runs down his back and off his brow as the intensity builds surrounding the military objective. His body reacts the same way every time he pulls the trigger on the .50 caliber rifle that can penetrate back-to-back concrete blocks more than a mile away.

His spotter, Dan, crouches low next to Joe sighting a set of binoculars perusing the dusty village pathways looking for Mr. Wrong. Dan Peters and Joe Tramazzo have been a Navy Seal sniper team for three tours in country successfully dealing out death in a single shot twenty-six times. A single shot taken from several thousand feet aimed at the sternum delivering a bullet entering the body one-half inch in diameter coming out the other side creating a hole the size of a grapefruit.

It's not a game of chance but a calculated mathematical formula administered like the precision of a surgeon. Surgical doesn't do Joe's abilities justice, he's missed one kill shot in three years and that target was moving in a closed vehicle more than a thousand meters away.

"Target is smoking a cigarette northeast of the water well… confirm your sighting." Dan relays without taking his eyes away from the binoculars.

Joe moves the rifle scope ten degrees to his left, locates the well and soon the target. The team goes into a countdown mode that eliminates most of the chance surrounding the shot.

Dan: "11 degree slope."

Joe: "Check."

Dan: "Distance… 2054 meters."

Joe: "Check."

Dan: "Please adjust the distance for elevation change -205 meters."

Joe: "Check."

Dan: "Wind south by southwest six miles per hour."

Joe: "Check."

Dan: "Fire when ready."

Joe: "Prepared to fire."

Joe heard a voice in his head long before he became a Navy Seal Expert sniper. The voice intensified since getting the nickname 'Grim Reaper' by his fellow Seals that spread to the Afghan countryside. To Joe the haunting nickname didn't have a foundation even though he's an arbiter of life or death. He's doing a job killing military combatants that would kill him or his fellow servicemen without the slightest hesitation. As Joe tightens the pressure on the trigger seconds before pulling it, the voice rifles through his head: "Joe, don't shoot the child."

Joe listens intently to the voice's frightening prediction and his finger moves away from the trigger.

Dan makes a prediction of his own. "We're going to lose him if you don't fire."

Joe refocuses the weapon on the cigarette smoking man squeezing off the .50 cal round and the voice returns: "Don't kill the child."

The bullet strikes the center of the man's chest killing him instantly. It passes through his body into a six-year old boy stepping into the line of fire behind the target. The voice tells the truth, the small, lifeless body is surrounded by relatives screaming in pain.

Dan gets up tapping Joe on the head.

"We have to go now, Joe, right now."

The two are extracted three hours later and Joe hears the jaded voice preach the sermon of his non-faith for his listening infidelity.

The team goes on several more missions but Joe pulls the trigger only once, mysteriously missing the target. The talk is intense about the killing of the boy and the voice warning Joe.

Navy Seals are hardened professionals living the toughest military training process in the world to prove elite status and any sign of weakness is frowned on at every level. Dan didn't want to hear about voices; hell, his demons inside talked to him constantly. Suck it up, be a man and do the job you're assigned to. Joe never felt so alone in his life, trying to serve two masters can justify the term "crazy." One of those two masters had to go.

Joe is out of the military eleven months later returning to civilian life troubled like many veterans having walked in and out of Hell's gates. The voice in his head didn't remain silent, giving him directions from time-to-time. V.A. doctors tell Joe it's a common complaint from solders coming home after serving in war zones. Joe knows the voice speaks the truth and will not disobey its directions again regardless what counselors and fellow war veterans say concerning "those sounds in your head."

Home is Southern California to Joe. He moves in with an ex-marine named David he knew from high school into a small but neat two bedroom condo. It's awkward at first; the ex-marine is a daily pot smoker and hates the military after two tours in Iraq. He bashes his country to anyone willing to listen.

Joe loves his country and can't stand cigarettes of any flavor. After weeks listening to the constant bitching, Joe picks David up and slams him to the floor. With a simple "Shut the fuck up about my country and smoke that shit in your room" firmly implanted in David's wide-open ear, they settle into a routine rather easily.

Joe rides a Harley to a large warehouse complex Walmart uses as a distribution center for a number of its retail outlets. Walmart has a work training program for veterans, and Joe's learning the nuances of running machines including giant forklifts. In route to work, Joe passes a quaint Catholic Church displaying a rose garden. He slows down to admire it every day. He grew up attending a Baptist Church but quit going as a teenager.

He stops on the way home and goes inside the church not sure why. As he walks down the worn wooden floor toward the front, the voice speaks to him: "Talk to the Father."

The church is virtually empty, only three people kneeling in various stages of prayer. It seems rather awkward to Joe sitting down in the pew glancing around. After a few minutes he moves to the front of the church searching for an entrance to the back of the building hoping to produce a priest. Two young choir boys walk out a door next to the stage to replace candles on the altar.

Joe approaches. "Can you tell me where I can find a priest?"

"I'll get Father Gentile for you." One of the boys replies and heads back through the door.

In a couple of minutes Father Gentile approaches Joe while the boy returns to his duties. "May I be of service to you?"

"Perhaps Father, but I must tell you I'm not a Catholic." Joe explains.

"Faith comes in many colors. I let God pick and choose the ones I listen to." The priest's voice is soothing to Joe's ears although he has no idea why.

"May I have a few minutes of your time?" Joe asks.

"Would a confessional make you feel more comfortable?" Gentile responds.

"That'd be great, thanks." Joe concurs.

The two men walk side-by-side to a small confessional room in the back of the church. Each could not be cut from a more different cloth, one a man trying to save lives/souls and one that tried to extinguish them. They settle into respective chairs, only a thin piece of black screen separating their voices and thoughts.

"My son, what troubles you?" The priest's voice drifts into the screen.

"I have done bad things in my life, Father, took many lives fighting for this country." Joe drops his head in shame.

"God judges us on where we end up in life not necessarily where we start... his forgiveness has no boundary." Father Gentile responds.

"Is it possible for God to talk directly to me... a voice in my head telling me what to do?" Joe continues.

"What do you think God is saying in your ear?" The priest asks.

Joe tells the story about the young Afghan boy and how he should get out of the Navy Seals for reasons unknown. The voice told him to stop at the church and communicate with a priest. "Is this possible," Joe asks. "Or perhaps I'm crazy like many lost souls, killing many in battle?"

Father Gentile remains silent for a few seconds deep in thought. "I don't know what to say giving you the truth of grace. God does speak to all of us in many indirect ways… if he's chosen you to speak directly to you, there's a cause of service none of us can understand."

"Thank you Father, I will see you this Sunday for sure." Joe breathes a sense of relief.

"Take God's blessing with you."

CHAPTER EIGHTEEN

Hell Hath Fury

JOE DIDN'T HEAR the definitive answer from Father Gentile about the voice giving directions but neither did he get the "monsters are in your head response" heard from others after sharing his innermost secret. The tiny church has an aura giving him warmth, something missing for a long time. He will follow this vein of hope to see where it leads.

He arrives home and David is piled on the couch, a large bag of Fritos in one hand and a bong in the other watching TV. When David sees Joe coming into the door, he immediately jumps up and carries the bong to his room leaving a trail of chips. Joe breaks out in a smile.

It's been a good day.

The next Sunday Joe attends church and the priest goes out of his way speaking to him after the service. For the next few weeks, he gains an inner peace going to the church and spends his days off working in the rose garden and doing needed repairs on the roof.

Father Gentile gets to know the troubled man who rides on his Harley and volunteers to help in any way the church needs. That inner peace is going to be turned inside-out when a stranger appears.

The strange man waves at Joe riding his bike to work from the church graveyard standing knee-deep in a newly dug grave. Joe waves back thinking it's someone he met at a recent service. He eyes the man from time-to-time, always in the graveyard digging a grave and waving at the passing Tramazzo.

Joe sits in a pew on Sunday, and when the service starts two hands grab his shoulders from behind. His military reflex tries to flip his way free of the hold and turn to face the aggressor now tightening the pressure around the neck. Joe comes close to blacking out when the grip is finally released and his breathing returns to normal.

The ability to move his body is taken away, only his eyes roll side-to-side and he sees a congregation and priest frozen in a fixed position, zero movement in the church.

The voice Joe heard all his life is standing beside him whispering in his ear, the breath of that speech falling on the side of his face. A voice that made one of the toughest soldiers in the world succumb to its wishes, now enters his life upfront and personal.

Joe has felt and witnessed fear few people ever experience, but his body now trembles in its helplessness. Forced to acknowledge the voice has a physical presence grips his sanity, and ultimately it has the right to dictate life and death. The voice speaks close to his ear, carrying the familiar smell of death hanging like a war scene mist around Joe's head.

"You have been a loyal soldier in my army, dealing death at my whim; for that a gift of everlasting life is yours. I'm trusting you on a mission of great importance, protecting and placing vengeance on any that will harm our master." The voice dictates.

The hands tilt Joe's head to the figure of Jesus on the cross behind the stationary priest. The cross inverts and Jesus is now upside down.

"Don't be confused by anything you see or hear from others. Our master is the Anti-Christ and your soul belongs to me. The kingdom you seek here doesn't accept into their gates the Grim Reaper. Both you and I dictate life and death; we've earned our Reaper status. There is no power like ours, and that stupid priest will feel the power today." The voice goes silent and the hands are released around his neck.

Motion returns to the room and Joe sees the priest raise his hands to the sky emphasizing a point to the congregation. Father Gentile falls to the floor experiencing a massive heart attack, dead before his body touches the wooden floor.

Joe's terrified of his own shadow the next couple of days. He reroutes his commute to work away from the church and hasn't slept from fear the last two nights. On Wednesday night, Joe finally falls to sleep from pure exhaustion and the aid of several sleeping pills. He sleeps until mid-afternoon, his boss asking him to work the third shift from midnight till 9:00 a.m.

Work starts out very intense with most of the large trucks being inventoried and loaded with product between 10:00 p.m. and 3:30 a.m. then dispatched to stores all over SoCal. Joe takes a break at 3:45, sipping on a cup of coffee and eating a frozen fruit drink concocted from bananas, apples, oranges, and celery. It's his power and energy source he is needing.

Joe returns to operating a forklift that can extend thirty feet into the air. He checks the loading manifest and repositions the forklift at a distant part of the warehouse to pull down a sporting goods shipment. The area is dimly lit compared to other parts of the warehouse, and he turns the headlights on to maneuver the narrow aisle. The forklift is extended to the twenty-five foot shelf when it happens.

"Go to the church immediately... it's death and life." The voice predicts.

Joe has never been afraid of anything in his life until the last three days and now he quivers at the directions in his head. The voice is specific but Joe didn't understand if he's in danger or someone at the church. That question is answered when he lowers the forklift and sees the outline of a woman's profile at the distant end of the aisle.

"It's coming for you, leave now." The voice didn't mix words.

As Joe lowers the forklift, twenty-feet of shelving loaded with tons of products starts to fall toward him, one shelf crashing into the next like a giant wall of dominos tilting over. Joe raises the forklift to its maximum height and when the wall hits the machine it knocks Joe onto the top of a shelf. Using his training to take punches, he rolls down the shelf and ends up against a walkway leading to a skylight.

Shots are fired beneath Joe and bullets are bouncing off the metal frame of the walkway. He reacts quickly, running across the walkway followed by a barrage of gunfire. A bullet shatters on the grillwork, shrapnel hitting the side of his face leaving a deep cut entering and exiting above his cheekbone. The right eye is hit and he losses vision on one side. The bullets stop flying temporarily and Joe knows someone is reloading their weapon. There is no time to figure out how to get the skylight mechanics working to open the window, so he throws himself into the glass and onto the roof. The glass cuts into his clothing, blood flows from numerous lacerations.

Joe is determined to get to the church regardless of the cost. A fire escape allows him descent to the ground and he runs to the bike starting the engine. In the background the tires of a car peeling across the parking lot heading in his direction shouts go. The bike's gear is engaged and he pushes the Harley to the max but the car gains ground.

The guarded front gate to the storage complex has a metal lift allowing entrance and exit; but Joe ignores the obstacle crashing through it. He hears the carburetor kick-in on the Mustang chasing him. Weaving in and out of traffic, he realizes it can't be outrun. Two shots whistle by his side reinforcing the idea that something drastic must be done to make the church and complete the mission's goal.

The Harley is topping 100 MPH but regardless of the speed, the Mustang inches closer.

He makes a decision of death and life by attempting to cut a corner sharper than the car can make. This will allow him to change directions and gain enough time to make the church. The bike is geared down and he leans into the turn with all his strength but the front wheel hits a small patch of sand and starts skidding on its side toward a parked truck. Joe hits the truck's rear bumper doing close to sixty and dies instantly.

Several police cars have lights flashing in front of the Walmart warehouse and Joe's supervisor, Chris Anderson, is being interviewed.

"What happened to cause Tramazzo to go off the deep end?" A cop asks Anderson.

"I don't know what tripped it. One of the guys working the same shift said he took the forklift… knocked down an entire shelf system of product then jumped out the skylight window. Crashed his bike through the front gate."

"Something must have precipitated that kind of reaction?" The cop asks.

"I checked the security video… happened just like he said. Several of the guys have expressed a concern about Joe… talked about voices in his head from time-to-time. He was in the special forces, which one I don't know because the State Department works with corporate to hire veterans and won't tell us. Nice guy... but the war must have been bad for him, complete nut job did this." Anderson gives his opinion.

"I'm going to need a copy of the video... we'll find him, get him some help. Anyone that's been in war deserves the help." The cop relays.

A second cop walks up. "Just got a call from the county sheriff... Tramazzo laid the bike down into the back of a truck. He's headed to the morgue."

CHAPTER NINETEEN

The Soul Man

JIM PULLS THE GTO into a parking space two hundred feet from the front entrance of the Benders Institute. Closer spaces are available, but he tries to protect the car from idiots using their vehicle to deface what he takes driving pride in. The rearview mirror helps him adjust the tie wrapped tightly on his neck, a purchase that Janey insisted he make for the interview. Jim never put one on before; he feels it brings a constraint like those the bulls wear at rodeos.

The jacket is also new and despite the loss of causal he craves, he enjoyed modeling for Janey at the store. She encouraged him to step up his dress code and even Rollie promoted the idea. Slick showed him how to tie the tie, now he wears a bit of pride in his appearance entering the Institute's door.

As Jim signs in at the front desk, four people sit around a board table file folders in front of them. Cindy Benders is head of the table. Behind her is a painting of the late Dr. Benders and a picture of the Lord's Last Supper.

Steve Hopkins hands out an additional file to the other three and returns to a chair. "Jim Cirmah is next, but I have reservations from his background."

Cindy looks at the file. "He comes highly recommended... seems to be the type of person we're looking for."

"I contacted an old colleague at FBI headquarters in D.C. ... he has a serious criminal past to consider. Spoke to him directly lining up the interview, wasn't impressed with his professionalism."

"This doesn't reflect in my report... what did he do?" Cindy asks.

"It wouldn't show up, he was a juvenile at the time... the information doesn't appear in normal channels." Steve continues.

"So, Steve Hopkins, what did he do, get a teenage girlfriend pregnant?" Cindy retorts sporting an attitude.

"At age thirteen, he killed his stepfather... sent to a juvenile detention center until his twentieth birthday. The charges were sealed because of his age... mother killed at a young age, even his sister committed suicide as a teenager. It all leads to a very unstable set of conditions." Steve fills in the blanks that on the surface paint a negative picture for Cirmah."

"Let's see, mother killed early in Jim's life... stepfather killed, sister commits suicide. Sounds like a whole lot of abuse on stepdad's part, including molestation on the daughter... I want to judge for myself. That said, William, what does the street have to say?" Cindy turns to William Bolensky, Chief of Security for the Institute and ex-County Sheriff for seventeen years.

"I talked to a number of bail bondsmen ... they rave about his ability to run people down and bring back in country or abroad. L.A. PD says he's tough but does things legally. He's rough around the edges from my personal standpoint." William lays additional information on the table.

Cindy stands up, a sign of her determination. "We're not looking for a stockbroker, I want to talk to him alone."

The other three stand up but Steve adds one more caveat to the discussion. "There are certain legal issues needing counsel present to discuss with Mr. Cirmah."

"Thanks for your legal advice, Steve, all duly noted… please leave gentlemen… have Mr. Cirmah join me." Cindy gives the final order.

All three men get up to leave the boardroom. Last at the door, Steve turns back to Cindy.

Cindy cuts him off. "It's alright Steve, I understand the legal issues well. You did your job, now let me do mine." Steve shuts the door.

Cindy walks to the portrait of Dr. Benders and opens a bar below his picture. She picks up a glass canister containing vodka and pours a drink. The glass is raised to her late husband. "My brilliant Doctor… give me strength to see all this through."

Jim opens the door as Cindy sips on the drink. She turns in his direction. "Mr. Cirmah, come in…join me in a drink?"

Jim approaches Cindy and she assumes the answer is yes. "Bourbon or vodka?"

"Bourbon." Jim answers, surprised at the less than formal interview expected but one he seems at ease with.

A drink is poured and the glass handed to Jim.

"I would like to salute my gifted but departed husband… Dr. Royce Benders."

Jim follows her direction and salutes the Doctor. Cindy digs deeper into the cabinet and retrieves a lighter and cigarette.

She offers one to Jim but he declines.

"Got a lot of bad habits… just not that one."

"Well, haven't had one in seventeen years…but the loss of my dear Royce, I need to get rid of a little pain." Cindy raises the drink and cigarette up at the same time. "Please Jim, have a seat."

Jim takes the drink and sits at the table. She sits across and looks him in the eye. "You see my hidden sins, what about you, Jim… any skeletons in the closet?"

Jim hesitates for a few seconds. "Everyone has something to bury."

Cindy realizes she doesn't have anywhere to put the long cigarette ashes. Jim throws down the rest of the bourbon and hands her the empty glass.

"Thanks… appreciate a man that can improvise." She flicks the ashes into the glass and turns back to Jim. "I'll cut to the chase…my husband was a brilliant man, a genius in DNA research and fertilization process… way ahead of his time in both fields."

"Is this about his death?" Jim asks.

"Actually, it's about the perpetuation of his genius life. In the eighties he fertilized the eggs of three women with his own DNA. He replicated himself as an experiment in vanity."

Jim glances at the Doctor's portrait and back to Cindy. "Sex by proxy… not my style, but I don't ever judge people. So, this experiment…don't see how I fit into the picture unless you want me to find out who killed him."

"The police are handling that aspect…I have something very important for you to do, but I have a need for full disclosure on your part." Cindy sips more of the vodka.

"I can be transparent… shoot." Jim says confident.

"My husband was completely intolerable of drug use…are you using any drugs other than bourbon?" Cindy asks.

"Occasional beer… nothing stronger." He responds.

"You'll have to undergo a drug test, snip a strand of hair and give it to Steve." She focuses her gaze on Jim's eyes.

"I can handle it, if not I would walkout right now not to waste your time or mine." Jim is strong in his offer.

Cindy finishes her drink and looks intently at Jim. "Why did you kill your stepfather?"

His senses go numb for a few seconds, a rush of emotion fills his body. The same feeling when reading his sister's diary and finding out the dirty little secrets drowning the so-called childhood home with evil.

Cindy can see his temporary mental struggles and goes to the liquor cabinet pouring a new glass of bourbon, returns and sets it in front of him.

He takes a drink. "That's painful... how did you know?"

"We have, shall I say, a unique set of resources to pull from." The woman knew how to angle those resources when she needed to.

"What does something I did as a thirteen-year old have to do with my ability to perform an investigation now?" Jim inquires.

"Jim, I'm not here to take the job away from you...rather, I'm trying to hand it over to you. But this is about the reputation surrounding my husband, his legacy and future financial abilities to keep this institution going long after both of us are dead and buried. We have plans to expand to Atlanta building a second facility; I won't let his death nor infidelities on unsuspecting families back in the eighties tarnish or destroy that path. You have what we need from all accounts... you're damn good at what you do and understand discretion when you complete the job. That's extremely important to us at this juncture." Cindy laid all her cards on the table for Jim to read.

"Jack Staymen pretended to be my stepfather, but the rock he crawled out from trailed too much slime to qualify. He molested my six-year old sister until her 10th birthday... all the while beating on me and my Mom. I shot him… I'd shoot him now if he walked through the door. If there's a hell, he's having a drink as we speak." Jim didn't have a hint of remorse in his voice.

Cindy gets up from the table. "If there's a hell, I don't think he can get the bartender's attention. Let's go see Steve… get the paperwork completed."

During the short walk down the hallway, Cindy lays out what the job is. "What we need is verification of the three people you track down, make sure they are descendants of my husband."

"How do we accomplish that?" Jim inquires.

"Simple, DNA testing…Steve will give you all of the details." Cindy confirms.

Cindy knocks on Steve's door and enters, Jim in tow. "Jim is our man…have him sign the non-disclosure document… the rest of the contract is filled out."

She turns to Jim and shakes his hand. "Steve will be your contact person. Any questions about any aspect of the job will be communicated through him."

She walks away leaving the two men together.

Jim hands him the file. Steve pulls an NDA from a desk drawer and places it in front of Jim.

"You will need to sign and date the Legal Non-Disclosure Agreement… I'll notarize it before you leave."

While Jim signs the Non-Disclosure, Steve glances through the questionnaire. "Do you understand what the job entails?"

Jim looks up from the agreement. "Not completely, I know about the three individuals that gave birth to the Doctor's offspring… I'm to run them down… report back to you."

"Find the three individuals genetically coded to Dr. Benders' DNA, get blood or hair samples for the Institute to confirm their heritage… that's the job description."

Steve isn't nice like Cindy, thought Jim. The incessant business approach on everything reveals a lack of personality.

"Why all of the secrecy?... If the Doctor left these people money, why don't you approach them with a check... wouldn't they cash it?" Jim asks what he thinks is a simple solution.

"There are immense legal ramifications that could arise from what Dr. Benders did... and we want to make sure these individuals are indeed related before we approach them with money. Dr. Benders wanted two things: one–make sure the experiment worked; and, two–take care of those genetically coded to his genes. So using great discretion, we find those eligible...get them the money without any connection to the Institute. Are you capable of discretion, Mr. Jim Cirmah?" Steve responds in his very dry approach to every subject.

"Torture proof...however, do you have suggestions on how to discreetly draw blood or get a lock of hair without them knowing?" Inquires Jim.

"Mr. Cirmah, you have been hired because of your no holds barred creativity. Neither myself nor anyone else connected to this company should be given the details of how you do it." Steve makes no bones about who should do what.

Steve goes to the cabinet, uses a key to unlock it and retrieves a series of files. He returns to the chair and sets them on Jim's side of the desk.

"Here are the individual files on the women giving birth in the experiment and their children's names. One is in L.A., one in New Orleans."

Steve hesitates and opens a file. "The last child lived in the St. Louis area. Where they are now is up to your investigative skills."

Jim takes the files, walks to the door and turns around. Steve is writing notes and never looks up yet anticipates Jim's question.

"A $5000 advance against your expenses will be deposited directly to your checking account tomorrow." Steve looks up. "Keep your receipts if you want to be reimbursed...there are no exceptions."

"Got it...expense receipts and complete autonomy are not discretionary." Jim loves sliding in the last word leaving his office.

CHAPTER TWENTY

Players Play

Part One

THE GTO PULLS into Jim's driveway and parked. He left the family files from the Institute with Rollie, the FBI will effectively run down the locations of Dr. Benders' children. With their addresses found, he can wrap the case up in two weeks max collecting the biggest payday of his life. Rollie gave him a little grief about using his "resources" to work on a case having nothing to do surrounding his extended empire, but Slick helps regardless of the case origination. The price for Jim is good natured bitching filling his ear, but a small cost to get the job over and done.

He feeds Winston then makes a hard four mile run finished by an all-out sprint the last half mile. Drenched in sweat, he slows to a walk the last block to cool off and sees the '73 Mustang driving toward him, long blonde hair flowing.

Deb Sweeney stops the car next to Jim. "You work up all that sweat walking?"

Jim leans on the passenger side window. "A little walking plus a four mile run will cause sweat to pour off a body... how about you, done any sweating lately?"

"I run a little... same kind of distance, but I've seen your pace...way beyond my stride. We're headed to your girlfriend's place tonight... heard about the really good food and beautiful women...are you going to be there?" Deb's Aussie accent encourages one of Jim's fantasies, climbing in the car to drive all afternoon listening to her speech.

"True on both fronts, but the women won't have anything on you." Jim wanted to gauge her reaction to old fashion flirting.

"You're too kind...maybe we'll do a little running together if the pace is slowed. Will I see you tonight?" Deb didn't react too strong to his throw out.

"Yeah, I'm headed that way... buy you guys a drink." Jim responds.

"Good...take you up on it. I understand it's amateur night; you might get a lap dance from me...bring plenty of twenties." The Mustang races off down the road.

Jim rolls his eyes itemizing the detail of a lap dance from Deb. It's a thought way beyond fun but Janey might not handle it too well on her turf. However, it firmly planted in his mind the realization he's not dated another woman other than Janey for the last eight months. Maybe it's time to do a little exploring on the side. Deb would make anyone think twice on self-imposed celibacy.

Jim showers, dresses, and warms up a burrito he buys from a local grocer in the neighborhood. He likes cooking but it's a hassle preparing food for one. The exception is Sunday night cooking a pile of pasta and chicken, he tailors flavor options depending on the mood. He feeds Winston and freezes the rest to be reclaimed later in the week. Bow-tie pasta trips the taste buds this Sunday.

He picks up the phone and dials Detective Fox.

"Well, well… you got any helpless Hells Angel types we need to pound tonight?" Fox answers.

"No, met my quota this month. Amateur night at the Booty Trap… come on by, I'll get you a beer." Jim replies.

"Got nothing better to do… why not. I'll come if you'll throw in a t-bone and large bake potato with the beer." Fox lays the parameters down.

"You just said you had nothing better to do… why am I bribing you?" Jim says half joking, half truthful.

"Because you always want to drain me for info on some asshole you're trying to rundown… deny that." Fox nailed Jim to the wall.

"Okay, get you a steak…buy you a beer, anything else comes out of your own wallet." Jim offers a compromise.

"Depends on the info you want." Fox counters.

"You better be full of information to get a lap dance tossed in. I won't commit until the info hits my ears." Jim did want to know something about the Benders' murder.

"See, you're a cheap date…I won't put out unless you spend cash on me." Fox announces proudly.

"Nothing new to that approach." Jim shuts off the phone.

Jim was not born a skeptic, but certainly raised one. His distrust for people didn't overpower his day-to-day actions, but he never buried it too deep to retrieve. He understood how self-serving needs shapes an individual's reaction to events in life and learned early to leverage it. The litigious test for entering his domain on a business or social level came down to: 'what's in it for them'? Right now he needed more information to clear up the Institute's picture.

It did make commonsense for the Institute to track the Benders' descendants without revealing their position. This insures the right people to eventually negotiate with. Keeping the cards close to the vest limits the risk of destroying the good Doctor's name by someone not related to him and getting blackmailed in the process. Jim is digging into Fox's head, maybe the murder is connected to the targets in some way? Expensive meal notwithstanding, inside info could help down the road.

Jim gets to the club early, but none of the players in his group can be found. The stripclub regulars are typically a late arriving crowd, but tonight is amateur hour and the club is getting filled already.

For the regulars, seems to be something more erotic when a non-professional goes into a bar, hugs a poll and takes her clothes off. A lot of husbands/boyfriends like the thought of seeing their woman take it off in front of other guys and have hot sex later that night.

One thing for sure it wasn't about the money, the club only put up $500 to be split by the top three "crowd pleasers." A crowd letting the amateur hear quickly how good or bad by cat calls or applause. The amateur better have a good body, a touch of the exhibitionist sprinkled with self-loathing to prance around naked getting verbally abused and/or loved at the same time.

The club management depends on this time honored amateur night; it's typically their biggest moneymaker of the month. The only thing bigger is bringing in a film porn star, let her strip on stage and take pictures with a hundred plus drunks one at a time. But porn stars are expensive, demanding and temperamental profiling their good side. So the amateur night rules until desperation sets in for the stripclub owner to buy a new car for an ex-wife as a payoff to visit his children. Or worse, bribe the local underworld types working their way into the owner's bad dreams by supplying the stripper talent free drugs in exchange for sex.

Jim looks around to make sure none of his guests are in the house and heads to the manager's office to ask a favor. Tony Joseph sees Jim heading his way through an open door and waves him back.

"Jim, how's the world treating you?" Tony likes Jim and is aware of his relationship with Janey.

"I'm doing well...need a favor if possible." Jim asks.

"Name it." Tony responds.

"I have three guests coming tonight...if the VIP boxes aren't full, could I get one?"

"Let me check it out." Tony pulls up a spreadsheet on his computer tracking everything. "Pretty slow night for VIP's... sure, tell Brandon to fix you up."

Brandon is head of security and leads Jim to a VIP room nicknamed the "skybox." It juts out directly over the stage, one-way glass giving total privacy. Jim didn't expect this kind of treatment, but isn't going to argue either. Walking to the bar, he catches a glimpse of Fox entering the front door and waits on the detective to catch up.

"Foxman, knew you wouldn't turn down a free meal." Jim deadpans.

"I'm a cop... free is a word we understand well," Fox retorts.

The two sit at the bar and Jim orders two beers. Janey is on stage in all her glory and Fox takes notice. He waves his beer toward the stage. "No way in hell a woman that good looking will stay with you much longer."

""Your jealous streak shows... may want to consider therapy?" Jim has enough confidence to shoot down the Foxman.

Fox shakes his head. "You're right... I'm crazy just like her. Before ordering my steak, what are you working on that desperately needs my input?"

"The Dr. Benders' murder..."

Fox interrupts Jim in mid-sentence. "Hold on friend, that's the biggest case in California since the Nicole Simpson murder. Not getting anything from me...steak or not. Besides, what are you working on connected to the Benders' case?"

"Not that much," Jim answers meekly. "I was hired by the Benders Institute to run down a couple of their former clients... not anything to do with Benders himself. Thought you might fill in a few blanks on what is going on?"

"Well, Doctor Benders was a great man...and most of the forensics we use on the force came from his DNA science. Worked on the Shroud of Turin...won a Nobel Peace Prize." Fox profiles the man.

"What is this Shroud thing?" Jim asks.

"The Shroud is the burial cloth Jesus was wrapped in when laid in the tomb...you're not much on religion I take it." Fox has no idea how bold his statement is surrounding Jim's background.

"Each to his own... just not for me." Jim answers. "Why do you think he was killed?"

"Had a lot of threats over the years, probably someone that hates Christianity." Fox continues.

"Could it be an inside job?" Jim raises his eyebrows hoping for a response defining the picture.

"If it's an inside job... not confirming by the way, I think the guy in charge of security might be connected. Something doesn't seem right about the man." Fox gets into detail he should never be revealing, but Jim isn't looking a gift horse in mouth.

Jim motions to the bartender, ordering two more beers waiting for the right timing. "What's the security guy's name?"

"David Sanders... an ex-cop from Denver. Can't trust cops you know." Fox adds.

"Can't argue the truth." Jim agrees taking the two beers and handing one to Fox. He makes a mental note of the name.

Jim clicks his bottle to the one held by Fox. "Here's to a good time... got the VIP skybox for all of us tonight."

"A touch of class unexpected... who is the 'us'?" Fox asks.

"My next door neighbor and his girlfriend... you'll like both." Jim informs.

Fox takes a sip of the fresh beer. "If you really want to dig deeper into the case, you need to see Captain Cyril... I really can't say anymore."

"The Captain owes me plenty, got him World Series tickets for the Dodgers... I'll give him a visit." Jim fully intends to follow up on Fox's suggestion.

The men move away from the bar. "These people are from your neighborhood... that's not a way to impress." Fox throws a barb.

"Come on asshole... let's go upstairs. Try to be tolerable for a change." Jim declares.

Heading for the stairwell, Deb's voice is yelling in the background calling Jim's name. He turns to meet Deb and JD.

Deb is stunning in a black, pleated miniskirt, tall stiletto heels and pulled back hair completing the high school girl look. Jim introduces her and John David to Detective Fox. Fox is impressed but holds his composure well.

The four climb the steps to the VIP skybox to begin the evening. New drinks flow in the skybox and soon the main topic rears its beautiful head, Deb's debut on the stage a few feet below. Deb is energized and not a bit intimidated. At least it reads that way to Jim. She smiles even after the intense kidding Detective Fox spouts about seeing under the short skirt. Fox's poking only makes her more giddy as the evening progresses.

Jim's eyes wander to JD from time-to-time gauging his reaction to all the attention Deb's getting, but all seems fine. It takes maturity or disconnect from a man's ego not to react negatively watching her take clothes off in front of a house packed with guys like Fox.

Jim eases over to JD at one point to make sure. "You okay with Deb doing this?"

JD looks at Jim and gives him a slight grin.

"Hell, all she's talked about the last few days is stripping on stage... fine with me, she's a big girl. I can tell you this, won't be any boos or catcalls from the crowd when she does her thing...she's a stunningly beautiful woman with or without clothes. Do you have any inhibitions when Janey goes on stage?"

Jim thinks on the question for a few seconds, he didn't have any emotion about Janey's chosen profession... it's a job. As the flash of the question races across his mind, Jim realizes he's emotionally attached to nothing in his life.

"Not really," Jim confesses. "It's her life... don't want to judge anybody's decisions."

The two men glance at the stage below, the first of twelve stripping 'virgins' climbs on the stage to start the party. Jim didn't really care too much about amateur strippers, but then he's never seen one like Deb Sweeney either. The u-shaped sofa seating everyone has Deb at one end, JD and Fox between them.

Jim watches the interaction, throwing in two cents when the timing is right. Deb looks his way on occasion, smiles displaying perfect teeth and deep green eyes piercing his mind. He felt a warmth between them, going well beyond instinct seeing her body language. Neighbor or not, Jim is feeling things for this intriguing woman rapidly moving to impulsively explosive.

Deb gets up to find the restroom as the crowd noise gets louder around the skybox watching the next amateur lady climb the stage to dance. Each girl chooses her music for the stage act. The blond is well built causing JD and Fox to walk forward in the skybox to get a better view.

Deb brushes up next to Jim's ear and whispers; "get high with me tonight." She kisses him lightly on the ear and leaves the skybox.

Jim's adrenaline heightens the moment's intoxication. He finishes the beer but feels it's inadequate to get the high directed by Deb. When the cocktail waitress makes her round, a Crown and Coke steps up the game. Janey comes by the skybox to check on the crew and is mildly surprised at Jim's Crown cocktail having never seen him drink anything but beer. She watches the stage listening to the comments by Fox and JD describing the action below.

Janey walks to Jim and takes a drink of the Crown. "High octane tonight…like your attitude. You planning on getting in trouble?"

"Why not," Jim explains. "Been working hard lately… you game?"

"Whatever you want, baby… I'm up for it." She kisses Jim on the cheek and starts to leave as Deb comes in."

Janey stops short of the door. "Ready for your big night?" Both women are inches from each other's face.

"Absolutely," Deb responds. "How about a kiss for good luck?"

Janey never hesitates, leaning over mouth open and passionately kisses Deb. Janey turns slightly back to Jim, winks and leaves the box. Jim orders a double Crown advancing Deb's goal of getting high.

The crowd is getting wilder by the minute. Freelancing ladies display talent at varying levels of success according to the hundred or so self-appointed smug judges screaming encouragement. But the crowd didn't have any idea how wild the scenery is about to get.

Deb is getting ready like a prize fighter going into the ring, kicking into the air and shadow boxing. It isn't lost on anyone in the skybox she isn't wearing panties, all focused on each outward swing of her leg in the short miniskirt.

Jim's emotional attitude in life for the most part is evenly keeled unless you did bad to someone he liked. He'd blow up until the wrong is righted. But when it came to events surrounding himself, his reaction rarely gets above room temperature; deep down he really didn't care. If it came his way he grabbed it, but rarely goes off the beaten path in pursuit.

His childhood made him grow up too fast and he's geared not to expect good things at the end of the day. But tonight something special is happening beyond getting high. High on Crown, high on Deb, high on life in general, whatever it is he wants it to go on and on. He can't remember a day without nasty thoughts of history rearing its ugly head to drain the energy from his soul.

John David leaves the box for a few minutes and returns carrying a backpack containing school books and a ruler. Deb checks the bag's contents to be used as props in her act.

Jim comes closer watching her position everything to her liking. "I can see where this is headed."

Deb looks up and peers into his eyes. "No you don't." A simple statement of fact delivered by the beauty. She closes the bag and heads down to the stage.

Jim takes a sip of the Crown and feels like his fighter is heading into the ring, a little anxiousness on their performance in his gut.

"Hey JD," Jim asks. "What song did Deb choose for her debut?"

John David turns back to Jim. "Dave Matthews, his remake of 'The Watchtower' originally put out by Jimi Hendrix."

Fox jumps in. "Hendrix, now that's a talent... no one played the guitar like him."

All three men move close to the front of the skybox waiting on Deb's name being announced.

"Is she going by a stage name or her own?" Jim inquires.

"Wanted to keep her name... doesn't seem to bother her, but nothing does." JD remarks.

Dave Matthews' voice is cranked up on the sound system and the stage manager introduces Deb. She leisurely strolls on the stage, the usual cheers from the fickle crowd turning on a contestant quickly if any flaws are perceived. This act or body did not have flaws.

Deb has the high school look perfected, carrying books walking home late after school. Sweet and innocent drives men wild with thought.

At the other end of the stage is Janey, dressed in a slutty looking outfit, leaning up against a stripper pole and smoking a cigarette.

"Damn, no one mentioned Janey getting into her act." JD blurts out.

"This isn't happening by accident." Jim adds looking down on the women. "Janey's never smoked a cigarette in her life."

Fox jumps in. "Not one of those swinging dicks knows that... this is going to be fun to watch."

Deb walks close to Janey, gets grabbed by the ass and kissed on the lips by Janey. The club gathering roars its approval, two women touching each other is a universal man's fantasy.

Janey hands the cigarette to Deb, and she accepts with trepidation, but takes a drag. The backpack is taken by Janey, thrown to one side except for the ruler. She uses it to spank Deb after ripping the miniskirt off. Dave Matthews never performed on this kind of stage before.

Deb tries to run away but is caught by Janey and more clothes ripped off. Several men try to climb on stage, spurred by excitement but security quickly restores order. Deb goes to one pole on the right and Janey takes her clothes off working a pole on the left. It's a dueling strip off, two beautiful women eliminating any doubt who the winner is in tonight's contest for best in show.

Janey moves off the stage to let her "converted" school girl finish the last two minutes of Dave Matthews' nine minute version of "The Watchtower". When the song is over she leaves to applause and chants of "more…more."

Detective Fox turns to Jim and JD. "Damn, I'm going to shoot both of you, neither one deserves that much woman."

"I'm going to stand here and let you." John David responds in agreement.

"Wow, that took some planning… did you know they were putting this together?" Jim looks inquisitively at JD.

"Not a clue… did you?" JD answers.

"Nope." Jim simply confesses.

The two girls come into the skybox excited and breathless hugging onto one another like the innocent school girl Deb played. Both confident it blew away the crowd including the men in the skybox.

The next couple of hours are drink filled and conversation in the box surrounds the performance. Tony Joseph comes to congratulate the ladies handing over cash and offers Deb a job. Deb says it's flattering and think about it. She does ask Janey a myriad of questions concerning the business side of stripping, all the pluses and minuses thrown around.

Fox leaves although Jim is not exactly sure when, he took Deb's direction of getting high to task. Things are slowing down for him partly from the booze and partly from his flirtation with Deb. Strangely, he feels both are being encouraged by Janey.

Food is ordered to the box, only temporarily slowing down the buzz taking place in everyone's head. When the food is finished, Deb pulls a joint from her purse, lights it and passes it along.

Jim does not do drugs, although some of his juvi-days were spent smoking weed with fellow inmates. Smoking a doobie didn't do much for making him high, so he never went out of his way to get it or stay around those that did. His acceptance is Janey's reaction, he's never seen her touch any drugs. To his surprise she takes a drag and hands it to Jim. With that endorsement the evening starts to get wild and dark.

TO BE CONTINUED

CHAPTER TWENTY-ONE

The Short and Winding Road

Part One

DAVID SANDERS SITS in a one bedroom apartment sipping on a cup of coffee in one hand and a book about "The Shroud of Turin" in the other. The empty file in Dr. Benders' office titled 'The Shroud' is bothering him, and the newly purchased book does little to shed any light on the Doctor's silence. David visits the publisher that found the Doctor's body. He maintains no knowledge of the new book's content.

Benders kept the transcript a mystery, only exposing to the publisher questions concerning distribution and available marketing dollars. Unlike previous book launches, the editor received no advance copy to review and Benders' willingness to help finance the marketing exposure came as a shock. Requests are out-of-character for Dr. Benders.

Dr. Benders, an extreme creature of habit, rarely had interest in the sale of his many books. It was about education in the medical or criminal justice field, never about money. This book represented a dramatic change in his approach, but why?

David called Cindy Benders and casually inquired about the transcript. All she knew about the book was "The Shroud thing" had something to do with his work in Italy over the years. No clue where the transcript might be didn't surprise David, but she promised to look and get back if anything turns up.

The apartment gave David a sense of emptiness, his direction of purpose and small circle of friends left when Benders died. He's getting tired easily and sleep didn't restore the energy. Many sessions staring at a psychiatrist over the death of his son and divorce painted a familiar picture of depression hanging in the apartment. Darkness appears, a viable alternative to light.

The gravity of haste to figure out the next chapter of his life pulls on his senses and it didn't include L.A. His father left him a small cabin near Vail. The thought of drinking wine dad bottled and sitting by a burning fireplace reading a book suddenly has great pull. Might have to get a dog to share the warmth.

A decision to get out into the night for dinner and jump away from the rut is made. He walks to his BMW noticing his car stands out in a parking lot filled with older vehicles. The BMW is five years old, just one more confirmation of his fall from grace. He pulls onto the street bound for Dean Anthony's, a small Italian restaurant serving great wine and food at the foot of Hollywood Hills.

A habit disconcerting to any passenger riding in the car is David's constant changing of the radio stations. It's an ongoing search for good rock and roll. Radio stations meet his music expectations no more than a couple of songs, compulsion drives him to find a different one. A lean to hit the dial facilitates a glance in the rearview mirror surveying the road behind. After several street turns and radio adjustments, he notices a car driving exactly the same path he's traveling. David is not the paranoid type, but cop instincts take over. He turns left at the next intersection and watches the car go straight through the light not following. His vivid imagination adds to the resolve of getting to the mountain cabin sooner rather than later. The pressure of life is making him bend the rules of reality. A U-turn is completed and he gets back on track.

The dinner at Dean Anthony's exceeds his expectations and he enjoys watching the sunset over Hollywood Hills finishing a bottle of wine. He calls his ex-wife, perhaps connecting to times past but only gets voicemail. He didn't leave a message, not really sure why the call was made.

David returns to the car putting the seat belt on. A vehicle parked a few spots away has two men inside. The feeling that something is wrong tickles his mind. He starts the BMW exiting the restaurant lot, the men pull out a short distance behind him. David speeds up to put distance between them, but the other car matches his maneuver. Staying on his rear end, it's obvious his active imagination didn't create their intent.

He pushes the BMW well past the speed limit, it now has become an all out game of cat and mouse. The single lane road winds its way across the rolling Hollywood Hills and the two vehicles reach a dangerous 80 plus. David drives the car trying to retrieve his pistol from the glove box with little luck. The phone is pulled out and he hits 911, but the signal is weak against the hills rising above on both sides.

An intersection approaches quickly blocked by a delivery van pulling onto the road disrupting his view of oncoming traffic. He makes a split decision, turning right sharply on the single lane road heading up Mulholland Drive and into the Hollywood Hills. Hoping to buy some time, get his gun and contact police from a higher elevation is the plan.

The road is pitch black except for the occasional mansion behind secured walls driving up the valley's edge. Valuable

ground is widened between him and the car allowing retrieval
of the pistol.

He hits 911 and the operator answers approaching a sharp
curve going way too fast. A turn into the road's bend reveals
two sets of headlights coming his way and side-by-side
vehicles taking up both lanes. His first instinct is turn sharply
to the right avoiding a head-on collision but the fear of driving
off the mountain is strong. David stomps the brakes, bracing
for the inevitable crash with headlights barreling toward him.

The BMW instead hits a wooden sawhorse mounted with
two headlights, not a car first visualized in his lane. The car
skids to a stop on the outside right lane short of a 300 foot drop
to a creek below. David gets out and sees how close he came
to driving into the valley, dead before he reached the bottom.
He catches his runaway breathing and notices a second
sawhorse in the far left lane, same two headlights mounted.

It dawns on him the rerouting by the delivery truck is part
of the plan to lead him up the mountain to fly off the cliff
avoiding another car's head-on crash. The ambush was
perfectly designed using the fake car headlights and only a
miracle of luck saved his ass. David shakes contemplating the
planning and professionalism it took in order to carry out such
an elaborate scheme, a murder meant to look like a terrible
accident.

The 911 operator is trying to get David back in conversation
and he finally responds. "I'm approximately two miles up
Mulholland Drive...please send the police ASAP... someone
just tried to kill me by running my car off the road...hurry, I'm
not sure if they are coming back."

David gets out of the car, pistol in hand and waits on the
police to arrive. He moves the remaining sawhorse to the side
of the road to avoid another car rounding the curve and hitting

him or driving off the mountain. The other sawhorse is broken and lying under the front wheels of the BMW.

A man approaches, a hoodie drawn around his head. David points the .38 at his chest and demands he stop. He's not sure who is trying to kill him and isn't taking chances.

The man's face is thin and hollow in the headlights but other features escape David's attention.

A deep voice comes from the hoodie. "Bad accident, are you alright?"

"This was no accident, someone tried to kill me." David fires back. "The cops are on their way."

"Cops can't help you David, but I can." The deep voice is soothing to David's ears.

TO BE CONTINUED

CHAPTER TWENTY-TWO

Players Play

Part Two

THE SKYBOX AT the club is out of control, Jim summarizes watching Janey and Deb re-enact their schoolgirl play minus Dave Matthews' golden voice. Not that he objects to beautiful women running around in various stages of nakedness, but his direct observation of Janey is somewhat perplexing. She acts like a cat with a new mouse toy named Deb, and didn't have an ounce of jealousy surrounding the group interaction. None of this is a negative, but it's almost too good to be true.

Jim decides to stop trying to make an analysis of Janey, simply walk the path and see where this strange evening is headed. Another drag from the intoxicating smoke makes the decision seem very right. It starts to separate fact from thought and in the end, leaves memory at the train station waving at the departing mind. At this point he didn't care if the next train ever arrives to catch his mind up to reality.

A group decision to leave all the cars behind and get into the GTO letting Jim drive is voted on. In spite of the fact he's way beyond drunk by anybody's standards. Self-justifying words are exchanged. Jim knows every cop in town and can talk his way out of trouble. Jim takes comfort in the gossip pulling onto the street, but drives the speed limit hoping the breathalyzer monster didn't rear its ugly head.

The two girls are in the backseat without a lot of clothes on, giddy toward the world at large. Jim glances at JD, seeing a look of helplessness concerning Janey and Deb's actions, one he shares. Jim simply shrugs his shoulders, along for the same ride JD found himself tethered to.

On occasion, everyone gets to an intersection when a single action seems to open the floodgates to doing things you know are wrong. Janey places her incredibly long legs ending in four inch stiletto heels on the front seat next to JD's face.

"I'll let you kiss all the way to my panties if you can tell me what kind of shoes these are." Janey challenges JD.

"That's bullshit." Deb jumps in. "You aren't wearing any panties."

"Exactly," Janey states. "It doesn't matter cause these two think everyone wears Nikes."

Deb puts her stilettos on either side of Jim's head. "Same thing goes for you but I have panties on. I am, however, willing to take them off."

Jim is worthless in this sexy new game Janey's thrown out and figures JD is also clueless. He has little interest in the shoe brand he's wearing and defiantly not into a woman's fashion.

To his utter shock, JD turns to the backseat and says.

"Your shoes have a red sole on the bottom, they're made by Christen Luberten."

As the girls scream in surprise, Jim and JD slap a high five.

"Very cool," Jim begs. "Now help me out."

JD leans over looking intently at Deb's shoes. "Bonics, you're wearing Bonics."

"Nope," Deb states. "But I'm still very impressed with the Christen Luberten lucky guess.

"Guess," JD responds. "That wasn't luck... my ex-wife owned a closet full of high end shoes. Give me one more shot."

"Yeah, one more shot." Jim adds.

"What the hell," Janey chirps in. "Give him another guess."

Jim is fully engaged on what's going to fall off JD's lips. Deb's long legs are propped up on the backseat and he is focused, looking at the beginning and end using the rearview mirror.

JD studies the shoes intently like a pitcher standing on the mound in the bottom of the ninth, a no-hitter riding on the catcher's signal. "Jimmy Choo's." He says authoritatively.

The confirmation came from the screams of delight in the backseat. Jim has no idea who Jimmy Choo is, but glad he makes four inch stiletto heels.

The ride home presents a vague memory and what's left goes up in a smoky haze at Jim's house. Jim gets up early the next morning for the bathroom and lying next to him is Deb. He sits up, looks at the green eyed beauty sound asleep and can only shake his head.

"Must have been one hell of a night." He says out loud having no idea where JD and Janey ended up. He didn't have a sense of guilt, it wasn't in his makeup and all involved are adults doing adult things.

Today he didn't have the time nor inclination to study the detail of a wild night no matter who is involved. The water hits his face from the shower head and helps the headache inherited from the skybox intoxication. He swallows several pills from an anti-hangover medicine bottle not having a label, but felt it would help.

Jim dresses slowly, not by choice but necessity. On the way out, he sees Janey and John David lying together in the second bedroom sound asleep. He's still not sure what kind of shoes Deb was wearing to spark all this craziness, but took his hat off to JD for knowledge few guys possess.

He leaves the house to the sleeping threesome and heads to the Pawnshop to pick up the researched files and start running down his $39,000.

CHAPTER TWENTY-THREE

Raising Heaven

JIM WALKS DELIBERATELY through the front door of the Pawnshop cradling a large cup of coffee and Drug Lord starts his routine in a much higher screeching voice. Conrad picks up on the sensitive nature of Jim's head.

"Late night?" Conrad asks guessing the answer in advance.

"Wouldn't believe me if I wrote a book." Jim answers, a smug look on his face. "Did Rollie get the files worked up?"

Conrad goes behind the counter, picks up a briefcase and pulls the files out. "Done and delivered."

"Let's get the L.A. man first." Jim opens the file on Joe Tramazzo. "Wow, a special forces guy. At least we don't have to cuff him."

"Don't think I'll be slipping up on him to cut some hair off." Conrad says in a serious tone not negotiable.

"That won't be necessary," Jim says confidently. "I'll figure it out.

Conrad points to the top of the file. "He's close...lives off Greenville Lane. Maybe twenty-five minutes from here."

"Let's pay the soldier a visit." Jim invites. "Give me a lay of the land to figure out the next steps."

The GTO pulls up in front of 2141 Greenville Lane and Jim faces Conrad. "Let me do the talking."

"It's all yours, Sherlock." Conrad snaps back.

"Damn," Jim states getting out of the car. "I've created a smart-assed monster."

"Simply following your lead." Conrad adds proud of his quick wit.

Jim knocks on the door and Joe Tramazzo's dope smoking roommate answers it.

"Is this about the rent?" David sheepishly asks.

Jim's smile presents a broad veil of ivory. "Nothing to do with the rent, is Joe in?"

David looks around and shuffles his feet to one side of the doorway. "Dude, Tramazzo slammed his bike into a truck two weeks ago... he's dead."

"Can't believe it...saw him a couple of months ago." Jim lies convincingly and offers his hand. "I'm Joe's cousin, Jim...this is Conrad."

"I'm David," he shakes Jim's hand. "We roomed together... really close, too."

Both men lie about their relationship with Joe.

"Say, did you keep any of Joe's things around...I would like to send them back to his family?" Jim asks.

"No...didn't have much, gave everything to the Salvation Army." David continues to lie, he threw away everything except a military knife and .45 pistol.

Jim offers his hand again. "We appreciate your help... such a shame, way too young to be dying."

David accepts the hand. "So true, dude... so true."

Jim and Conrad return to the car. "Damn it, can't believe this BS." Jim relays pulling out his phone to call Steve Hopkins from the Institute. "Steve, we have a problem with Tramazzo."

"What kind of problem, Mr. Cirmah?" Steve responds.

"He went and killed himself in a bike accident two weeks ago...I'm going after the second person on the list." Jim declares.

"Mr. Cirmah, you were hired because of creativity... being dead doesn't change our need to confirm the DNA match one way or another."

"So," Jim questions. "You want me to dig the guy up?"

"I don't really care what you do... get the job done. And, Mr. Cirmah...don't include me in your plans." Steve shuts the phone off.

Jim gets back out of the GTO and returns to the front door knocking on it. Soon David comes back and opens up.

"I need to pay my respects to Joe, where's he buried?" Jim questions.

"That Catholic Church off Harrison...a cemetery out back." David answers.

"Thanks." Jim returns to the car and starts the GTO.

"We have some digging to do tonight... pick you up at midnight."

"What are we digging up?" Conrad inquires confused.

"Joe Tramazzo." Jim says determined.

"Cool." Conrad states in a surprising tone.

Jim keeps his thoughts private roaring away in the GTO dropping Conrad at the Pawnshop. After leaving Conrad, he gets a call from Wayne Davis finally recovered from the induced coma. Jim heads to the hospital and a reunion with his old pool playing friend.

The conversation is short lived. Wayne is still suffering the aftermath of the drugs and needs sleep. He listens to the story about Jim going into the Hells Angels' bar and taking care of the two goons that put him in the hospital. Wayne laughs at the absurdity of Fox firing his pistol into the ceiling and Jim pounding them in the parking lot. Jim is proud of the response and Wayne knew it would end that way, it simply defines Jim and his friendship.

The meeting is brief but Jim feels good seeing his friend and realizing his full recovery. On the way home, Jim receives a call from Janey and doesn't dance around the previous night's activities. "So, we alright with last night?"

"Yeah," she responds. "I went into it very open minded. You completely unwound last night... I went along. The three of us talked about it over breakfast this morning... no one's feelings are hurt. Are you okay?"

"Other than a headache and a little problem with the Institute case, I'm fine... it was one hell of a night. Still can't believe John David knew what kind of shoes you guys were wearing."

"He definitely deserved something after that performance... catch up with you this weekend?" Janey asks.

"See you Saturday night." Jim turns the phone off, pulls into his driveway and sees JD moving lumber to the back of his yard. JD waves as Jim approaches.

"What are you building, Mr. Shoe expert?" Jim asks looking at the various piles of wood.

"Building a fence...tired of the jacked up poodle sharing his dog food a couple of hours after eating it on my yard."

Jim notices a piece of machinery setting next to the porch. "Is that what I think it is?"

"Posthole digger... my days of dripping sweat may not be over, but are limited." JD relays.

"Could I use it tonight... got a little project?" Jim asks.

"Sure, what do you need it for?" JD asks.

"Well... a case I'm working on." Jim replies sheepishly.

"Take it." JD responds. "I'm not going to do anything until Sunday anyway."

The digger is placed in the car's trunk and Jim retreats in the house to contemplate his "project" later tonight. Unlike Conrad, he didn't have the same amount of enthusiasm digging in a grave to snip hair off a corpse.

It has nothing to do with the fear of getting caught, Jim has ice water in his veins and stays calm under the craziest of circumstances. Digging up a dead man is different, this will test his fortitude and resolve. To stay loose, he runs six miles to distract the thinking but it does little to dispel the image in his mind.

Getting to midnight seems to take days not hours for Jim. When Conrad finally pulls into Slick's parking lot, Jim is ready to get the job over and done. Jim came to the Pawnshop two hours early, listening to a Cubs/Dodgers game waiting on Conrad to arrive.

Conrad is full of energy and talks every mile of the drive to the church while Jim is silent. Finally Conrad stops his yapping after parking a block behind the church. "What's wrong, Jim?"

"Look, I'm a little uneasy about this." Jim relays. "Not too keen playing in a dead guy's grave. Let's get in… get out."

Jim retrieves the posthole digger, two shovels and a flashlight. The two find Tramazzo's freshly dug grave easily.

"Maybe we should use the shovels instead of cranking up the noisy engine?" Questions Conrad.

"Not going to be here all night." Jim responds pulling the rope to start the engine.

In a couple of cranks the posthole digger comes to life and Jim drills down into the dirt piling up loose ground next to the grave. After less than a minute the digger has extracted a large mound of dirt, Jim shifts his attention to the center of the grave repeating the process over the full length of the coffin.

Jim looks around to check if lights come on from the church, but all is calm at this point.

"Damn," Conrad admits. "That took no time." He jumps down in one of the holes, starts to remove additional dirt while Jim digs at the opposite end.

Conrad hits the wooden coffin first and taps it a couple of times. "Got it here."

Soon Jim hits the top of Joe's resting place at the other end. They start throwing dirt out working toward each other, finally meeting in the middle.

"Okay," Jim jumps out. "We need to find the head of the coffin...get it open." He shines the flashlight into the hole and points out the hinged cut at the top of the coffin to Conrad. "There it is...can you pry it up?"

Conrad moves the last bit of dirt from the top of the coffin and starts to disengage the hinge. Jim fills the grave with light. Jim's head moves in several directions expecting flashing sheriff lights at any moment rushing to the cemetery. The night is silent except for Conrad clawing at the top of the coffin using a knife to get face-to-face with Joe Tramazzo.

Jim does not feel good at this moment. It could be the coffin, the hangover or even the faded memory of his dead stepfather lying on the front lawn wearing his shredded Target shirt. His sense of control has left, thrown in a coffin like the one being violated and burying it six feet deep. He turns to the church, not for answers but a diversion of thought.

"Damn," Conrad screams out far too loud for Jim's liking.

"Keep it down...get the hair... let's get the hell out of here." Jim demands.

Conrad looks directly into the flashlight's ray and then moves closer to Jim. "It's empty... no body... no one's in there."

"What," Jim questions. "That's crazy."

"Look for yourself." Conrad says climbing out of the hole.

Jim jumps on top of the coffin and sticks the flashlight into the opening. Only the lining to the coffin stares back. His eyes follow the flashlight into the opening but Conrad spoke the truth…empty.

Something reflects off the flashlight in the corner two feet from the opening. Jim takes a small freezer bag from his pocket then uses a pen to place an earring into the bag. After sealing the bag, the grave is refilled.

Jim is hoping the earring has enough DNA to satisfy Steve and the Institute. He's not too disappointed the body is missing and his headache is gone for the first time since this morning. Joe Tramazzo's absence did present a riddle to Jim, but in his wildest dreams he never imagined the answer to that riddle.

CHAPTER TWENTY-FOUR

The Gift

THREE TWELVE-YEAR OLD boys stand on the ledge of an old bauxite quarry pit and thirty feet below is a lake created after it was abandoned. It's the summer of 1996 in Southeast Missouri and cousin's Sam Wallace, Blake Rogers, and Ryan Jessey look down at the water. The boys discuss a long leap to the still waters below reflecting the sunlight on this June morning.

Blake is the undisputed band leader of the cousins. Sam and Ryan do whatever Blake's creative mind dreams up. It's usually no more than a mischievous prank like putting a greased piglet into a neighbor's house. Whatever Blake imagines is endorsed and performed by the other two. Not today.

Blake decides the young trio should climb a six-foot fence put up by the Reynolds Aluminum Company that quit mining the property for bauxite a few years before. He thought it would be great fun to jump off the cliff of the old pit, swim back to shore and climb the hill to do it all over again.

When they get to the pit and look down on the water, Sam says he won't jump. Blake is calling him all kinds of twelve-year old insulting names trying to make him jump but is getting no response. Blake knew if Sam didn't jump then Ryan wouldn't either.

Sam is focusing on the water below and really can't hear Blake flinging the colorful verbiage even standing only a couple of feet from one another. When Sam goes into this trance the world around him is completely blocked out.

He concentrates on images going to happen in the future. It's a frightening gift to a young mind starting at five when witnessing the car accident killing his grandmother six days ahead of the actual event. He never spoke to anyone about the future vision, he didn't think anyone would believe and his strict father might beat him for being strange. Something he witnessed first-hand, his older gay brother being constantly harassed.

What Sam sees is Blake jumping off the ledge, plunging three stories into the water and smashing his skull on a rock less than four feet from the surface. He looks at Blake trying to open his mouth about the impending doom but nothing comes out as Blake backs up a few steps.

Determined to show his cousins how easy it can be done, Blake gets a running start ten feet from the edge making the leap head first. He never surfaces.

Sam doesn't reveal his darkest secret to anyone over the years. He excels in school graduating at sixteen from high school and enrolling at the University of Missouri in pre-med conquering in less than two years. Genius is used often to describe Sam Wallace's rise in medical school at Vanderbilt, and at twenty-three he's the youngest resident doctor at Memorial Hospital in Cape Girardeau only nine miles from where he grew up.

More talents for Sam surface quickly beyond a very high IQ. His training includes diagnosis on many patients having a wide range of ailments. By simply touching the individual, he can assess their maladies and never be wrong. His reputation is growing as someone special, and is contacted by major hospitals in New York, Chicago, and Boston to serve his residency at big city facilities. He's flattered by the attention but a small town man at heart.

Ryan Jessey, the other cousin that fateful day when Blake died at the bauxite pit, has moved through life at a slower pace. He's a Cape Girardeau cop, starting a family at nineteen with wife Amy and twins, Melinda and Ryan, Jr.

Although the two cousins don't see each other often due to Sam's eighteen hour days at the hospital, they stay connected by text and phone calls. The two share a passion for sports especially college football, basketball, and beloved St. Louis Cardinals. A sports bar called 'Prime Time Sports' is a common destination when schedules allow.

By Sam's twenty-ninth birthday he is the Assistant Chief of Staff at the hospital and a skilled surgeon. He and Ryan plan an afternoon at the sports bar to celebrate his birthday and get caught up on life in general.

Sam is first to arrive shortly after 2:00 and has his pick of the tables, the lunch crowd being dissipated. A booth in the corner lines up several large screen TV's for the Saturday basketball games and Sam likes his timing and seat options. The menu is read to pass time waiting on Ryan's arrival, it hasn't changed in two years and Sam's tried everything at least twice. He orders a beer and watches the opening tipoff between the Arkansas Razorbacks and the Missouri Tigers, a heated rivalry for boarding states. The beer is an added treat. Sam never drinks alcohol when working. This afternoon his scheduled rounds have been turned over to an associate.

Ryan walks in finding Sam in the corner and compliments his choice of seats. An envelope is laid on the table, a birthday gift Ryan knows will please Sam. After a little guy talk about the basketball game, food is ordered and Ryan offers his beer to Sam's celebration.

"To my cousin and dearest friend, Dr. Samuel Eugene Wallace...Happy 29th Birthday, my man." The mugs click together, a drink taken.

"Thanks for the salute, you're a dear friend...not sure on the cousin status with all the shenanigans going around your side of the family." Sam relays tongue-in-cheek.

"The sad part is, I can't refute the statement. I can, however, point out your side made as many reckless choices as mine." Ryan counters.

"Touché." The cousins click the glasses together once more. "I have no comeback for your counterclaim." Sam states.

Ryan moves the envelope toward Sam. "Open it ...didn't go cheap this time." Ryan brags.

The envelope contains a birthday card stating something about Sam's bad golf game and four tickets to the Cardinals and Braves game in early May.

"You did bend that crusty wallet of yours... Cardinal tickets. I'm super pumped about the game, thanks." Sam's eyes light up in appreciation.

"Third base dugout seats... premium tickets." Ryan adds to the impact.

"Four tickets... besides Diane, I'm at a loss to figure out who gets invited to the game." Sam rubs in the fact Ryan and wife, Peggy are expecting to be in those seats next to Sam and his girlfriend.

"Let me know when you figure out who to invite...if it's not Peggy, you'll have to deal with a terrorist." Ryan states as a pure fact.

"Peggy gets one of the tickets, at a loss on the fourth one." Sam can't let the opportunity pass not having fun at Ryan's expense.

"You better give it to the one wielding a loaded pistol ready to use it on unfaithful cousins." Ryan throws it back into Sam's lap.

"If that's the case, do you happen to have the day free?" Sam offers up.

"I need to check my calendar...going to the bathroom." Ryan gets up and heads to the other side of the restaurant.

Sam stares at the game catching a glimpse of the basketball score. A tall man opens the front door and walks to the bar behind the TV hanging from the ceiling. Sam goes into a deep trance envisioning a young man entering the restaurant, pulling a weapon and shooting patrons at will. The man draws a second weapon from his jacket, continuing the shooting rampage on people screaming in fear and panic. Individuals are running in different directions, many falling in a hail of bullets striking their bodies.

Sam hears a distant voice familiar to his senses. His name is spoken long distance, from the other side of a long tunnel but can't understand who is trying to get his attention. Ryan shakes Sam's shoulder, speaking his name over and over hopefully bringing him back to the real world and out of the trance.

"Sam...talk to me. What's going on...are you sick?" Ryan again shakes Sam's shoulders trying to regain a responsive cousin. Sam finally comes back into the moment, fresh from the shooting running like a DVD on a big screen in his mind seconds ago.

"It's okay... I'm fine." Sam repeats a couple of times. "There's nothing physically wrong."

Ryan's mood went from celebratory to cautionary around Sam's unusual behavior. "Alright, if it's not physical, that leaves mental. What are you keeping from me?"

Sam realizes the shooting spree will become a reality and needs to do everything possible to stop it. He's sitting in front of a cop that happens to be his cousin, it's time to tell Ryan about the gift. For the next hour Sam paints the frightening picture of the things witnessed before occurring.

It's painfully personal when Sam profiles what happened in the bauxite pit years ago after cousin Blake died in the jump. Sam's lived the guilt ever since and now Ryan knew the deepest blackness of his soul.

CHAPTER TWENTY-FIVE

Re-Gifted

IT'S BEEN NINE days since Sam made his prediction on the sports bar shooting. Everyday Ryan made it a point to circle the bar in case there's validity to Sam's vision. Ryan admired and envied his cousin's many talents, Ryan played sports in high school and grades were not his priority. Simply getting by was enough for him. At the same time Sam blew through high school and college, not only great academically but always top of the class. Sam was number one, and the truth be told, number two a very distant second in IQ and focus.

Ryan didn't tell fellow officers about the prediction. In fact, he didn't say a word to anybody. He witnessed the event at the bauxite pit and the death of his cousin, but Ryan buried the incident deep in his subconscious to block out the pain. It's not he didn't want to believe Sam, but the memory is now a clouded distance. It's viewed from an altitude of thirty thousand feet leaving little room for detail.

The unmarked police car is parked a hundred yards from the sports bar in an adjoining shopping center lot. Just in case a crazy man carrying a gun shows up, he didn't want to scare him off. Ryan is a non-uniformed detective but all the locals in the restaurant know he's a cop the moment he enters. It would have to be a stranger not to recognize the situation. All these decisions are buzzing inside his head opening the sports bar door, his right hand leaning on his .38 Smith & Wesson. He tries to be discreet glancing around the interior.

Nothing greets him but a twenty-year old blond waitress that thinks he's cute and pays a lot of attention to his needs. His flirting isn't hidden, it comes natural and a little fun. The smell of fried food permeates the building and Ryan's thoughts move from a shooting stranger to wings and chili.

Dr. Sam Wallace sits in an early afternoon staff meeting, anxious to leave to check on an eleven-year old boy he performed surgery on yesterday morning. The procedure went as planned, but he's more comfortable attending his patients than listening to new government pricing guidelines for Medicare. Money is not why he became a doctor.

Sam looks at his watch and it reads 1:07. A flash of fate races into his mind, he visions the shooting to start in minutes at the sports bar. He places Ryan in the middle of the carnage. A dash out of the room to his car and a madman's drive to the restaurant ensues.

The cute waitress lays the check next to Ryan smiling broadly. "I'll take it when you're ready."

Ryan pulls his credit card out, laying it on the small tray holding the bill. He returns the smile. "Thanks".

She walks off carrying his VISA card intent on running the charges and getting a nice tip Ryan always gives. His smile makes her day.

Ryan has a habit of looking at his tie after a meal for good reason. He sees a chili stain lying comfortably halfway down his shirt. It's not surprising, spilling food on clothes is a family tradition. Another tradition is getting a friendly ribbing from his wife trying to get the mess out. The bathroom is only a few feet to his left and an attempt to neutralize much of the stain as possible beckons him. He opens the door, grabs paper towels, wets them from the sink and begins to rub.

A tall young man is sitting in the last bathroom stall drinking straight from a bourbon bottle and downing several 'uppers' to gain control of the moment. Both his parents lay dead in a pool of blood at home and there's a determination to go out of life creating the biggest bang possible. The only reason to select the sports bar is love for their French fries and apple pie he finished eating ten minutes ago.

He reaches into a backpack pulling out two pistols. The .22 is stuffed in his waistband and the .40 caliber held in one hand. The other hand grips the backpack containing three hundred rounds of ammo for both weapons. The stall door opens and he takes two steps toward Ryan, the pistol aimed at his back. Ryan senses trouble, turns and receives the .40 caliber slug to the left center of his chest. Ryan falls to the floor fighting for breath and life, losing at both.

Sam gets to the sports bar, jumps from the car as the young man erupts from of the bathroom firing at anything moving. People are running out the three exits, shots are sprayed in every direction, and no quarter given to anyone in the line of fire. One man throws a chair through a large pane glass window and the shooter fires twice in his direction but misses. The pretty blond lies in a pool of blood, lifeless from a shot to her head. Four more are dead and several dying in various parts of the restaurant.

The shooter pulls out the .22 firing into turned over tables and approaching eleven trapped staff members and customers that fled to the back of the kitchen. As he shoots his way around the corner, Sam goes into the broken window and his medical instincts take over. He helps an elderly couple get out and goes to the waitress checking for vitals but she's dead.

He can hear the shooter returning from the back room and decides to avoid fire by hiding in the bathroom. He finds Ryan, blood pouring from his chest wound and Sam realizes the grave situation for his cousin. Ryan's shirt is ripped off and Sam makes a bandage trying to compress the wound. A check on Ryan's vitals brings the dark of death to Sam's gifted hands, no pulse or life is left.

The door flings open and the shooter stands no more than eight feet from Sam and death. Ryan's gun is in the holster and Sam could defend himself if he grabs it and fires. Instead Sam lifts Ryan's head up, hugs him close to his chest unwilling to take the gun. Sam doesn't fear dying at this moment, settled with the thought of death holding his friend and cousin.

The young shooter raises the weapon and points it toward Sam, their eyes meet for several seconds in lockstep. Sam accepts his fate of death watching the shooter leaning down, the gun pointed at his face. The young man stands up, places the pistol on his temple and commits suicide.

Sam closes his eyes seconds before the weapon goes off holding Ryan close to his heart and praying for a miracle.

Realizing the kid shot himself, Sam lifts Ryan from the floor and takes him out as SWAT rushes into the restaurant. Sam can feel Ryan's heart starting to beat again just before the paramedics place him in an ambulance for a ride to the hospital. Sam never stops working on him and Ryan does survive the chest wound. The miracle he prayed for occurred twice in the span of an hour.

CHAPTER TWENTY-SIX

Collecting Your Due

THE POSTHOLE DIGGER cranks up in JD's backyard a little after 7:00 a.m. The noise wakes Jim from a deep sleep, not happy he goes to the window looking at JD's fencing activities. The window is slammed shut. Out in the night grave digging until 3:00 a.m., he needs more shut eye before attacking the day. So much for John David starting the project on Sunday. A return to the bed produces little other than buzzing of the digger doing its job. He decides to start the day early, not by option, but annoyance.

Jim has an 11:00 a.m. meeting with Steve at the Institute to produce the DNA sample of Joe Tramazzo. Tramazzo's absence in the grave didn't exactly shock. He figured the funeral home placed the body in the coffin for viewing, cremated Tramazzo collecting military insurance money to do the burial. It wouldn't be the first time short cuts are taken in the funeral business.

With the early start dictated by JD's fence building, Jim calls Steve to pass the DNA sample off early. Steve is cranky but agrees to a 9:00 a.m. meeting. Jim pulls into the Institute parking lot, more casually dressed this time and more confident in the environment.

He knocks on Steve's door, not waiting for a response he goes in. Steve looks over the top of his glasses at the rude entrance, but says nothing. A ziplock bag is pulled from Jim's pocket and sat on his desk. Steve picks it up, closely examining the earring inside.

"We prefer several strains of hair, not an earring that may not have a sufficient amount of DNA for identification." Steve states with authority.

Jim didn't want to detail the empty coffin; in his mind the job is completed. "Tramazzo shaved his head... love you but not going to pull the boxers off a dead man for the required hair. Hey, you guys are the best in the world at extracting DNA."

"Flattery gets you zippo with me... I'll submit the earring to the lab for analysis." Steve says bluntly.

Steve passes an envelope across the table to Jim that slides into his back pocket. "Thanks." Jim responds casually, gets up and goes out the door without any response from Steve. All pretty much expected at this point. Steve's coldness is inherent to his personality, and nothing Jim says will interest him enough to change it.

Once inside the GTO Jim opens the envelope to verify the content. He focuses on the $13,000 posted in the check's right hand corner to verify the happiness. The happiness is replaced by a flowing shower of bright red flooding his consciousness and dominating the senses.

Seconds go by. Jim imagines an object falling from the sky into the red walls surrounding his body. He tries to identify the descending mystery but can't visualize what is slamming into the middle of his mind. He recoils in the seat, ducking from something thrown from high above.

The red cloud lifts his blinded sight, he leans forward in the GTO stunned and confused. This is the second time he's fallen into a mental crevice and it's frightening. The key is turned over and the car moves away from the lot slowly. Driving alleviates the fear and clears his mind. Maybe Janey was right, he might need to see a doctor? A concussion is a serious condition, being macho is giving him major problems.

The most amazing or worst talent Jim possesses is his resiliency; a byproduct of childhood abuse and the loss of all those close to him. Maybe being a hard headed character adds to the texture, but two miles down the road his optimism is growing and health fears subsided. Instead of a doctor, he goes to see Detective Fox intent on digging a little deeper into Dr. Benders' murder. His dealings with the Institute is based on the intimacy of a fractured childhood, now he needed to know all the dirt on them. It festered in his mind that everyone at the Institute reeked of control, one thing he deplores the most. His stepfather's control shaped this thinking.

Fox is heading out of the station when both meet in the hallway.

"Foxman, where're you going?" Jim asks.

"Headed to court...testifying on a domestic violence case that turned really ugly... can't stand a man beating up on a chick. What are you doing at the station?" Fox inquires.

"Came to yak at you, but we'll connect later," he answers.

Fox continues down the hall but turns back to Jim. "Hey, the Captain wants to talk about Dodger tickets... he's in now."

Jim pulled a rabbit out of the hat for Captain Cyril when he scored four Dodger tickets to the World Series from Slick Rollie. The Captain would throw Jim in jail if he discovered the tickets were negotiated from a substantial Mexican drug lord. The tickets became available when said drug lord tried to cross the border from Canada to see the game and got detained.

Slick learned early the political power sporting event tickets possess and brokered all types including the Super Bowl and NBA finals. He owned a box at Dodger Field for business dignitaries, a revolving group sitting virtually every time a home stand played. The irony surrounding the event tickets, Rollie cared less about seeing any sports. It's strictly playing the 'owe me' game very well.

The Captain likes Jim's bounty hunting reputation, the tickets and signed baseballs only adds to the fondness. Captain Cyril's gruff reputation keeps most people at bay, but Jim rolls into his office like the governor looking to get answers.

"Captain, heard you needed to see me." Jim states picking up a signed baseball on Cyril's desk, tossing it in the air, catching it and repeating the process.

"Jim," the Captain states shutting down his computer. "Caught any bad guys lately?"

"Been a little slow, but can change quickly… you know that better than anybody." Jim answers.

"Our business has a neverending chain of characters having no willpower… the only thing that changes are the faces. Say, my ignorant brother-in-law is coming to town this weekend…he's awkwardly a Giants fan but is married to my sister so I have to forgive. Think you could rustle up four tickets?" The Captain leans heavily across the desk, elbows supporting the question.

Jim sets the ball back on the desk. "Box seats on the first base side… would that work?"

"Hell yeah, that would be a beautiful thing," the Captain endorses.

"I'm sure Slick's box is open… call you to confirm." Jim gives him the news he wants to hear. "I could use a little help."

"Name it." A benevolent Captain responds.

"Doing a little work for the Benders Institute, what can you give me on the Doctor's murder?"

The Captain leans back in his chair. "You dogging my case?"

"Not really, running down past clients of the Institute. Just want to know what I'm dealing with... his death may undermine the direction I take. What's your feel for the staff over there?"

"Can't say much, Jim... this goes way beyond the normal murder in SoCal. Politically it's off the charts, even the Feds contacted our office. The last time that happen was the O.J. trial. Will say this, that's a strange bunch over at the Institute... starts with his widow. She doesn't seem too upset over the murder, guess some people don't have a lot of outward emotion. Getting plenty corporate cooperation...financials, computers...most anything we've asked for." Cyril relays.

"What was the Doctor like... why would someone nail him to a tree? Just killing the guy wasn't enough?" Jim questions.

"When you figure that out, you'll probably have the killer. The guy was king of DNA science... big in the Catholic Church, more than seven million in contributions the last couple of years. Knee deep in helping the church with the Shroud of Turin over the years... a lot of Muslims hate what it stands for. This takes our list of suspects international, which I have gladly handed over to the FBI. You can do me another favor... your contacts on the street, keep your eyes open." The Captain asks for Jim's cooperation.

"Sure, Captain." Jim commits extending his hand.

Both men get up and clasp hands. Jim turns to head out of the office.

"Jim, one more thing," the Captain adds.

As he opens the door, Jim turns back. "What's that?"

"Bring everything back to me, no one else," the Captain demands.

"I understand." Jim eases back into the office. "By the way, word on the street is the guy in charge of security... David Sanders might have a role in all this. Any basis for that?"

"Off the record... doesn't add up. Nothing in his background gives credibility to that premise. Hell he worked for the man more than nine years. Somebody did try to run his ass off the road the other night... don't think it has anything to do with this case." The Captain responds to the contrary.

"Fair enough...catch you later." Jim leaves.

CHAPTER TWENTY-SEVEN

Sanders Dollar

THE .40 CAL FIRES, recoils and fires again. Jim finishes the clip off with four more shots hammering a tight pattern of holes in the paperman thirty feet down the firing range. He reloads, retrieves the target checking the bullet pattern and replaces the target sending it back down the range 35 feet. He checks the ear plugs, unloads the weapon duplicating earlier success peppering the chest area with every shot.

Slick Rollie taps him on the shoulder and Jim takes the headgear and safety glasses off.

"Stop wasting my ammo, you're not going to get any better." Rollie kids Jim concerning his shooting prowess.

"You should mask the jealousy a little better," Jim responds.

"Haven't fired a weapon in ten years… can still outshoot you," Slick brags.

Jim turns the pistol around butt first and offers it to Rollie. "Shoot 'em up cowboy… it's all black and white when the firing is over."

"I'm here on company business… don't have time to show out fortunately for you." Rollie hands a file over to Jim. "Here's the workup on Sanders… the security guy for Benders."

A look at the file and back to Rollie draws a smile from Jim. "Can't argue with business… especially when it's business for me." He holsters the weapon and both walk out to the front of the Pawnshop.

"My generosity knows no bounds, however, when are you getting over this Institute case… need my boy back?" Rollie asks.

"Be done ten, maybe twelve days max… then I'm all yours. By the way, Captain Cyril asked for your Dodger box seats next weekend…any problem?" Jim asks.

"Cyril, huh?" Rollie responds. "That old horse thief… why not, I like it when power needs my help."

"Why did you call him a horse thief?" Jim inquires.

"There's always a blurred line between good and evil… word on the street has it when the Captain was a rising star he busted Eugene Cunningham for a large quantity of cocaine. Worked out a deal on the side that got him probation instead of serious jail time."

"Who is Eugene Cunningham?" Jim looks puzzled.

"Cunningham Publishing… largest book publisher on the West Coast. It seems Cyril wanted to write a real book, so Cunningham suddenly became interested in the manuscript, advanced him large dollars for a rag not even his relatives read. Published author he was anointed, helps him break the ice at all those Hollywood parties he's a regular at."

"Gives new meaning to honest cop…he's bad like the people you bail out, people like we both deal with." Jim relays.

Rollie puts his arm around Jim's shoulder walking over to the office.

"And they call me, 'Slick'."

Jim looks over the file getting a read on David Sanders. The phone rings and Janey is on the line.

"Got you a flight out Sunday, back on Tuesday to St. Louis," she relays.

"Perfect...should be able to wrap up in two days. Never been to Missouri, have you?" Jim asks.

"Nope, but we've got a new girl at the club from there... couldn't wait to get out," Janey answers.

"Won't be doing too many tourist attractions...see you Saturday night." Jim turns the phone off.

Jim looks closer in the file and sees Sanders' phone number. He dials it.

"Sanders here," David answers.

"Mr. Sanders, my name is Jim Cirmah. I'm a P.I. doing a job for the Benders Institute... do you have time to talk this afternoon?"

"All I have is time...where?" David answers.

"There's a Starbucks on Central and Vine...see you at four?" Jim sets the location.

"I can make that...see you then." Sanders hangs the phone up.

Jim goes out to the front counter. Conrad is eating a pizza. He grabs a slice under duress from Conrad. "Hey, the extra pizza is my dinner tonight... get your own."

"How many times have I fed you...didn't have time for lunch?" Jim picks up a second slice.

"You owe me." Conrad continues the pizza defense. "When are you traveling to Missouri to check on the Doctor? What's his name?"

"Doctor Sam Wallace, he won't make house calls out in L.A." Jim starts on the second slice. "Going on Sunday, be gone a couple of days. I'm headed to meet the security guy for Dr. Benders...want to come?"

"Can't, no one to work the front desk...Lance had a dental appointment this afternoon." Conrad relays.

"Alright, was going to buy you Mexican food afterwards, but that seems out now." Jim teases.

"I can meet you at 7:30." Conrad quickly responds hoping to get a trade out on the pizza.

"I'll call you in a little while to confirm." Jim winks at Conrad leaving the Pawnshop. Conrad knew the Mexican was Jim's favorite, too.

David Sanders looks at his watch sitting in Starbucks. It reads 4:06, his hands start to perspire. Little can be done about the anxiety but wait for Jim to show. He decides to leave at 4:15 if Jim's not made the front door, but doesn't exercise the option. Jim walks in two minutes before the deadline.

Jim pretends not to know what David looks like but has a photo in the file. He walks up to David sitting by himself.

"Excuse me, Sir," Jim asks. "Are you David Sanders?"

David looks up, glad he didn't leave early based on his time obsession. "Yes...you're Jim...?"

"Jim Cirmah." He extends his hand to David and both hold firmly.

David picks his coffee up. "Buy you a coffee?"

"Sure." Jim agrees and the two go to the counter returning with a new coffee.

Something refreshing about David thought Jim immediately. He's patronly, almost father like to a man never experiencing someone in that role. The connection is mutual on David's part, perhaps for no more reason than his son would be the same age as Jim and his personality is protective naturally.

"So," David asks. "Why did you call me?"

Jim peers out the window, sips the coffee and looks back to Sanders. "To be honest, not sure why...I know a few cops in my line of business, one of them investigating Dr. Benders' death told me about your connection with the Doctor. Got this job at the Institute…keep brushing up against the Doctor's legacy. Something I can't put my finger on, but it seems to lead me to you. Crazy, huh?"

"Probably, but sometimes you have to follow your instincts. What are you doing for the Institute?" David asks.

"First, why did you agree to meet me?" Jim has the same curiosity.

"Frustration, even some fear…I allowed Dr. Benders to change his security schedule the day he died, it was my fault. I want who did it bad. A team of individuals tried to run me off a mountain…very professional in their attempt. Those kind of people are paid a lot of money to orchestrate an accidental death. Am I that close to finding real evidence, my gut tells me yes? My gut also thinks you can help me." David responds.

"Fair enough, let's compare notes about the Institute." Jim fills in the blanks surrounding his list of people he's running down. It felt good like a church confessional. He even breached his NDA with the Institute by telling David the story concerning Benders' possible descendants and the DNA confirmation.

David sits stunned.

"I was around Dr. Benders for more than nine years, no way in hell he would get anyone pregnant outside of strict protocol…that's not him, ever."

Jim listens to the homeless man's story attempting to kill David in the theater and the tattooed man's intervention. He did leave out the part about the homeless man getting killed in the process.

"What kind of tattoo did the guy have?" Jim asks. "Run across a lot of tats in my line of work."

David places his finger on the side of his neck and moves it down to his shirt collar. "A military looking knife that drops low on his neck."

"Your guy 6-1, around 210 pounds...dark headed, very short cropped hair?" Jim is connecting the dots.

"That's the man... do you know him?" David leans on the table intently waiting on Jim's answer.

"Sorta," Jim states. "His name is Joe Tramazzo... special forces dude. Never met him but have a picture and a background profile. The only problem... he supposedly died in a motorcycle accident three plus weeks ago which means he either has a twin or someone is playing both of us for fools. He was the first target on my list for the Institute. Is the guy still in custody?"

"After he blew his face up on the glass at the precinct they took him to the emergency room, but after he got stitched up he overpowered the cop escort disappearing." David explains.

Jim shakes his head. "Listen, I'm not sure what this means but it stays between you and me right now. I'm following up on the second target in Missouri over the next few days... it may reveal more of the puzzle pieces. We'll get back together next week to move the train further down the track. You stay low for now...don't expose yourself."

The two men stand up and shake hands. "I can stay low...we'll get to the bottom of this soon enough."

Jim heads to the GTO content for the first time in a while but not exactly knowing why. David left the meeting thinking he isn't in this thing alone. They have no idea how deep each must go to find the bottom.

CHAPTER TWENTY-EIGHT

Pin Tail Donkey

THE PLANE TOUCHES down in the St. Louis airport on schedule and Jim picks up his rental car. Janey has everything lined up including MapQuest directions to Dr. Sam Wallace's home and a second one to the hospital from the airport. The drive to Cape Girardeau lists 115 miles, but road construction demands more than three hours to get there.

Janey isn't just a pretty face and a great set of legs, she's smart. Jim explained the Institute case and need to recover a DNA sample from the three targets. There are several ways to accomplish the objective without the person knowing and giving up the sample voluntarily. One is to follow them around, waiting until the subject discards a touched item like a cigarette or coffee cup. Another is go through garbage and find a contact item such as a toothbrush. These require a great deal of patience, something Jim didn't have 2000 miles away from L.A.

Jim's plan is a lot more direct and illegal. He wants to pick a lock when the target isn't home and retrieve an item. But to succeed he needs to get a look at the home's alarm system keyboard to understand what he's dealing with.

Janey's idea is to approach the home telling the subject he's a friend of a former high school classmate having interest in Amway products. The friend tells Jim the target is an Amway distributor and can pick up product from the subject. Janey even researched Dr. Sam Wallace's high school yearbook and got Jim a classmate's name to use. Simple thought Jim, but brilliant.

The FBI file workup on Dr. Wallace states he lives with a girlfriend, Diane Hatters that works at the same hospital as a nurse. Jim is hoping they don't work different shifts leaving someone home at all hours. Dr. Wallace is a surgeon up and gone well before daylight during the week. To find out Diane's schedule, Janey calls the hospital various times looking for her. Turns out the Doctor's schedule is similar, Diane getting home mid-afternoon and the Doctor arriving back early evening. Janey's research saves Jim time observing the couple's schedule and made the job easier. It didn't, however, lessen the fact it's dangerous and something he could go to jail for. As a thrill junkie, all this intrigue made Jim feel alive and wanting to jump in headfirst.

No time is wasted once Jim gets to Cape Girardeau, he drives to the Doctor's house to assess the target and determine the next steps. It's after 4:00 p.m., Diane should be off work and home. After circling the neighborhood, Jim parks in front of the house and goes to the front ringing the doorbell. He waits 30 seconds and rings again. Diane comes to the door.

"May I help you?" Diane asks in a soft southern accent.

"Is Doctor Wallace in?" Jim asks.

"No, may I deliver a message?" Diane replies.

"Yeah, I'm a friend of Dave Wilcox that went to school with Sam. Dave told me I could get Amway products from Sam...

I'm new to the area… usually get my supplies through a local distributor." Jim explains peering inside the door but not seeing the alarm system.

"Must be some mistake, Sam doesn't have anything to do with Amway." Diane's voice is delicate.

Jim needs to review the alarm keypad and tries to gain access into the house. He pulls his cell phone out. "Been on my phone all day…it's dead. Could I use your phone one minute to call Dave, I'll be quick?"

Jim feels 99% certain he'll be turned down, and if asking that question in L.A. the door would be slammed in his face. To his surprise Diane lets him in and hands over the house phone. The phone is dialed to a make believe number without gaining a dial tone. A quick look reveals no alarm pad. Jim can't believe the home didn't have an alarm system, but clearly it didn't. He's not used to this much trust shown by his fellowman, but not familiar with a small southern town where half the homes didn't bother to lock the doors at night.

Jim pretends to communicate on the phone about the Amway situation and quickly comes to a conclusion handing the phone back to Diane.

"Thanks," Jim smiles in his best actor face. "Must be some kind of misunderstanding…have a good afternoon."

He drives away figuring an easy get and go opportunity early in the morning, he won't miss his flight from St. Louis tomorrow night. That evening he calls Janey to relay the success of her plan. Jim senses a little mental distance and gets off the call faster than normal. Last night she worked a double shift and needed the sleep, Jim took her word and shut off the phone.

The television inside Jim's hotel room is channeled on Sports Center and he drifts in and out of sleep. The flight, drive, time zone change and securing the target plan delivers him to the bed watching baseball before 9:00 p.m. He nods off within a few minutes.

The air conditioner inside the room roars a deep-throated noise demanding Jim's attention the first couple of times, but soon he ignores its labored workings succumbing to the begging sleep.

Time passes not counted by a clock, only the heavy rolling wave of dreams filling his head with abstract visions rarely recovered in the light of day. Jim sits up in bed, a bright light flooding the confines of his mind and bleeding over to his surroundings. Sports Center Station is gone, replaced by a red lava-like flow dripping down the walls. The ceiling retracts to an open sky, objects tumble toward the bed in a freefall. The instinctive reflexes take over for Jim, hands flying up to protect himself from the impending doom raining down.

Jim, not awake not asleep, is fighting against the red liquid like a salmon swimming upstream, his lungs flooded and fear griping his attempt to escape. Jim fights, not understanding what monster wants his soul, but little doubt the dark demon is no longer patient in its demands.

The cool evening air fills his lungs, giving him relief from the suffocating red liquid. Jim bumps into a parked car, locked and silent. He's barefoot, walking outside his room in the hotel parking lot clad only in boxer shorts fighting the confusion. The door to his room is shut, he stands in front measuring it. He's bathed in doubt never experienced before. A stranger opens a door down the hallway and embarrassment makes his hand turn the doorknob to duck out of sight.

Sleep nor the monster returns to Jim's room the rest of the night, only the cranky air conditioner. The red numbered clock on the stand next to the bed states 6:30 a.m. Jim showers, packs and dresses in a jogging suit with a hoodie. A strong cup of coffee gives him a caffeine lift, he'll need more for the job ahead.

Dr. Wallace and Diane are gone before 7:00 a.m., Jim drives by the house shortly after 7:30. He stops at a distance surveying the neighborhood, everything seemingly quiet. The car is driven a few blocks away, parked and Jim jogs an alleyway behind the Doctor's home. His weapon was left in L.A. It's a pain to clear airline security even though Jim has a permit to cross state lines with the gun. This isn't the first time he's broken into a home or place of business, but without a pistol he feels vulnerable.

A run to the front door and subsequent knock makes sure no one is home. He slips around back to work his touch using a lock picking device on the backdoor. He acquired the skill set from an old locksmith that happens to be a longtime friend of Slick Rollie.

The door is quickly opened and Jim wastes no time heading to the second floor and the master bedroom. A 'His and Her' bathroom is separated by a large shower. He looks for a hairbrush on the Doctor's side, but only a comb without hair meets his stare. Rifling in one of the drawers, he notices a box containing toothbrush heads used to replace the one attached to the electric toothbrush plugged in next to the sink. Jim removes the used toothbrush and replaces it with a new head bagging the old one.

The DNA prize in pocket, he turns to leave the bedroom determined to get on the airplane and return to L.A. Exiting the hallway, he starts down the stairwell. Two uniform police officers step out of the living room, weapons drawn.

Jim freezes and places his hands behind his head.

"Move... you will die." One of the cops screams.

Jim knew when to be defiant; this is not one of those times.

The same cop gives more directions. "Lay face down on the floor."

As Jim follows directions the second cop handcuffs him then helps him to his feet. He is led to the couch and seated. The cop doing the talking holsters his weapon, walks around the corner to the kitchen making a call on a cell phone. Jim is surprised by the move, but maybe cops act differently in this tiny southern town?

Words are exchanged over the cell, but Jim can't link into any discernible sentences. The other cop continues to point the weapon at him handcuffed, not following police protocol.

What triggered the cops to make entry behind him, perhaps motion detectors?

How could he miss something so obvious?

A look around the living room and hallway doesn't reveal motion detectors, so the mystery deepens.

The cop returns from the kitchen and nods to the cop standing close to the couch. Jim is expecting to be placed in a squad car, delivered to a jail cell and hopefully get out on bail when Slick gets a phone call.

The cop closest to Jim makes a strange request.

"Lay face down on the couch."

Jim looks up totally confused. "Do what?" He questions.

The second cop moves his weapon close to Jim's head. "Do as you're told, asshole."

Countless scenarios are blitzing into Jim's mind, but is helpless, no option other than doing what he's told. He lays face down on the couch and feels the distinct penetration of a hypodermic needle into his buttocks. Within a few seconds he's out cold.

Jim lays unconscious on the couch, one cop leaves while the other takes the cuffs off and flips him over. The cop returns carrying a finger printing pad, paints several of Jim's fingertips and pulls off each print on a piece of clear tape. They load him in the back of an SUV in the backyard and drive away.

Jim looks into a blue sky and moves a hand to cover his eyes. The brightness causes him to squint, adjust his line of sight and line of thinking. He's lying in an alley next to a dumpster behind a Kroger Grocery Store. He tries to stand up but only gets to one knee, stopping to gather his strength. Grabbing the dumpster, he pulls himself to a full stand. His back reacts to what feels like a kidney beating. A homeless man approaches, hitting Jim up for money.

"I've had a bad day... take it elsewhere." Jim says, little passion in his voice.

Jim walks out of the alley and reaches for his wallet not expecting it to be there. To his surprise the only thing missing is his driver's license. He still has money, credit cards, and a Rolex Watch given by Slick for his 25th birthday. Walking the street he is confused, hungry, tired, and sore. The fastest way to get past this nightmare is taking care of each need one at a time. Hunger is satisfied at a small diner converted into a restaurant from an old Pullman Railroad Car.

He peers out the window chewing on a bite of a hamburger steak watching the traffic make its way from one side of the rotary road circling toward the courthouse setting directly across the street. He remembers the toothbrush and reaches into his pocket to confirm its existence. It's still there.

Many questions circle his mind like the cars on the rotary. He moves a fork load of gravy and onions to his mouth and notices a chemical smell on his fingers. On closer inspection, a distinct odor of bleach comes from both hands. Why would anyone take the time to bleach his hands? None of this made sense. Those two are not cops, what is the object of the drill?

Jim finishes the last fry, pays his bill and catches a cab to the rental car. The drive to St. Louis is faster than remembered,

the blame placed on a heavy footed accelerator. He wanted
out of Missouri, it seems to be the land of evil. The evil cares
nothing about Missouri, it only has interest in Jim Cirmah.

CHAPTER TWENTY-NINE

Who Bugs You?

THE PLANE RIDE is non-stop and Jim sits next to a window wrapped in a blanket, sound asleep the entire way. To his relief, security in St. Louis accepted his P.I. photo license instead of his driver's license. Getting off the plane he's reminded of the trip, a soreness not going away soon. After arriving at the terminal he grabs the carryon and goes straight to the GTO, no temperament for waiting at this juncture.

He arrives home wishing Winston was there to greet him, but Janey took the dog for the trip. Missing Winston told Jim how alone this moment felt in his life. The trip has been bad, getting home is not much better.

Jim unlocks the backdoor walking into a mess. His house has been ransacked. Numerous items are missing including his computer and flat screen TV. A check upstairs reveals his pistol hidden between the mattresses is gone also.

"Damn it." Jim talks to the walls, but silence offers no solace.

The iPhone is pulled from his pocket, flipped to his recent call column and hits David Sanders's number.

"Jim, how did your trip go?" David answers, thinking he'll get the standard retort from Jim.

"Miserable is selling it way too short...I'm back at the house... someone turned it upside down taking electronics, got my pistol. We need to talk tomorrow." Jim relays.

"No problem...where?" David questions.

"Booty Trap on Sims and 65th Street at noon." Jim answers.

"I'll be there." David hangs up his phone.

Jim thinks someone is in the house several times during the night and gets up to investigate finding nothing. Nights without sleep follow him around much like trouble.

Jim is not late for the meeting, he's twenty minutes early. David finds him at the table talking on the phone with Slick. Jim smiles at David pulling a chair up to the table, but continues the phone dialogue.

"Yeah, bastards got my pistol... computer, TV too. Do you have a .40 cal at the shop?" Jim waits on an answer. David listens to one side of the conversation.

"Perfect... I'll come by to get it in a couple of hours. Thanks, Slick." Jim shuts the cell off and turns to David.

"Replacing my gun and TV at the Pawnshop," Jim explains.

"Isn't there a two week waiting period on getting a gun in California?" David smiles knowing the answer.

"For most people a true statement." Jim responds.

"Nice to have people in high places." David understands how the game is played.

"If a high place, I couldn't get my gun for two weeks." Jim smiles at a rule playing Rollie, the first taste of humor chewed on in a while.

A couple of beers find the table. Jim waits until the waiter gets well away and leans to David.

"Alright, time to pull our dresses up to show all." Jim glances around the room hoping one of the staff doesn't come to greet him. "I do things other P.I.'s don't. That's why the Institute hired me. I told you about Joe Tramazzo... got his file from a top government agency... totally bought and paid for illegally. When I found out he died... never hesitated to dig up his grave for a hair sample to get my cash from the Institute. The problem is Joe Tramazzo's body wasn't in the coffin." Jim is bent on gaining a partner in this twisted chain of events.

"Whose body was in the coffin?" David looks like he saw a ghost.

"There's no body in the coffin... found an earring in the lining, happy to collect my bounty turning it over for DNA analysis." Jim feels compelled to get a number of things off his chest and in turn get as much as possible from David.

"Are you wearing a wire?" David's eyes focus on Jim's face.

"What?" Jim's not sure where this came from.

"You heard me...are you wearing a wire... are you a cop?" David is really setting a hard tone.

Jim pulls his tee shirt up to his neck revealing nothing. "I'm far from being a cop as you can get... are you wired?" A back in your face question by Jim.

"Nope, not a cop anymore but have to ask the question to further this conversation." David stands up and lifts his shirt. "No wire on me either."

Jim takes a deep draw from his beer realizing David did the right thing for both under the circumstances.

"You're right... it needed to be done." Jim states.

"When you hear my story, you'll understand. I was being tortured by the homeless man in that hellhole theater. He tied me up, rolled a chamber with one bullet pulling the trigger pointed at various parts of my body. Death was imminent when Tramazzo blew his head off... saved my life. He cut my bindings, turned and left. Not a word exchanged." David is relieved to deliver the story.

"That's a wild story. I can see why you have an affinity for Tramazzo," Jim assesses.

"The rub is, I didn't report it… he saved my life, didn't want to put him in jeopardy over a crazy bum. Being an ex-cop, the book could be thrown at me," David confesses.

"You're a boy scout compared to some of the things I've done." Jim states a left-handed compliment. "This trip to Missouri, I picked the lock of the target, go in to grab a toothbrush for the DNA. On the way out two guys dressed like cops cuff me, flip me over shooting a drug in my ass knocking me out cold. I end up next to a dumpster in an alley… took nothing from me but my license. I flew back totally confused… what was their angle?"

"Did they take the toothbrush from you?" David asks.

"Nope," Jim responds. "Nothing but the license… didn't touch my Rolex, money, credit cards. Funny thing, my hands were washed in some type of chemical… maybe bleach?"

"They lifted your prints," David answers.

"What for?" Jim knows the answer will not be good.

"Probably to plant at a crime scene would be my guess. That's CIA/KGB stuff… someone sophisticated knew you were going to be there. Someone having a lot of money hires that kind of talent. It doesn't come cheap." David being an ex-cop recognizes the business of deception well. "A car didn't try to run me off a cliff, two sawhorses rigged with headlights I thought was two oncoming cars appeared. I ditched to the right almost driving off into a 300 foot ravine. That's not amateur hour but highly paid pros."

A glance at his hands gives Jim a feeling of helplessness at that moment. "Where do we go from here… want to run from the Institute, my life was good until I took this job?"

"Emotionally, running away may seem to be the thing to do, but logically you need to finish the project… that buys us time to dig deeper, get answers," David explains.

Jim looks to the bar expecting to see Janey appear any moment even though her shift didn't start for a couple of hours. "The only person knowing my schedule is my girlfriend… can't believe she's involved."

"That could be it, but your house might be bugged… listening to every conversation going on," David summarizes.

Jim instantly travels back to the ladder incident justifying his paranoia.

"I know exactly when they got in the house."

"Do you have access to a debugger device…scan your home proving it one way or another?" David offers.

"Actually one was pawned at Slick Rollie's several months ago…we made jokes the IRS was bugging Slick's house. Probably still there." Jim seriously wants to disprove Janey's involvement quickly.

"Got a suggestion," David injects. "If you find a bug leave it alone… whoever installed it won't know you're on to them. Could give us an advantage."

"Excellent idea, I'll figure it out one way or another this afternoon." Jim concurs.

"Everything points to the Institute, but is it a corporate conspiracy… was Dr. Benders killed because he didn't want to go along with something?" David asks.

"We need to break into the boardroom, plant a bug to play the game." Jim jokingly adds.

"That's it… we need to get inside to figure it out." David likes the suggestion.

"The place is secured like Ft. Knox… I've been known to break into a house from time-to-time, but that's way over my pay grade." Jim confesses.

David asks, "Do you have anybody that possibly can tap into a computer system?"

"Hell yeah, my bud can hack anything. He works at Geek Squad during the day, but plays with the big boys at night. All he needs is an access point." Jim is talking about his pool playing buddy, Wayne Davis.

"I might have an access point on my Mac; it may still be connected to their server. Even got Dr. Benders' computer coordinates." David thinks this is a way to breach the security.

"I'll get a meeting with Wayne ASAP...he'll have the answers." Jim insists.

The two new partners eat lunch and part ways. Both leave convinced it's only a matter of time before the tide is turned in their favor. Even a good tide can drown you.

CHAPTER THIRTY

Computer Genius

SLICK ROLLIE IS not at the shop when Jim arrives. He has a contractor home to design electronics for his game room already having a ten foot screen and sound system a Hollywood director would kill for. Jim arrives not his usual chipper self and Conrad notices right away.

"You don't seem upbeat about your trip." Conrad shares his thoughts.

"Could have gone better…but got what I needed." Jim didn't want Conrad knee deep in things that might come back to bite either of them.

Conrad pulls a .40 cal in a carrying case from under the counter. "Rollie said you'd be looking for this. What happened to your pistol?"

"Someone broke into my house… to remind me how much I need Rollie and this place." Jim still has a little sense of humor left.

"And me?" Conrad asks.

"Sure… you and that talking Drug Lord are needed." Jim responds. "I'm going to get a flat screen, too…what's in Rollie's inventory?"

"We have a sixty inch somewhere in the back," Conrad answers.

"Way too much TV… need like a forty inch HD." Jim checks around the shop to see what electronics are available.

The phone rings but Conrad and Jim ignore it thinking Drug Lord is playing the phone ringing game. It wasn't Drug Lord and within a few seconds Conrad's cell rings.

"Hello." Conrad's eyes tell Jim whose call was missed.

"Why did the store phone go to voicemail… where are you?" Rollie questions.

"Sorry Uncle Rollie…thought Drug Lord pulled his phone thing on me, won't happen again," Conrad explains.

Jim motions to get the phone. "Rollie, it was my fault…we both thought that damn bird called. Say, do you still have the debug device?"

"Yes…a bargain at fifteen hundred. Who wants it?" Rollie lays out the economics.

"Actually, need to borrow it this afternoon… think something may be happening at my house." Jim admits.

"No problem… put Conrad on the phone," Rollie instructs.

Jim hands the phone back to Conrad.

"Conrad, go to the holdover shelf in the back… you'll find a debug unit, it looks like a metal detector setting on the shelf. Give it to Jim. Now, answer the phone next time. Gotta' go." Rollie hangs up.

"Watch the front, I'll get the metal detector thing." Conrad leaves the desk while Jim breaks his new pistol down, puts it back together and loads it.

Conrad returns and Jim takes the debug unit home. In route he calls Wayne Davis.

"Wayne, how you feeling?" Jim knows he's not completely in the clear yet.

"Feeling better, just a little bored. I've been cleared for work tomorrow, thank goodness. Got a pool game we can jump into?" Wayne begs.

"Name the night...we'll chalk it up, have a beer." Jim does miss his friendship. "I need a favor if you're feeling up to it?"

"Not ready to help whip any biker ass, but guessing it's something a little less demanding like fixing your computer." Wayne shoots back.

"It does have something to do with computer work; however, it may be slightly illegal." Jim is not exactly sure what kind of response the 'illegal' part is going to get.

"Damn, you took me from bored to excited...what is my man up to these days?" Wayne questions.

"I'll give you the shady details tonight...how about 7:30, bring the beer and pizza." Jim offers.

"Pepperoni and cheese...like it simple." Wayne counters.

"Simple it is...hey, text me your address. It just dawned on me I've never been to your house," Jim asks.

"When you get here you'll understand why... 7:30, don't be late. I have to be in med-heaven by 10:30." Wayne instructs.

"Be there carrying a smile, beer...pizza." Jim hangs the cell up.

Jim gets to the house and goes to pick up Winston at John David's. Janey left him with JD before going to her shift at the club. Winston licks his hand when Jim reaches down to pet the rather large neck. It's more affection than he expects; Winston isn't exactly heavy on the emotional side of things. Jim is pleased, a little love from anyone is appreciated right now.

The two walk back to a house still turned upside down from the ransacking. Winston doesn't mind, he settles on the couch for a nap as Jim plugs in the bug finding device to charge it up. After a forty minute run and straightening up the mess lying around in piles, Jim uses the debugger upstairs but finds nothing.

He moves to the first floor and the machine lights up around the landline phone mounted on the wall. A second bug is planted on a light fixture in the living room.

Jim is mad and relieved at the same time. The thought of Janey helping someone hurt him is devastating and this proves how his actions were tracked in Missouri. The bugs are left in place following David's advice. He will adjust to being under constant surveillance, perhaps he could misdirect whoever is listening when the time calls for it.

A hot shower lowers his emotions for the time being. He goes downstairs in his boxers to grab a beer and notices how peaceful Winston appears on the couch breathing heavy. Jim never takes a nap but his watch says David won't come to the house for another hour and half. He lies next to Winston, setting the wakeup alarm on his phone and falling into a deep sleep immediately.

David gets to Jim's house twenty minutes early. Jim apologizes for the home still having a lot of work to do before it looks like a home again. He asks David to call a local pizza restaurant to order a couple of large pepperoni's to go while he finishes getting dressed. He grabs two six packs from the refrigerator and heads to Wayne's house full of surprises.

The GPS on Jim's phone issues directions to Wayne's home and it takes them through a less than flattering neighborhood. The GTO pulls up in front of the house and the first thing noticeable is a wire mesh screen on each window decorated by a sign stating in direct terms: 'WARNING'. Getting closer to the fine print on the sign, it becomes readable and not misunderstood: 'Windows Are Electrified'.

Jim looks at David approaching the front door. "Damn serious signs there."

David shakes his head in agreement. "Can't argue."

The front door is covered in the same metal mesh and an additional warning pinned in the middle of the screen.

"I'm afraid to push the doorbell," Jim states calling Wayne on his cell. "I'm on the front porch. If you want the pizza, let me in."

The porch light comes on and Wayne opens the door. What comes out of his mouth surprises both. "Jim, who the hell is this?"

"This is David Sanders, a friend and business associate." Jim answers feeling like he didn't know the guy asking the question and apologizing for David's presence.

"I don't know him...he can't come in." Wayne says matter of fact paralleling the warning signs plastered all over the outside of the house.

Jim is stunned having never seen this side of Wayne before. Now he understands why he's never been invited to come over to Wayne's house witnessing this kind of paranoia dripping off his tongue.

"What the hell's wrong with you, Wayne? He's my friend... now you need to act like a friend. Let us in or we're both leaving."

Wayne glances back toward the interior and then returns to Jim. "Alright, you can't bring a cell phone in... leave them in your car."

"What's going on... leave my cell phone?" Jim is ready to explode but hesitates thinking Wayne has lost his mind taking the beating and heavy medication.

"This is not personal, have things I don't want strangers to see... your phones could be damaged on my electronics, sorry for the mystery. Put your phones in the car...come on in." Wayne paints a strange picture.

David and Jim lock the phones in the trunk and return to the front door.

David looks over at Jim.

"We're not going to see hookers hanging upside down dripping blood from the ceiling are we?" He's half joking, half serious.

"I'll shoot him personally if he does." Jim answers telling the truth.

Wayne stands at the door holding it open and the guys walk in. There is a living room off to the left, door shut and secured with rather large locks. Wayne points to the framework around the front door, to the naked eye it looks no different than any other doorway in anyone's house.

"A very strong built-in magnetic bar outlines the frame of the door. Any device containing stored data will lose it going or coming, that's why your phones couldn't be brought in." Wayne explains leading the guys to the kitchen breaking out the beer and pizza.

"Are those windows really hooked up with juice?" Jim asks taking a bite of the pepperoni.

"It works like a large bug zapper." Wayne says matter of fact. "Two guys have already found out how well it works trying to break-in."

"Didn't the cops have a problem?" David asks.

"Didn't have the signs up first time... got a warning. The second guy didn't believe the sign, cops didn't say a thing. Look, it doesn't kill them...just knocks them out cold unless they have a pacemaker. Got cameras all around the house hooked into my laptop going off if someone comes into the field of view. Saw both idiots get lit up like a roman candle... called the cops to pick them up. They weren't going any place for the next hour or so." Wayne tells the story with a great deal of pride.

"What is so important in here to bug zap these guys?" Jim is thinking he could use the same system at his house.

"I'll let you see something, but have to promise you won't tell anyone." Wayne demands.

"We're good with that." Jim answers.

Wayne turns to David staring him down.

"Hey, pretty much fine to anything but a bathtub filled with a dismembered body." David at this point is preparing for something dark.

Jim smiles but Wayne doesn't. He gets up and leads them to the living room door dialing in a few number combinations opening two locks. The door is swung open, behind it is row after row of computers stacked to the ceiling. All powered up and appearing much like the NASA Center on launch day. Wayne shuts the door locking it behind and returns to the kitchen.

"Wow, what are you doing with all those computers?" Jim asks ignorant to what Wayne needs 100 plus computers for.

"I monitor outside systems to see what illegal activity might be going on." Wayne states.

"Then what happens?" David questions.

"I work for a number of agencies that go after people doing bad things." Wayne answers.

"Feds?" Jim tries to grasp the full picture.

"Sometimes…sometimes I do things for private companies," Wayne adds.

"So what's flying around in the air you can monitor?" David asks.

"Six miles away is a large apartment complex housing four hundred tenants. A computer hack lives there, adds 20 cents to every credit card transaction anyone makes in the building. You buy a beer at the ballgame, he adds 20 cents to your bill deposited in an offshore account. He collects several thousand dollars a month, no one questions 20 cents on their bill. Zapped his equipment the first time but was back in business two months later. Turned him over to the FBI." Wayne tells the story amazing Jim and Wayne.

Jim had no idea Wayne is a computer nerd superhero on the one hand and a pool playing, beer drinking buddy on the other. All of this information bodes well for his ability to help Jim and David but creates massive doubts on his willingness to do something illegal.

"You never shared a word of this." Jim is a little hurt to be completely caught off guard.

"No offense... even my family doesn't have a clue. It's too dangerous to share." Wayne eases a little of Jim's hurt feelings.

"Well," Jim stands. "What we need done is way off base for you, don't think it's exactly legal."

Wayne laughs, chases the last bite of pizza sipping on a beer. "Jim, nothing I do is legal chasing a scumbag stealing from old ladies on their VISA purchases. I do access sites that would land me in jail if I could be tracked, but they can't. No one has ever taken up for me like you did on those bikers... I will forever love you for it. If breaking into systems at the White House will help you, that's what I'll do." Wayne clears the air quickly.

Wayne leans toward Jim his beer extended and clicks the bottles together.

For the first time since getting to Wayne's house, David and Jim have a sense of relief on what Wayne can and will do. The next twenty-five minutes Wayne hears the details surrounding Dr. Benders' murder and the string of events following Jim and David. Every step drags them deeper into the dark abyss generated by the Institute.

David provides access to the Institute's system using Dr. Benders' computer number, although Wayne laughed at the premise he couldn't breach their system on his own.

"Once I'm in, any key words or sentences that should be pulled linking specific documents?" Wayne inquires.

"Yes," David quickly responds. "The Shroud of Turin. Dr. Benders had a manuscript on the Shroud that's missing... I believe it has a direct link to his murder."

"Give me a couple of days to worm my way around... see what pops up." Wayne is confident in his abilities.

Jim and David are excited about their new ally and feel confident moving forward. The GTO is optimism driving back to Jim's house.

CHAPTER THIRTY-ONE

Movie Magic

JANEY IS AWAKE before Jim this morning and that's usually not the case. He ended up at the club last night and followed her home. Janey could tell he's totally exhausted mentally and physically, going to sleep within minutes after hitting the bed. No sex for Jim spoke volumes.

Janey is at the stove cooking bacon, eggs, and biscuits in various stages. She has good culinary skills and is looking forward to the day when stripping at the club is in the rearview mirror and she can be more home focused. Children would be nice, but Janey isn't naive to think Jim is ready to jump into that space. She isn't completely sure Jim is the right guy, so domestic plans are still off in the distance.

Bacon, egg, and cheese is stuffed into several biscuits and taken to the bedroom to get Jim moving. He smiles at the breakfast in bed gesture and for the next thirty minutes rids himself of outside distractions. The cell rings, he starts to ignore it keeping the morning headed in a different direction without distractions. A glance at the caller I.D. makes him answer it.

"Wayne, how's your first day back at work?" Jim is a little surprised Wayne Davis is contacting him so quickly after the meeting last night.

"Happy to be back, I'm only working half a day the first week but it's good to see the crew again. Didn't take my meds last night, wanted to do something for our little project." Wayne explains.

"Didn't need to jump in too fast, but I certainly appreciate your efforts...what's going on?" Jim asks.

"Rather talk in person, think you will be happy seeing the results. Can you come by customer service at Best Buy?" Wayne has far more than Jim ever expected.

"Sure, 2:00 work?" Jim asks.

"Perfect...listen, when you get in the parking lot call me on the cell... I'll come to your car wagging a box of happiness." Wayne makes a bold prediction.

Jim is excited by Wayne's optimism. Since he took the job little has gone right except collecting a thirteen thousand dollar check. The second check will be picked up at 11:30 this morning when Sam Wallace's toothbrush is handed to Steve. Jim would gladly trade both checks to have normal back.

After breakfast Jim goes home to feed and walk Winston. On his way out, Janey asks about arranging a trip to New Orleans for the third target, a Miss Gayle Kidd. In spite of Jim's respect for David's decision making ability, he's tired of chasing people trying to snip a lock of hair and go running back to the Institute for a check.

He'll buy time pretending to play the game but fully intends not to make the trip to New Orleans. Jim shares this point of view with Janey who expresses relief his exposure to danger is limited.

Winston moves slower than usual placing him just short of a limping glacier. Jim peeks at his watch, if not moving toward the Institute in the next ten minutes he'll be late for his meeting and Mr. Personality. He tugs the large neck at the end of the leash, but Winston has plenty sniff and pee on his mind. Jim, not very patient to begin with, picks him up and deposits him in the house. It didn't upset Winston, he decides to pee on the floor thirty minutes after Jim leaves.

The DNA/check exchange with Steve went by having little fanfare and even less conversation. That's just fine by Jim. Something's evil in the Institute and Steve didn't do anything to dispel the image.

Jim gets to the GTO, check tucked away and a hesitation to open it. It could lead to a repeat of the Red Sea rushing into his world and a complete loss of control. If it's going to happen again, it will occur in the teller line at the Wells Fargo Branch when Jim deposits it.

He looks at the balance of his checking account and rolls his eyes. Never has Jim seen this much money under his control, he will solicit Rollie's advice on what to do.

A text to David confirms Wayne's meeting and possible progress breaching the computer system at the Institute. Jim promises an update later in the afternoon.

The traffic is bad heading to Best Buy and Jim's hope of stopping for lunch is a lost exercise. A call to Wayne in the parking lot gets him to the GTO a few minutes later carrying a taped box.

Wayne is all smiles cutting the tape and sets a new Toshiba laptop on the car seat next to Jim.

"I have two surprises," Wayne admits. "This computer is for an old pool playing buddy. Thought you might need one after the Devil visited your house the other night."

"Wayne, this is too much...certainly need the computer, but I will pay you. We're friends but this is business." Jim states authoritatively.

"All duly noted... now let me feel good about giving you the Toshiba, it's a great product." Wayne counters. He opens the computer, turns it on and pounds the keys in lightening-like quickness. He turns the computer to Jim. "Watch this."

Jim concentrates on the screen and is amazed. He sees a video feed of himself getting the check from Steve earlier in the morning exchanging for the toothbrush. Wayne rewinds the tape a few seconds and replays to illustrate the control features.

Jim looks at Wayne. "How the hell did you do that?"

"A little reverse engineering turning his computer into a video cam. I'm obviously in...so now the fun begins. Meanwhile you can see and hear what goes on in Steve's office getting a step up on insider information." Wayne does more than a little bragging.

"I'm floored," Jim says humbly.

"As you should be," Wayne says revealing no humility. "I've got a project to clean up, but shortly no secrets will be buried in your beloved Institute."

"I'm in your debt... David won't believe this, thanks." Jim states.

"You are in my debt... figure a couple games of pool... add a six pack, that's the minimum I'll settle for. My talents are not cheap." Wayne likes to help Jim and showcase his talents at the same time. He now feels equal in the friendship and it's not always been that way.

The drive to David's apartment is restoring Jim's energy armed with the new tool Wayne has installed. The world appeared to cave in on Jim but a renewed sense of optimism is giving balance to his actions, and just as importantly control seems to be restored.

The phone rings and Jim answers. "David, got the beer on ice… be there in five minutes."

"It's been cooling down since your text…you still have that debugger with you?" David asks.

"Yeah, in the trunk…Rollie doesn't care how long I have it." Jim answers.

"Perfect, bring it in to my apartment…we'll clear my place before playing the computer." David has walked down a lot more paths of evil than Jim and is thinking from experience.

"Good idea…that's why we're partners." Jim is impressed.

The debugger is waved in and out of every crevice of the apartment but remains silent proving the area is clean of intrusion. Jim sets the computer in motion and beer in hand watches the boring activities swirling around Steve's office minute by minute. Nothing more than a loud fart by Steve making both nearly spit beer laughing so hard was of any interest.

The action is recorded on a disc to be replayed, watched and listen to at their leisure. The fart is replayed a couple more times for cause and laughing effect breaking the boredom.

David retrieves a couple new beers and returns. "Can't wait to see what else the mad scientist brings up next…if I had this kind of accessibility being a cop, the job would have been a hell of lot easier."

"The problem is, none of it's admissible in court." Jim waters down the enthusiasm.

"True, but when you know how people conduct themselves in private it takes a lot less investigating to put the puzzle together."

"And we have it." Jim clinks his beer onto David's.

The new toy soon loses its shine and the two decide to hit happy hour at an Irish Pub down the street from the apartment. Steve's office activities are boring except for the random fart and everything is recorded for view on demand at a later time. Nothing will be lost.

Jim stays conservative on the drinking having a long drive home but David feels little pain leaving the bar at 9:45. After dropping David off Jim heads home, the computer wrapped in a blanket, placed on the floorboard to protect its vital nature. A couple miles from his house Jim drives through a residential neighborhood. A cat bolts from the side of a yard into the path of the GTO. The brakes are slammed, but Jim feels the car rollover the helpless creature.

He gets out distraught over the accident; it couldn't be avoided but little compensation for the death of an animal. Jim lost his compassion for many in the human race, but always has a soft spot in his heart for animals.

The trunk is opened by key, the blanket removed from the computer and the lifeless small body wrapped and placed in the trunk. His thoughts drift to Winston and how he would feel if killed by a car. The cat is collarless and he didn't want a small child to find his pet flattened in the road by many vehicles tomorrow morning.

The GTO pulls into the driveway and he decides to bury the cat in the backyard, the least to do under the circumstances. A key is inserted into the trunk and turned. Jim lifts the trunk lid and the formerly dead cat springs to life, jumps to the ground disappearing in JD's yard.

CHAPTER THIRTY-TWO

Can't Handle the Truth

WAYNE DAVIS SITS down in front of the endless rows of monitors and focuses on various screen savers bouncing up and down on the thoughtless cubes of white. A power is gained directing these lifeless flashes of light to perform and tell their story crafted by Wayne. Few truly understand how to control this intelligence at such a high level and point the power on a subject. He completely strips away all the varnished lies and layers of rusted cover-ups hammered in place by individuals that have everything to hide.

The keys on the master board scream under the constant pounding Wayne administers. It makes the adrenaline pump into his body linking a sequence together polishing away the tarnished layers and uncovering the truth brightly shinning on the screens. It's always been Wayne's substitute for sex, and tonight he's going to bed down a Victoria Secret's Model.

For the third night in a row Wayne ignores the sleeping meds, instead chasing the sexy Angel's Wings in his mind.

Computer hacking is part skill, science, and intuitiveness. The skill aspect deals in the mechanics of breaching the system and not being detected; but if you do get caught not allowing the target trace who you are and where you come from. Wayne is one of the best on the planet when it comes to probe, extract, and disappearing into a keystroke black hole.

Wayne stops hitting the keys and settles his focus on a screen directly in front of him. A smile leads to a clap of his hands and he hits print. As the printer spits out the magic, Wayne peeks at his watch reading 1:37 a.m. He calls Jim hoping to interrupt sex, drinking or better yet, both.

"Was hoping to wake you up." Wayne wants to create suspense.

"Hate to disappoint…I'm at the club waiting on Janey to get free. Can snore on the phone if it helps the mood?" Jim throws back.

"Give my apologizes to Janey for interrupting her evening, but I have something you need to see ASAP." Wayne confirms.

"Should I get David?" Jim questions.

"Wouldn't want to leave him out," Wayne answers. "It is worth your time."

Wayne hangs up, pulls a printed stack of paper from his printer, reloads more paper and starts reading as the printer continues its job.

Jim pulls the GTO behind David's car in front of Wayne's house and parks. David beat him to the surprise and Jim can't wait to share the excitement that must be important. Wayne lets Jim in and smiles ear-to-ear.

"You're not going to believe what I found." Wayne gives Jim a high five as if running the table on an eight-ball game. Jim returns the excitement but has no idea what the exchange is about. The two go into the kitchen, David sits reading a stack of papers and his excitement is not hidden either. He looks up.

"This is unbelievable, my friend." David only adds to the intrigue.

"Enough," Jim states. "What's going on?"

Both Wayne and David start speaking at the same time clearing up nothing only adding to the confusion.

The talking stops and David points his hand palm up to Wayne. "You found it... tell him."

Wayne starts talking with a focus. "A couple hours ago I yanked the missing manuscript written by Dr. Benders from the bowels of the Institute. Not through it completely, but the people you're running down for their DNA are descendants of the man covered by the Shroud of Turin. The Doctor took blood from the Shroud, inseminated the DNA into several women being treated at his clinic in the mid-eighties to facilitate the Second Coming."

"Second Coming of what?" Jim stands confused.

"The Second Coming of Christ." David breaks into the conversation. "The Shroud covered Jesus after his crucifixion in the tomb... he bled on the linen cloth. Dr. Benders' genius is bringing him back to life." David is giddy with excitement.

Jim sits in a chair looking at his copy of the manuscript a little numb to the revelations being tossed back and forth. His religious stance has always been 180 degrees away from the Bible his stepfather made him carry to school in the second and third grade. The only thing it ever got him was harassed, picked on and beat up on more than one occasion.

"Doesn't Jesus do miracles...where are the miracles?" Jim struggles to measure the entire width of what is being spoken.

"Did you meet the guy in Missouri? What is he like?" David asks.

"Not really...met his girlfriend, went into his house but never saw him. He's a doctor, but no miracles. Wouldn't miracles be on CNN?" Jim asks, a sense of innocence bleeding through.

"Very little is known about Jesus before he got into his twenties…maybe the miracles are coming shortly?" David adds.

"I was raised a Catholic, but haven't gone to church in years so I'm no expert." Wayne jumps in. "But I can tell you this, reading Dr. Benders' words sure makes me want to believe again."

"If you knew Dr. Benders like I did, you would believe a man of his faith and scientific skills could help make it happen," David adds.

Jim's mind drifts away from the table as the conversation goes back and forth between Wayne and David. His early life poisoned any openness to the possible truth of religious values much less being close to this so-called, 'Second Coming.'

How could there be a God if he allowed the horrendous things oozing out of Jack Staymen burning his family to the ground with only Jim as a scared survivor?

He can see a genuine excitement being bantered between David and Wayne. There is a need to share what seems to be a charged moment, but Jim can't make the old demons disappear.

Wayne directs his attention to Jim, sensing no connectives to the revelations laid out in the manuscript. "What did the file say surrounding the third target the Institute handed you?"

"To be honest, didn't pay a lot of attention. But I don't think it's the Second Coming," Jim responds.

"Why?" Wayne asks.

"It's a woman…she's lives in a mental institution." Jim profiles.

David takes exception. "Who's to say a woman can't be someone that produces miracles."

Wayne jumps in.

"That mental institution thing might be a slight hindrance… doubt she can do a lot of healing confined."

The possible presence of a holy woman brings a lively debate among the three. Jim is in the conversation, but his mental image drifts to younger days when the term 'Bible Belt' had a literal meaning of beatings and mental brutality. His existence was bad, but he can't imagine all the suffering his little sister endured.

The revelation presented by the manuscript certainly puts a new spin on what Jim is doing for the Institute, but to him it didn't explain away the Benders' murder or the strange events surrounding what happened to himself or David. Nothing has been simplified nor identified that makes him want to go back to Missouri or head to New Orleans searching for miracles to change his life. Jim has always survived by believing in himself, and not a stained glass church nor a robed person is going to change that. He left Wayne's house at 4:00 a.m. tired but not impressed.

CHAPTER THIRTY-THREE

Game Changer

THE ALARM WENT off at 9:00 a.m. and Wayne gets up slowly to make his way to the shower. The adrenaline rush of finding the manuscript has been replaced by stiffness he still suffers from the beating. He takes a tablet that calms his headache down for a few hours, a pain in the head rarely subsiding unless medicated.

It was a sweet night of success using his talented fingers to help the guys out; and it subdued an inferiority complex spent in life shielding from others. He suffers from a burden of doubt in everything until hearing accolades from multiple sources. All those confirming voices are needed to drown out the screams of failure his mother nonchalantly peppered on him daily as a child.

By the time he arrives at Best Buy at 11:00, the store is humming with activity in the customer service line due to computer malfunctions or consumer ignorance in its use. Most of the time the problem can be solved within a day or two, or fifteen minutes if Wayne does it himself. He isn't paid to fix things although he prefers to do just that. His job is getting the tech-crew out in the streets to repair or install electronic equipment of every description for Geek Squad, a national company booming in a vertical that outside the service angle is thin on profit and flat in sales.

Geek Squad has twenty-seven techies in greater L.A. Wayne keeps moving in a sophisticated customer touch point system. It's state of the art surrounding appointments, tracking, billing and customer follow-up. Wayne started as a techie in the field and likes to get away from the office management when staff doesn't show for work. Today he's tired before starting the in-store balance of complaining customers and phone nuisances about techies being late for appointments.

Sheila is the office manager and informs Wayne two support crew members are sick and asks if he could make a1:00 street call. He jumps at the chance and helps an older couple install their first desktop computer taking them through a short course on how to do the basic functions. Wayne can't believe anyone doesn't have an e-mail account but neither has ever sent or received an e-mail. The couple is so happy with Wayne's patience and guidance that he leaves the house carrying a large piece of homemade apple pie he eats in route back to the store.

Sheila calls Wayne in the middle of a large pie bite and he swallows the evidence before answering the cell.

"This is Wayne." He hopes the chewing isn't noticed by anyone from the office.

"When you finish lunch, can you do a call in Beverly Hills… they requested you by name?" Sheila wasn't fooled by the forced bite.

"What time?" Wayne responds.

"3:30." Sheila answers.

"Always in public demand…how do I say no to my subjects."
Wayne never misses a point of bragging if given half a chance.

"The address is 2206 Candice Way." Sheila relays ignoring
Wayne's love for his own abilities.

"You know the rules…text me the address with a confirm
number. I can set it in my GPS thus giving you a trackable
ticket." Wayne does follow the guidelines.

"Coming your way in a few seconds," Sheila confirms.

Wayne eats the last bite of pie and hears the text beep on
the cell. With a touch or two on his iPhone the GPS coordinates
pop up on the screen and he starts heading to Beverly Hills.
It's 3:10 when he pulls up in front of a very high end property
and parks his car halfway around the driveway. A note is
written on the time to generate an invoice used to do the billing
when all is done. He hits the doorbell but gets no response for
thirty seconds or so. The fact he's early might mean a wait in
the car.

Wayne can hear movement on a wooden floor behind the
door and can sense someone looking out the peephole. He's
expecting someone older to answer the door; it's rare for a
young person to own this type of expensive housing unless a
movie or pop star. Wayne spent two days installing a fortune
in electronic gadgets at a house once belonging to Clark Gable
but never met the new owners…maybe he'll be luckier this
time?

The door opens and a beautiful black-headed woman with
stunning blue eyes stands before Wayne.

"Are you with the Geek Squad?"

The wonderful voice travels to Wayne's ears like a gentle
stream filled with Rainbow Trout. Wayne offers his hand. "Yes,
Wayne Davis…here to install your computer.

The tall woman shakes his hand. "I'm Diane Rogers, come
in."

Wayne steps into the house completely void of furniture and looks around in the emptiness. It's not unusual to pre-wire homes and equipment before new owners move in and Diane explains it away.

"I don't move in for ten more days but like to have my computer functional for business."

"Sure," Wayne responds. "What kind of business are you in?"

Diane turns away and starts walking to a hallway that seems to go on forever without answering the question. She stops in front of an open door and turns to Wayne.

"I'm in real estate…perhaps you're looking to upgrade your home?" Diane points her hand leading Wayne into the doorway.

Wayne rounds the corner of the door and a man shoots him in the forehead with a .40 cal pistol having a silencer. He instantly crumbles to the floor. Two more shots are placed in the middle of his back to complete the overkill.

CHAPTER THIRTY-FOUR

Stand Alone

SLICK ROLLIE SPENT little time in the Pawnshop during the last ten days handling the renovations going on at the house. The involvement of Rollie on day-to-day operations continues to decline at the Pawnshop as time passes; not because he doesn't want to work in the store but because other projects are distracting his focus. A vast portfolio of real estate made up of residential and commercial properties needs his attention along with a sizable stock and bond account.

Jim is really close to Rollie, looking up to him for advice and forever grateful Slick took him under his wing when he first arrived in L.A. desperate for work. Rollie plans sometime in the near future for the management of the Pawnshop and bond business to be turned over to his nephew, Conrad, on the operation and accounting front and to Jim Cirmah on the personnel and marketing side. That speaks to their strengths and let's him concentrate on other business interests. Along with the shared management responsibilities comes money and stock, making them wealthy over time if smart with their money.

When Rollie comes into the Pawnshop he's not prepared for what's going on in the life of his soon to be new partner. Jim gives him all the dirty details on the Institute including the Benders' manuscript brag about the Second Coming. A guarded man on his emotions and rarely jumping to conclusions, Rollie advises Jim to take a deep breath and not trip over wires causing a blowup in his face.

Jim's fragile state of mind is carried on his sleeve. Rollie's never seen it before. He tries to instill confidence and get the old Jim back. Rollie goes to his safe, opens it and pulls out two cell phones.

"Look, not sure where any of this is headed but we'll get through it together. You're young… I have unlimited contacts and money…that's one hell of a combination." Rollie hands Jim one of the non-branded cell phones. "Keep it on you at all times. If anything goes really bad, call me on this. The phone can't be traced or tapped under any conditions. We're a team."

"Thanks Rollie, makes me feel like I'm part of a team. Not going to chase this Institute shit anymore." Jim relays what Rollie wants to hear.

"I gave Franklin a bond jumper a few days ago named Henry Denisson…if he doesn't have him back in jail in the next forty-eight hours, he's all yours." Rollie knows the sooner Jim gets back into a routine the faster things will return to normal.

"Thanks Rollie…won't let you down." Jim hugs Rollie and goes out of the Pawnshop feeling better for eight minutes down the road. Then the call came from Detective Fox.

Jim glances at the cell and sees who is calling. "Wolf-man Fox, what brings you out this early in the day?"

"Don't know how to say this other than saying it…Wayne Davis was murdered yesterday afternoon…I'm truly sorry, brother." Fox seems to have a genuine interest in the pain going into Jim's body.

Jim pulls over in a parking lot and stops. "What happened?"

"All we know right now is he went on a tech call around 3:30 in Beverly Hills...someone shot him three times," Fox relays.

"Was with him a couple times this week... it just can't be," Jim states.

"Be back when I know more...if you need a drinking partner, don't hesitate to call." The cell goes dead leaving Jim to fight a losing battle, tears rising from his soul.

After lowering his emotional state, Jim drives to David's apartment sharing the frightening news. David is floored over the loss of someone he didn't know well, but respected Wayne's abilities and his willingness to get involved.

David surprises Jim, a reality check he'd have to cash. "What are you going to do now?"

Jim already made up his mind to drop everything pertaining to the Institute's myriad of problems. "I've done my last job for the Institute...walking away."

David leans across the small kitchen table. "Something tells me it won't be that easy, but wish you all the luck in the world."

"What are you going to do?" Jim asks.

"Wayne's death is the last straw for me... if I stick around there's no doubt how it will end, going back to Colorado. Got a cabin in the mountains, few know where it is...be safe there." David lays out his plan.

Jim's reflects on the FBI file he received profiling David. "Look, the workup file listed the location of your Father's cabin in the mountains. If I have it, so do the people hellbent on hurting you."

"Thanks for the advice, but believe the advantage is mine in the woods." David gets up, offering his hand. "Don't play it too macho...what we're facing is organized, lots of money behind them."

"Good luck, my friend." Jim shakes the offered hand and turns to leave.

Both arrive at the door and Jim gets one last piece of advice.

"I've been thinking how the bastards knew about Wayne's involvement...better check your car using the debugger, it's the only place left."

"Thanks, man... I'll check it out," Jim responds.

CHAPTER THIRTY-FIVE

Family Reunion

DAVID'S PREDICTION PROVED true. Jim found a bug in the GTO. His emotionally charged mind didn't allow rational thinking. He rips the bug out throwing it in the trashcan. He also takes the bugs from his house doing the same. This seems to put distance between Jim and his problems mentally.

The next few days come and go blindly. Wayne's funeral interrupted a drunken binge Jim took pride in. Janey tries to stay close and help him weather the crisis, but his focus is self-mutilation and needs to give him space. Janey takes Winston off his hands to eliminate one more responsibility.

Jim is mentally and physically alone; left to his out of character drinking spree, but something committed to. At his lowest point a distant ray of light calls out of the blue, his Grandfather Denzel.

Sporadic communication has been the trend between Jim and Denzel over the years, but did nothing to curb the love Jim has for the man. Throughout his life, the best times remained on the rice farm in Arkansas; hunting, fishing and sitting next to a log burning fireplace listening to Denzel's words of wisdom.

"Jimmy, how the hell are you doing?" Denzel's voice whispers over the phone, the only person on Earth to call him Jimmy and get away with it.

"Grandfather, more importantly how are you doing?" Jim forgets his problems instantly hearing his Grandfather's voice but senses something wrong.

"I'm calling about my health, thought you needed to know." Denzel relays.

"What's wrong, Grandfather?" Jim asks.

"In a little battle with Prostate Cancer... afraid I'm losing the fight. The doc tells me I've got six, maybe eight months left to roam my farm before the Good Lord takes me... hoping you might fly back to Arkansas, spend a few days with me?" Denzel paints a less than positive picture.

Jim never hesitates. "I'll be on the first plane out of L.A."

"That would be wonderful... can't wait to see you, been too long." Denzel is excited over the prospect of Jim coming to see him.

"I'll call you on my flight information shortly."

The event minimizes his personal problems and diverts his energy to someone he loves.

The next day Jim flies to Little Rock and makes the short drive to his Grandfather's farm. It brings back good memories even though the trip is bittersweet. A sense of guilt washes side-to-side in Jim's mind; he should visit his grandparents more often. He pushes the negative away driving the last five miles to the farm. He's here to spend quality time with Denzel and Eva.

Time has shied away from the farm ignoring the need for changes. Jim drives along the gravel road only a mile from the paved highway to the front door of the house. Numerous lakes surround each side of the road filled with wildlife. A Bald Eagle rides air thermals in the distance looking for fish. Jim assumes its one of a mated pair nesting in a giant cypress tree around the next bend year after year. Rounding the corner the nest comes into view and an eagle hatchling chirps at the sky demanding dinner. He can only wonder why it took three years to come back and see this beautiful landscape and Grandfather.

Pulling up to the large ranch house, Denzel is moving back and forth on a swing and waves at Jim opening the car door. Denzel struggles to get off the swing, even cane aided, to meet Jim walking to the porch. It hurts to see his Grandfather, once a strapping 6-4, 220 pound man, struggle to pull himself to his feet.

The hug is special, longer than usual. Jim can feel his thinness, losing the cancer fight. In spite of his frailty, his eyes are bright shinning on his grandson's appearance. Eva, Jim's Grandmother, comes out of the house to share the hugs. She has lost noticeable weight in the fight, too.

"You've grown up to be quite the young man," Eva states sizing Jim up. "Come in this house, got to be starving." She turns back to the kitchen door.

Denzel eases close to Jim for support to walk the porch. "You better bring your appetite or she'll be pissed." He states loudly wanting Eva to hear.

"Can't wait to jump into some good country food," Jim responds.

"See", Eva explains. "Jim likes my cooking even if you don't."

Nothing has changed, Denzel and Eva's bickering brings back a flood of memories, it's been a way of life for fifty plus years. Jim eyes the table of food, quantities large enough to feed six people.

The room is full of attention and adulation for Jim watching the sunset outside the living room window across a distant lake. Frogs jump to attention, their bass throats bellowing in the early evening reminding Jim of holidays past listening to the night song falling asleep.

Jim tells P.I. stories and the trials chasing down bond jumpers. He makes it sound more romantic than reality, every sentence absorbed diligently by the gentle souls sitting next to him. It feels good to smell the clean air and hear the country sounds generated by tiny voices. It's a far cry from the L.A. screams by millions of people unhappy in life. Jim's issues feel distant, absorbed by something good and caring.

The next day Jim and Denzel visit a favorite bass fishing spot. Denzel watches Jim walk the shore throwing a spinner bait next to fallen trees in the lake and catching fish after fish for two hours. Jim keeps six bass to fry tonight and throws the rest back into the lake.

Jim sits close to Denzel cleaning the fish on the bank of the lake, the thought of his Grandfather not being part of this pristine landscape rips him apart. He drifts back to the night Wayne found Dr. Benders' manuscript. Could David and Wayne be right concerning the descendants of The Shroud performing miracles? His Grandfather needs one now.

That night after the fish and hushpuppies have been consumed, Jim helps Eva wash the dishes and briefly talks while Denzel reads a book in the living room.

"Think I can help Grandfather beat his cancer," Jim says out of the blue, not sure why it came out of his mouth. Once the sentence settles in her ears, Jim is committed.

A dish falls from Eva's hands hitting the bottom of the sink and shattering. Eva leans over and starts crying. Jim hugs her, feeling the terror of losing her mate to the evils of cancer. Eva wipes the tears away, recomposes, and tries to regain the strength not to waver facing adversity. She has been strong to protect the mental health of Denzel, but Jim's words made the emotion jump to the surface.

"How," she asks. "How can you do that, Jim?"

"A friend told me about this woman down in Baton Rouge… she's able to do miracles, helps people like Grandfather." Jim didn't want to reveal the entire story.

"That would truly be a miracle, I love that old bastard. Can't stand to see what's happening to him." Eva leans over and kisses Jim. He's given her hope and it felt good.

Jim tells Denzel the plan to visit the woman in Louisiana; he readily agrees to the trip.

CHAPTER THIRTY-SIX

The Good, Bad, and Beautiful

DAVID'S BEEN AT the cabin for a couple of days and his radar is wide open to the surroundings fearing someone might come after him. He walks the property several times a day carrying a .306 scoped rifle his father used deer hunting, but doesn't find signs of anyone roaming the landscape. The closest city is Vail but would take police forty plus minutes to make the cabin if needed. The ability to reach the police is questionable, the cabin has no phone and his cell doesn't work nestled in mountain ranges on three sides.

The cabin is secure in many ways, his dad worked hard to prevent break-ins when no one was using it. He's slept little, keeping one eye open and the rifle within reach just in case. The only activity are hummingbirds drinking from the feeder and a neverending supply of chipmunks attracted by sunflower seeds placed on one end of the porch.

A neighbor hikes up to his property more than a mile away to say 'hi' seeing David drive by a couple of times getting supplies. James Rouse says he misses David's dad, a good man to have around that could fix anything. David misses him too, but not near the carpenter his talented father represented unfortunately.

David adjusts to the surroundings, a little less fear and growing to like the seclusion his dad enjoyed so much. A good book from the extensive cabin library and soaking up the sunshine made him happy. Little is missed not having a TV, although he did like to jump on-line from time-to-time, a luxury not available.

Late in the afternoon David makes chocolate chip cookies to treat himself, and much to his surprise, feed the chipmunks easing ever so closely to him on the porch. He makes a promise, only eat two cookies at a time or else all will be gone in one afternoon. A chipmunk named Bull possessing daring behavior sits next to his hiking boot waiting on a bit of cookie to come its way. Most of the other fur balls take a bite of food from David, run under the porch to hide and eat. Not Bull. He takes a piece of cookie off the boot top and sits on the laces eating. Bull looks up from the shoelaces waiting for the next handout patiently.

David reaches for the cookie pan setting on the guardrail made of a pine log to grab the third cookie. He smiles at his optimism eating two, takes a bite and leans down to share with Bull. As he ducks a bullet fired from a high powered rifle strikes the cabin wall only inches above his lowered body.

Instinctively he rolls off the porch and pulls his pistol out. A look over the porch's edge at the high bluff reveals a streak of sun bouncing off a metal barrel three hundred yards away in an outcrop of boulders.

Anticipating another shot, David goes to the back of the cabin, crawls into a window and retrieves the rifle with an eight-powered scope. A series of gunshots ring off the hills and David hears different weapons engaged. Hidden behind the cabin, he pumps a bullet into the chamber and works to the edge of the porch. A single shot is fired in the distance but nothing comes his way, adding to the confusion.

Peeking around the cabin corner, David sights the scope to the bluff focusing on the origin of the metal flash appearing earlier. A rifle barrel can be seen. Strangely, it appears to never move from its previous position. That could mean the shooter is down or a stupid hit man hiding in the rocks. A professional, once he missed David, would change his position to confuse the target. The people after him are not stupid but he locks onto the rifle for the next few minutes to make sure. No movement or sound comes from the rocks. David works his way north of the bluff by circling ridgeline cover and looks down at the shooter.

It takes twenty-five minutes to leg up and around the rocks to get a clear view of the rifleman below. The .306 is rested on a large boulder and focuses on three bodies in a clearing less than a hundred yards in the distance. David takes his time, surveys the clearing for fifteen minutes thinking something will move or another person appear. Someone has to be left standing after killing these three and David's determined to take them out before exposing himself.

Satisfied no one is appearing to retaliate, David climbs down to the crime scene and uses his detective skills to figure out what happened. The rifleman was shot long distance, a high caliber weapon instantly killing him. David checks his pockets finding an I.D., but it doesn't ring a bell on the identity. Thirty feet away a struggle ensued, two bodies embraced after a fight to the death. David is wrong, a fourth person didn't facilitate the other deaths.

A .50 caliber rifle sets next to the bodies indicating one of the two fighting shot the rifleman firing at David. He rolls the bodies apart and shocked to find the tattooed man, Joe

Tramazzo, has a bullet in his chest and one in the hip. The other body surprises David even more, he takes a baseball cap off and long blond hair falls out. Upon closer examination, all that hair surrounds the face of a beautiful woman. She evidently shot Tramazzo after he disposed of the rifleman using a long distance shot and approached not aware of her presence. The woman shot Tramazzo in the hip and rolled Joe over getting a seven inch blade shoved into her chest. Dying, she fired one final shot into his heart.

The Navy Seal once again saved David's life.

CHAPTER THIRTY-SEVEN

Hear No Evil

JIM LOOKS IN the rearview mirror and sees Denzel sleeping under a blanket in the backseat. His Grandfather needs to stop frequently for a bathroom break and keeps apologizing for the inconvenience. Nothing Jim says keeps him from doing so. Jim makes a joke to shut him up after crossing into Louisiana when Denzel asks to stop.

"You need to pee again, we can't make any time doing this." Jim, a serious look on his face, can't keep the smile off very long.

"Don't pay any attention to me, I'll just piss down the back of the seat next time." Denzel shoots back.

Both burst out laughing, sharing a moment only two men understand.

Central Arkansas is a rolling hill landscape but the farther south traveled, the land gets lower to sea level. Jim's never been to Louisiana and his first impression is all the water drains off Arkansas onto the Cajun state line creating swamps. Things are laidback in Arkansas and Louisiana compared to L.A., and

Jim is starting to like the difference. The people continue to amaze, springing a nice attitude and the food is great. Denzel directs him to a small hole in the wall restaurant, and they pull away chewing on a PoBoy Sandwich containing shrimp and hot sauce.

Denzel sleeps much of the trip, the advancing cancer sapping energy at a rapid pace. Something has to come from this yellow brick road miracle or his Grandfather may pass sooner from the long drive stress.

The car hits the Baton Rouge city limits and Jim follows the phone GPS to a large brick building. A rambling yard, giant oak tree filled and layered with Spanish moss completes the picture. Denzel is asleep. Jim rolls the windows down and makes way to the front door alone.

A small reception area ends in a glass window and a fat man sits behind it reading a SI Swimsuit Issue. Finally the large man sets the magazine in his rolling lap and looks up at Jim.

"Can I help you?" The staff member asks.

"Yes, here to see Gayle Kidd," Jim answers.

"Are you a relative?" The fat man asks indifferent to the response.

"Does it matter?" Jim can tell where this is headed.

"If you want to get in without advance clearance by the court or legal guardian it does," the fat man answers.

Jim reaches into his wallet pulling out a $100 dollar bill and pushes it under the glass opening. "Relative," Jim answers.

"Brother, I take it," the fat man states. "Can see the resemblance. Fill out this form, brother." He slides a piece of paper back to Jim and a pen.

The pen moves across the form and shortly Jim returns it to the fat Benjamin Franklin.

"Someone will escort you back in a minute." The hot Swimsuit Models are raised up to eye level behind the glass.

Even two thousand miles from greed and glitz, some things never change. He waits on the inner sanctum to open. He looks at the office walls and notices paintings depicting Bible scenes like the 'Last Supper'. A closer look by a non-trained eye tells Jim it's well done.

The SI man speaks out the glass. "You want to buy a painting?"

"No thanks, not cultured unfortunately," Jim informs.

The door opens and a smallish, middle age woman takes Jim into a maze of hallways and turns his paperwork over to an older black gentleman in front of a locked door. Jim's optimism is waning, getting Denzel close to any miracle this deep into the dungeon walls.

The black man eyes Jim up and down. "Brother, huh?" He turns, unlocks the door and Jim follows him down another hallway finally stopping at a door. A second key is inserted and the last door is breached.

The room is small, a window in the corner visibly barred on the outside. The whole process reminds Jim of a trip to the zoo experienced as a sixth grader years ago.

Out of habit, Jim turns to the black man. "Thanks."

He starts toward Gayle Kidd sitting on a chair next to the window, her back to the door. She intently focuses at a canvas applying a brush stroke paint loaded. Jim instantly recognizes whose talent penned the paintings in the office. No doubt she received nothing for the art performance but confinement.

The black attendant moves quickly catching Jim and grabs his shoulder. "Sir, excuse me, you can't get near Miss Gayle… please talk from a distance."

Jim turns to the attendant. "I need to speak in private."

"That's not possible. An attendant must be present at all times. You can't get any closer." The black man is firm in his speech.

"Is she sick?" Jim questions. "I'm her brother...we need some time alone."

The attendant places his hand on what Jim guesses is a mace gun on his belt. "I don't make the rules, but you will obey them or leave."

"Alright...we'll play by the rules." Jim states pulling a chair from the end of the tiny bed and straddling it backwards. "This okay?" Jim holds his hands up frustrated.

"That's fine." The attendant takes one step back and stands slightly behind Jim.

Jim returns his attention to Gayle and watches her gifted hands work across the canvas using delicate but sure brush strokes. "Gayle, it's Jim...can you take a break, talk a little bit?"

The slender hands keep moving and Gayle is completely disinterested in any conversation. Jim didn't know what to expect. She looks ordinary like a neighbor not someone who walks on water or cures human suffering.

"Gayle," Jim tries again. "I brought Grandfather along to see you... he's got cancer, really needs your help."

Gayle finally looks at Jim.

"He's very sick." At this point Jim figures there's nothing to lose. "Would you like to come out to see him? He only has a few months to live."

Without a word in response, Gayle turns back to the painting as if Jim isn't in the room.

"We drove a long way to see you." Jim's in a begging mode. "Please don't let us down."

The black attendant touches Jim on the shoulder. "It's time to leave, Sir. Miss Gayle can't help your Grandfather."

Jim gets up and returns the chair to its previous station. He's angry at this shithole mental institution, the jackasses working here, and this Gayle chick that can't open her mouth to say "go fuck yourself." Jim could handle a 'go to hell' better than dead silence. Most of all he's mad at himself for taking his Grandfather on this wild goose chase, believing in something so remote a commodity as a miracle.

The black attendant walks Jim out of the facility and to the front door. Jim peeks at the fat guy behind the glass, hoping his expression changes in the slightest. It would trigger his frustration to the point of pulling him through the glass, pounding his head and taking the $100 back on principle.

The air outside is refreshing to Jim heading to the car. There is a dread facing Denzel, giving him nothing more than a long drive and a PoBoy Sandwich for the trouble. The only way to relay the disappointment is direct and tell Denzel it's all a mistake on his part. Jim gets to the car but Denzel is gone. Knowing he can't go far, he looks around the property and heads to the side of the building.

Jim smiles openly seeing Denzel leaning into the bushes urinating on the side of the complex. He walks close to his Grandfather, unzips his pants and joins the urination fun.

"Great idea," Jim says relieving himself on the wall.

Their business finished, Jim laughs walking Denzel to the vehicle. From the corner of his eye, Jim sees the black attendant moving quickly toward them. He and Denzel can't make the car before being overtaken. Jim stands his ground ready for the man to say one word about peeing on this dreadful facility. It will be over quickly, a pure fact considering Jim's current emotional state.

"Sir, I take it this is your Grandfather," the attendant states.

"Yeah, what about my Grandfather?" Jim is wanting the wrong word to come out of the guy's mouth.

"He can be helped," the attendant surprisingly states.

Jim cocks his head to one side expecting the other shoe to drop. "What do you mean helped?"

"His sickness...he can be rid of it." The black man looks nervous. "I gotta' go, but you need to be in Neville tomorrow night at 9:00...'bout twenty-five miles from here." With that the man walks back to the building and disappears.

"What the hell does that mean?" Denzel asks perplexed.

Jim continues to the car. "Don't know, but we'll be in Neville tomorrow night."

The two find a hotel cheap but clean. A pizza place fifty years old gets their attention and the food justifies their choice. The two share a few beers, many miles apart generationally, culturally and physically, yet closer than ever before. Denzel tells the story about catching a ten pound bass along the same stretch of bank Jim had fished the previous day. After the beers, stories and pizza, directions are obtained to Neville for their journey Friday night.

Nothing is said surrounding the help Denzel might get in Neville, only talk about fishing for giant bass when they return to Arkansas.

CHAPTER THIRTY-EIGHT

See All Evil

THERE'S NOT MUCH to do in Neville, Louisiana, unless you're a shrimp. Then the entire populace spends all waking moments figuring out new ways to boil, fry or steam the tail into a format never eaten before. The town couldn't be farther from the sprawling City of L.A. having a population of less than 3,000.

Boredom attacks Jim waiting on the hours to peel off like the three dozen boiled shrimp sitting in the middle of a picnic table between him and Denzel. The picnic decor is not in a local park, but a restaurant calling itself Bazaar Cafe containing all kinds of eclectic furniture and a price tag to purchase on each piece. Jim eliminated the picnic table as a carryon option for the return flight.

Denzel takes a nap after lunch in the motel room, and Jim calls Janey to get caught up. She says Winston misses him, but Jim doesn't believe her for a moment. Janey also admits she wants him back soon and Jim confesses a desire for some Janey and L.A. He says nothing concerning the magical mystery tour tonight, been enough embarrassment and disappointment on the subject already. Time will bleed the truth soon enough.

The need to keep moving has always been an annoying trait for Jim. He's incapable of sitting still and enjoying the view and has a need to drift his feet and explore the surroundings and witness the kind of trouble available.

Neville is circled within an hour and the only thing of interest is a small bar flashing a couple slot machines in the corner and a large chunk of rounded cheese. Jim has never seen cheese elevated on a chopping block displayed next to the pool table. Jim shoots pool, only two other patrons drinking beer on opposite sides of the bar having no interest in life much less a West Coast pool shark looking for a game.

Every time Jim moves toward the side of the pool table displaying the cheese, he takes a drink of beer and cuts off another piece from the block. He's never tasted cheese like this and certainly can't get enough. Beer/cheese, then more cheese/beer. After the third beer, a calmness comes over Jim part alcohol, part mystery. Three beers are several short of getting high, but his mental drifting is pleasant and he can't stop slicing the damn cheese.

The door to the bar opens and a beautiful young woman enters, exchanging a smile and going to the bar for a drink. She grabs a beer, walks over to the cheese and cuts a piece off as Jim rolls a ball down the table.

"You've found the cheese post, Jim, like it?" She states flashing a perfect smile and dark eyes.

"Like it, about to ask it to marry me." Jim didn't notice she called him by his name or didn't care in his heighten state of bliss.

"Have you come to town looking for a game?" Victoria lights up the dark room, moving closer to Jim taking the Q-ball away from the end of his stick.

"Could be," Jim states slyly. "Do you play, Victoria?" Her name slides off his lips without an internal hint why.

"No," Victoria answers. "But Mr. Creighton does."

She points to a man at the far end of the bar. Victoria hops on top of a bar stool located at one end of the pool table and her short dress flies high on her thighs hiding no secrets. She doesn't move the dress down and catches Jim's attention.

While she advertises panty-less and Jim noticing the Victoria brand, Mr. Creighton walks to the other end of the table. The weathered face has a darkness beyond a tan, and Mr. Creighton wears a long sleeve shirt and sweater that seems out of place in the warm climate.

He startles Jim with his proximity and bellowing, heavy Cajun accent. "You want a game, Mr. Cirmah?"

Jim turns to Mr. Creighton and as usual, sizes up who wants to get on a table with him. The man is nondescript, small in stature and certainly not intimidating.

"Sure, what are we playing for?" Jim asks, a sense of innocence he can turn on and off.

Mr. Creighton roles the Q-ball to the other end of the table; like a medieval slap in the face, the game is on. He pulls a deck of cards from pocket fanning them out on the worn, green cloth covering the table.

"That depends on the cards, Mr. Cirmah." The voice is deep, accent so strong Jim must pay close attention to understand Mr. Creighton.

"What do cards have to do with it?" Jim asks what he considers a reasonable question.

"Everything," Mr. Creighton answers. "Pick one."

"Sure." Jim agrees to what must be a local custom. He pulls out the Ace of Spades and flips it on the table face up.

"My, my Mr. Cirmah," Mr. Creighton acknowledges. "You are one lucky young man."

"So, what does the Ace mean?" Jim asks.

"You came to Neville for what, Mr. Cirmah?" Mr. Creighton turns the question into a question.

"That has nothing to do with this fucking pool game." Jim throws the pool stick on the table and starts for the door.

The day turns to night and a hallowing wind whips the small town slamming the door shut. The only light visible in the bar is the glow hovering over the pool table. Jim twists the handle on the door but it won't budge. He pulls back his size twelve shoe and hammers the door creating only a glancing blow.

Jim is out of breath more from frustration than exertion. A few steps from the pool table, a temptation to start pounding Mr. Creighton's head using a pool stick erupts deep inside. Something tells him to cool down and play more than the pool game.

"I came here to save my Grandfather from the cancer raging his body." Jim states calmly.

"The Ace insures playing for anything you want...perhaps you'd like something else in your life, Mr. Cirmah? Denzel is old, the best you can buy is five, maybe six years cancer free. Care to raise the stakes?" Creighton is obviously negotiating with Jim to go beyond Denzel's health.

The maddening dream has to be over shortly. Jim will wake up in his bed, Janey lying next to him. He can't be in a rat-hole Neville talking to a devil wannabe. That's the only plausible explanation for this nightmare. But there's a sense of realness trapped in the beer hall, fed by cheese creating an out-of-body participation like a stoned college freshman at his first frat party.

Jim came looking to find a miracle for his Grandfather, maybe this is the process he must go through? No miracle books are sold on Amazon to read mapping out the journey. His jaw line tightens, deep down is a pissed-off attitude boiling up and a need to hurt and humiliate someone.

"Mr. Creighton," Jim says reaching for his stick. "Rack 'em."

Mr. Creighton doesn't do the honors, but Victoria 'No' Secret slides down the bar stool and racks the balls. Jim didn't appreciate the loose rack and tightens the balls down with precision.

Mr. Creighton notices the correction. "Mr. Cirmah, I like your attention to detail.

"Let's be clear on the rules," Jim states.

"Absolutely, couldn't agree more," Mr. Creighton retorts.

"Straight pool, first one to 125 wins… scratch brings your ball back on the table, a loss of point. Balls are racked when 14 go down leaving one on the table." Jim plays the pool game well.

"Excellent," Mr. Creighton agrees.

Jim moves close to Creighton and towers over him trying to fully intimidate. "This is your town, your bar, your whore, your table… if someone cheats, the game is forfeited.

"Can't stand cheaters…must be an honest game." Creighton confirms all of Jim's terms.

"Don't want to be completely ignorant, how does the card fit into the game?"

"The card determines how much you can wager on the game; the higher the card value the more you can bet," Creighton answers.

"So if I drew a three of hearts, I couldn't play for my Grandfather's health?" Jim asks.

"Precisely," Creighton agrees.

"But the Ace of Spades justifies my soul being wagered if I wanted it all." Jim adds, a slight 'fuck' you smile on his face.

"Something else is important surrounding the card, you must place it near your Grandfather's cancer to rid his body if you win. I can feel a double or nothing coming down the line perhaps?" Creighton's inviting smile counters.

"Perhaps?" Jim teases.

The two men take a ball and side-by-side hit their respective balls to the other end of the table. Each ball bounces off the far side and lags back to their end. Creighton's ball is closest to the table's end and gains the honors breaking the rack and starting the game.

The racked balls explode, Creighton hammering the Q-ball into their midst and two balls falling into pockets. Jim anticipates Creighton is good but now decides that's a major understatement. He runs three racks and scores 43 before running into trouble, leaving Jim an impossible position on the Q-ball leave.

Having no choice, Jim plays defensive and runs the Q-ball kissing the four ball tucking it against the corner. Creighton tries an impossible shot but almost pulls it off. If that shot went in, Jim would concede the man is simply better. It didn't. The table is wide open and Jim runs four plus racks putting 67 on the board. His Q-ball leave isn't perfect and he pays. Creighton seemingly rolls balls into pockets on the table forever. Before he sits, Jim is down 114 to 67, the Q-ball well protected in the corner.

Jim glances at his watch and time has flown by, the hands resting on 6:50. If the game goes past 8:15, he could lose the chance for Denzel to meet Gayle Kidd. Perhaps that's the real intent of the game he's playing now?

Jim has one shot opening and it's extremely risky. His only play is to chip the Q-ball making it hop over the seven and giving the Q reverse spin knocking the seven in a side pocket. The odds of making the shot and not scratching is one in five, but to win he must attempt.

The Q jumps the seven, reverses its path and kisses the seven dropping it into the pocket. Victoria jumps up screaming admiring the shot, but is quickly subdued by a Creighton stare.

Confidence grows in Jim's stick, two racks going down around the table but is left a tricky double bank shot to keep the streak going. He takes and makes it. Soon his total is 119 and the table perfectly aligned to take Creighton out.

But a problem exists, his watch reads 7:55 and Jim has little time to close the game out. He chalks the stick and starts to knock in the thirteen ball when a woman from the bar walks toward the table, her head lowered and face hidden. She walks closer, dropping her purse spilling the contents a few feet from Jim apparently drunk and unable to coordinate the steps.

Creighton moves in her direction but ignores the plight, going to the mystical cheese and sharing with Victoria.

Jim leans over to help retrieve the fallen contents and looks into the face of his sister somewhat startled. She smiles and speaks in a low voice.

"Nice treehouse, thanks for letting me stay."

Only Jim and his sister understood the content of that fateful day years ago. Brenda winks at Jim and gets closer.

"You must lose the game to save Grandpa Denzel… everything Creighton says is a lie."

"You playing pool or walking her home." Mr. Creighton says, a grumpy tone coming beyond the table.

Brenda opens the front door, leaves the game behind and Jim to his thoughts. Confusion abounds around the game on how to play and handle the gamble regardless the path he chooses to follow. A part of him wants to shove it in the little man's face, but another wants to believe in good not evil and the game is pulling him closer to the dark spirit all around.

The Q-ball sets two feet from the thirteen ball and the corner pocket is just twenty inches behind that. Jim has made the same shot a thousand times to wrap up another pool game, but when the Q jumps off his stick, it bangs into the thirteen off line by less than an eighth of an inch. The thirteen lightly touches the nine ball on its way down the table and then goes into the pocket.

Mr. Creighton jumps from his bar stool and shouts with joy. "You didn't call the kiss off the nine ball, that's a lost shot."

Not a word of response comes from Jim, Creighton is right by the rules and he did lose his turn.

He watches the cranky old Cajun run out the table and claim victory, but for the first time in life he feels really good and losing didn't matter. A calmness takes over his body and knows Denzel will be alright regardless of what happens tonight or six months from now.

As Creighton celebrates the win with Victoria, Jim looks skyward seeing the Ace of Spades floating down by the thousands from the ceiling. The heavens open up, pounding his brain on the truth. No one sees this truth but Jim.

Jim walks the table to the cheese where Creighton set the deck of cards after Jim pulled out the Ace of Spades. Creighton thinks Jim is circling to offer his hand in defeat, instead Jim picks up the cards and throws them on the pool table face up. Each of the cards is the Ace of Spades, Creighton cheated to start the game.

Jim picks a couple of the Aces up and throws in Creighton's face. "I owe you nothing...you owe me nothing." Jim exits into the early evening air hoping he made the right decision for once in his life running to the room getting Denzel.

He places Denzel in the backseat of the car and starts driving looking for Gayle Kidd. It doesn't take long. Outside the high school stationed on the football practice field is a large tent, people pouring in from many directions. Jim's never seen any kind of religious revival before and Denzel tries to educate him.

"It's an old time tent revival... used to see them all over the South but didn't think they existed anymore."

Denzel and Jim walk toward the tent, the sound of gospel music heard blaring from speakers and the masses clapping in rhythm singing along. Jim notices the crowd is principally black, older and many infirm being helped to what they pray is salvation and healing.

The line forming to get into the tent grows steadily and the two ease forward finally making the entrance. No admission fee is charged but several individuals hold baskets for donations. An older black woman stands to the right, Jim drops a hundred dollar bill into the basket.

"Bless you, young man, bless you." She speaks to Jim, a genuine appreciation and heavy Cajun accent.

Denzel and Jim find a seat close to the back of the tent facing the stage, a choir on one side and a podium on the other.

Jim leans over to Denzel. "What church is this?

"Not sure," Denzel responds. "Could be Baptist...could be Methodist."

A man in his forties well dressed and in control appears on stage. The crowd claps loudly and Jim sits before this strange scene uncomfortable, flashbacks of his church going days firmly anchored in fear and loathing for the event tied so closely to his stepfather. Talk of God and salvation showers the tent walls, sharing time singing gospel songs and thunderous applause. Shouts of "Praise Jesus" are randomly thrown at the stage by individuals standing in the audience. Time crawls by for Jim reliving the past hateful days he blamed on Jack Staymen.

God gets Jim's biased hate for letting Staymen use his name to inflict the pain.

Denzel gets up and Jim thinks he's heading to the bathroom. He helps move Denzel to the center of the aisle. He glances at the stage and several more individuals have joined the man including Gayle Kidd. A line is formed and Jim realizes he's standing in it, working toward the woman and the moment of reckoning near.

Getting closer to the stage, Jim feels Denzel's hand tightening his grip and body tensing. The finality of the moment sinks into Jim's mind, this is Grandfather's last hope before death comes knocking on his door. An odor permeates the air around the line of people, a mixture of the unwashed and a fear miracles only happen to others.

The stage is only a few feet away, a man is helped from his wheelchair by several and Gayle Kidd hugs his body. The crowd grows silent in anticipation. Jim sees the man's legs are emaciated from years of inactivity and watches intently to what this woman can do. She lifts him upward, still silent without talk and gently sits him back into the wheelchair. Several seconds go by, nothing more than a "Praise Jesus" in the background when tears start streaming down his face. He moves one of his legs upward a few inches and the second one follows suit.

The crowd goes wild in a pounding applause. Jim figured if the man walked off the stage it is being faked, legs inactive for any length of time take an extended effort to regain strength and the man would have to learn to walk all over again.

Jim helps Denzel move up the stage steps and the well dressed man asks him questions surrounding his ailment spotlighting Denzel's voice over the microphone. Denzel says stage four prostate cancer and the crowd adds a moan to their collective response. Gayle gets close to Denzel, wraps her arms around his body and Jim holds him up anticipating a passing out in the process. Her arm lays next to Jim's shoulder and a sudden volt of electricity shoots into Denzel and Jim at the same time.

Everything slows in Jim's mind, his line of sight moves from the audience to the tent's ceiling. He views the open sky, red liquid pouring on his face and body. This time his view is clear, Jim sees the outline of a man on a cross crucified and his blood falling on the stage.

Denzel and Jim fall to the wooden platform, the crowd screaming in the background.

CHAPTER THIRTY-NINE

The Blame Game

DR. SAM WALLACE intently watches a colleague finish bypass surgery on a woman he's known since childhood and a close friend of his mother. He's not the lead physician on the operation, but asked to be part of the team to placate mom. She called him incessantly until he agreed subject to her doctor's permission.

The surgery is textbook in Sam's mind and he didn't lift a finger or shout directions at any point showing great restraint. The lead physician is a golfing buddy and a round of golf bet on Sam's inability to keep his mouth shut. Sam's next round is free.

The last patient round is completed and a gnawing sensation in the pit of the stomach reeks of something wrong but intuition can't detail the circumstances. No panic ensues but he drives home faster than normal antsy to see Diane.

Sam walks in the backdoor and hangs his keys on a mounted hook in the kitchen. He shouts for Diane but gets no response. The table is set for dinner and Sam thinks Diane is gone to the store to pickup something to finish cooking.

A bouncing step up the stairwell and Doctor Sam Wallace is in the master bedroom facing two men, weapons drawn, and Diane bound and gagged on the bed. Sam is tied up and placed next to Diane. He felt helpless witnessing the fear in Diane's eyes but is confident it's about money and soon to be over. He is wrong.

A .40 caliber weapon is silencer fitted and two brilliant and vibrant people are shot in the head dead.

CHAPTER FORTY

Connecting the Dots

THE RETURN FLIGHT to L.A. leaves Jim's head swimming with anticipation. Denzel has a doctor's appointment in Little Rock in two days and the optimism is riding high for Denzel, Jim and Eva. Even when he touches down in trouble laden L.A. and leaves the airport in the GTO, he's energized about his own life and the people around him. A conviction of faith driven home by the Neville experience lays a path to follow although Jim isn't sure where that direction leads.

Ten minutes from the airport the phone Slick Rollie gave Jim rings in the GTO glove box. He retrieves and answers.

"Are you in the car?" Slick asks.

"Yeah, just left the airport. Why?" Jim answers.

"Pull over, get something to take notes." Rollie seems very serious.

"Now?" Jim questions.

"Jim, you're in a lot of trouble. I'm trying to help." Rollie summarizes.

"Hold on, pulling over now." Jim finds a convenience store lot and pulls in. "What the hell is going on?" Jim asks searching for a pen and paper to take notes.

"The cops found the murder weapon that killed Wayne... it's your old pistol covered in prints... yours. An APB is issued for you, can't go home...need to dump the GTO." Rollie lays out a series of intimidating issues.

Jim's head sinks in emotion, the thought he had anything to do with Wayne's death is painful. "Rollie, how do I handle all of this?"

"Go to the bowling alley between Dayton and Suggs...in the bathroom you'll find a key taped under the sink on the far right. Take the key to locker 231... you'll find $25,000 in cash, directions to my storage unit with the code to get in. Take my '65 Corvette...leave your GTO. I need time to get you out of the country...do you have a safe place for the next three, maybe four days?" Rollie asks.

"Could go hide out in the mountains with David for a few days. How do I get out of these charges?" Jim asks.

"I'm working on that, but if you stay in the U.S. more than a few days, you'll be caught. We can buy a lot of time if you go to South America...we'll get you out of this come hell or high water." Rollie completes the plan.

"One thing, look at David's file then text me directions to his cabin in Colorado," Jim requests.

"Can do. Last suggestion...contact no one, Janey, Conrad, your Grandfather...throw your cell away, the feds can ping towers to locate you."

Rollie waited. He knew Jim was trying to recover from the initial shock. After no comment from Jim, he continued.

"Drop your credit cards in a service station bathroom, maybe someone takes off on a spending spree. Only talk to me on this phone. Do you truly trust Janey? If so, I'll let her use my phone sometime over the next 48. Is this all clear?" Rollie wants to drive all the points home.

"Perfectly, don't contact Janey...I do trust her but don't want to get her in trouble," Jim answers. "Can't thank you enough, Rollie."

"It's easy for me, you're the son I never had. You didn't kill Wayne, no one risks his life going into a Hells Angel bar to take up for the guy then shoot him...time to right the wrong." Rollie hangs up.

A wild swing of emotion flies around Jim driving east toward Colorado. One moment he's high on life, the next he's running for that life.

He's smart enough to know Rollie spent years circling the outside edge of the law and will do anything to get him out of this mess. Little doubt on who set all of this misery in motion, but someone will have to crack the inner circle of the Institute for Jim to be cleared.

A single stop before the California State line is taken to get gas and a few things to snack and drink. Cash is used for payment. He places his credit cards in a bathroom stall.

Jim is impressed with the Corvette and its massive horsepower setting under the hood. Rollie spent an enormous amount of time and money restoring it, and Jim would like nothing better than hammer the accelerator to witness the 160 stated on the speedometer matching his frustrations. That kind of speed puts his life at risk in the mountains, playing close to the edge nothing to lose. A scary concern to most sane people, but a comfort zone to Jim. It took a great deal of restraint to keep the classic car around the speed limit. It could be disastrous attracting a cop for a speeding ticket and exposed to an outstanding warrant.

The next morning Jim drives the dirt road to the cabin and sees David standing on the front porch, the .306 in one hand

and a Leggo waffle in the other. A distrust in David's eyes stares at the strange black Corvette parked until Jim gets out.

David comes off the porch to give him a hug.

"What did the cat drag up now?" David jokes after letting Jim free from the hug.

"You never know, could be a big rat," Jim throws back.

"Man, I've been thinking about you a lot, but don't get too excited, nothing else to do up here but think." David relays.

"Went back to see my Grandfather...turns out he's only got a few months to live with cancer." Jim gives a brief description of the last couple of weeks.

"That's terrible, how is the family handling it?" David inquires.

"Terrible...I took him to see Gayle Kidd in Louisiana. Can't be sure yet, but hopeful she helped him get rid of the disease." Jim smiles for the first time in the last fifteen hours.

"That's phenomenal...so you think Dr. Benders pulled it off?" David questions.

"With what I've seen, I'm a believer. My Grandfather is the last piece of the puzzle if cancer free." Jim profiles.

"Come in," David demands. "We've got a lot to talk about. Like some breakfast?, I need a reason to cook for someone other than me." David tells the truth. He doesn't cook often.

"Love some...been driving for more than thirteen hours virtually nonstop. Could you stand a little company for the next few days?" Jim asks.

"Are you kidding? Sounds crazy, but all I've been talking to is a chipmunk...could use company to get caught up on the outside world." David heads into the cabin.

Over breakfast Jim drops the bomb surrounding Wayne's death and his blame.

"You're an ex-cop, if you want me to leave I'll go now... keep you out of harm's way connected to me." Jim does not want to bring harm to his friend.

"Neither one of us are surprised on the trumped up charges; doesn't bother me, I know the truth. We're in this together, far deeper than you know now." David fires back. Jim appreciates his loyalty but feels David has something to add.

"You holding out on me?" Jim asks.

"Sniper tried to kill me on the front porch couple days ago... heard an exchange of gunfire running to the back of the cabin. Worked around to outflank them, to my surprise found three dead...a young, beautiful woman and your Navy Seal, Joe Tramazzo. Man saved my life again." David describes the events.

"Did you call the cops?" Jim asks.

"Hell no, buried where they fell...cops would make this far more complicated than it is," David relays.

"What did you do with their vehicle?" Jim inquires.

"Drove it off in a mountain lake three miles from here...more than 400 feet deep. Found their I.D.'s...maybe you've seen them around since we have a common enemy?" David goes over to the fireplace and reaches inside recovering the I.D.'s.

"Was going to get a contact in the Denver Police Department to run a background check, then throw them away...know these two?" David hands Jim the I.D.'s.

"Son-of-a-bitch," Jim yells and heads to the window light to get a better look. "Can't believe this," he says excitedly.

David follows to look at the I.D. next to the window. "What, who is it?"

"This is an Aussie chick that dated my next door neighbor. Her name is Debbie Sweeney...going by Carol Davidson here," Jim says with conviction.

"Are you sure?" David questions.

"Sure," Jim states with emphasis. "I slept with the girl."

David cocks his head to one side, without saying anything Jim anticipates the question.

"Long story…we have plenty of time over the next few days to get the dirty detail down. Can't believe she's in on this shit happening to us." Jim states, a questionable look coming over his face.

David picks up on the look. "What are you thinking? I can see the wheels turning."

"Need to see for myself if that's her…where are the bodies buried?" Jim asks.

"Not doing anything this afternoon, might as well dig something up," David answers.

David retrieves a shovel and they hike up the hill to do exploratory digging. Once at the site, Jim grabs the shovel to dig up a second grave in less than a month.

Soon the man shooting at David is unearthed and moved to one side. Deb's body is uncovered next. Jim goes down on one knee looking at the once beautiful and fun loving woman lying in this nondescript hole in the ground unceremoniously.

Jim turns to David.

"That's her, that's Deb. In hindsight I can see the premeditation of why she broke into our circle. Damn, she probably planted the bugs in my house. What a waste…say, where did you bury Tramazzo? Jim asks.

"Here," David answers. "Buried him here."

"There's not a third body in here," Jim declares.

David grabs the shovel from Jim and exchanges places. He digs into the loose dirt in several directions but Tramazzo is not in the ground.

David stops digging for a moment, looks up at Jim, panic in his face. "Do you think someone found the grave?"

"Don't think so, but damn sure find it interesting," Jim answers nonchalantly.

"I find it frightening…man, I fucked this up. Hopefully, we'll be in adjoining cells." David bemoans his choices at this point.

"David, let's put these people back in the ground where they belong," Jim suggests.

"Easy for you to say." David starts shoveling dirt back onto the bodies.

"Listen, Tramazzo was the first on my list, right?" Jim asks.

"Right," David answers.

"He gets killed, buried and I dig him up... except he's not in that grave either?"

"Damn, I see where this is headed...Tramazzo is a descendant of the Shroud, he's being resurrected." David looks to the heavens. "God bless Dr. Benders, the man sent me a guardian angel."

The grave is refilled and the guys return to the cabin. Jim tries listening to David go on and on about Benders but total exhaustion overtakes him and he falls into a deep, dreamless sleep.

Jim sleeps until late morning the next day. Around 10:00 he gets up, not believing the time and looking for David but the BMW is gone. He finds himself starving and after rummaging around the cabin finds a couple of Pop-Tarts to stay off the hunger. David wasn't lying about the lack of cooking skills or at least the desire. A trip to the porch finds Bull eager to share the Pop-Tart and Jim complies finding the chipmunk amusing.

The air is full of busy silence; breezes tickle the tree branches and a woodpecker taps its way to a meal somewhere in the timber not far away. Jim feels a resentment for the city noise forced on his senses in L.A. He desires replacing it with the non-combative sounds pouring in and around these rocks. Comparing rural Arkansas and the Colorado mountains, Jim determines he's a country boy.

The BMW pulls up, loaded with a trunk full of groceries. After lunch David suggests a hike around the property, a habit he does twice a day looking for signs of strangers. Jim tries the cell Rollie gave him but finds zero service in the area.

"How far do you go down to use the cell?" Jim asks.

"The cell works in town, but don't you think you're pushing the envelope using one from a tracking standpoint?" David understands the exposure.

"Rollie bought this non-traceable phone somewhere, but it loses coverage if you call any other phone," Jim answers.

"Rollie's got his shit together," David states. "That's pretty impressive."

"Been thinking how to resolve this dilemma we have... need to go directly to the top of the tree, talk some sense into her," Jim states.

"I'm assuming you're talking about Cindy Benders... she's a tough bird, strong business mind. Don't think she'd be very receptive," David responds.

"Is there a possibility Cindy isn't behind all that's going on... someone at the Institute circumventing her input?" Jim asks.

"She knows," David explains. "Nothing goes on without her fingerprint on it."

David stops close to a cliff, in the distance a lake is spotted in the clear, blue sky. David turns to Jim. "That tree is the wrong one to bark up."

"Maybe, you being in charge of home security in a previous life, how would you get into her house to pay a visit?" Jim forms a slight smile with the question.

"That's easy," David throws a rock off into a deep ravine. "She likes to sleep with the sliding door open in her bedroom on the second floor... a large oak tree next to the house allows access to the balcony. She turns the first floor alarm on, but with the door open can't do the same on the second floor. If the bedroom window is open, there's a damn good chance she's sleeping in it." David starts back on the trail to the cabin, Jim throws a rock in the same ravine then follows.

CHAPTER FORTY-ONE

She Loves Me

ROLLIE SITS AT Detective Fox's desk waiting on him to get out of a department meeting and his patience is running thinner by the moment. People wait to see him not the other way around. He came down as a favor to Fox, a promise it wouldn't take long, and thirty-five minutes past the appointment time he stares at a string of hookers being processed and booked from the night before.

Fox finally appears apologizing for the inconvenience. Truth be known, Fox is intimidated by Rollie and his reputation, but the Captain wanted to contact him for information on Jim. Fox is following orders he realizes are worthless.

"Rollie, got more bad news for our boy...that doctor in Missouri." Fox looks at a piece of paper on his desk. "Sam Wallace was murdered and his girlfriend. Killed with a .40 caliber slug that matches the same one we pulled out of Wayne Davis. Jim is up to his ass in a triple homicide. Help me get him before some rookie cop unloads on him."

Rollie leans on the desk getting closer to Fox's face. "You so-called friend... you know damn well Jim Cirmah had nothing to do with any of this. You need to get your cop ass over to the Benders Institute; they're framing my boy."

"Nothing connects the Institute to any of this...bring me something, and we'll take them down together. It hurts me to put Jim in this position...he's my friend, Rollie... just doing my job." Fox tries to explain.

Rollie gets up to leave. "If I see him...let you know."

Fox hands Rollie a card. "Call me when he contacts you."

Rollie throws the card back on the desk. "I know who you are, where you live, who you fuck...who fucks you." Rollie walks out of the station and Fox is scared of the truth.

Rollie pulls in and parks in front of the Pawnshop. He gets out of the car, and Janey zips in next to him jumping out, Winston on a leash. It was only a matter of time before she turned up concerning her man.

"Rollie," Janey shouts. "We need to talk."

Slick looks around the lot and across the street checking for cops trying to be discreet.

"Not out here, come inside." Rollie voices and leads Janey and Winston to his office.

"I want to talk to Jim, know damn well you can contact him." Janey isn't asking, more of a demand.

"Look, the pot boiling Jim's ass just got a lot hotter. That doc in Missouri has been murdered along with his girlfriend. Coincidentally by Jim's stolen gun. I'm sure he wants to talk to you, but maybe it's in your best interest if we sort this whole thing out, get him away from this mess." Rollie sees the pain in her eyes rapidly filling with water. He takes a Kleenex from his desk and hands it to her.

"Damn it, Rollie... I miss him. We both act so independent, but I...I can't stand the thought of him not being around. What you say makes sense…I don't care if something happens to me. His voice is what I need to hear. Don't you understand?" Janey wipes away the flow of tears.

"Have the cops been to see you?" Rollie asks.

"Yeah, Fox and some other detective came by the club last night…told them what I know, nothing," she replies.

"Look, your phone is going to be tapped… you'll be followed, every move scrutinized. Let me work magic over the next few days, drill down deep to see what 'ole Rollie can do. I have the feeling Jim is safe, would love to talk. Patience, I need a little more time to earn this name "Slick." Rollie tries to buy time.

Janey gets up. "Tell him I love him…please."

"That's a real possibility, I'm sure he feels the same about you…say, how's Winston taking all of this?" Rollie reaches down and pets the large Winston head.

"He's not quite in the same mood, but can tell something is bothering him." Janey also gives Winston a rub behind the ears.

Janey hugs Rollie for a few seconds and starts for the door but turns back. "Tell him I'll be waiting." She closes the door behind her.

Rollie waits a few minutes, takes a baseball cap and goes to a fenced-in lot behind the building. Covering his mouth and phone using the hat, he dials Jim's cell but he doesn't pick up. He goes back into the storage area retracing his steps when the phone rings.

"Hold for 30 seconds," Rollie tells Jim. Once back outside, Rollie engages the conversation.

"Janey wants to talk but I bought some time… that young lady loves you."

"Think about her a lot, but we can talk later when things get fixed," Jim states.

Rollie has more bad news.

"A lot more has happened since we last communicated. "Your gun conveniently killed Dr. Wallace and his girlfriend. I'm flying Franklin out tonight to do some snooping among the locals to determine our next options." Rollie is determined to get to the bottom of every detail.

"When was he killed?" Jim asks.

"Just pulled the FBI case file to help Franklin's trip...he was murdered four days ago," Rollie relays.

"I was in Arkansas four days ago," Jim fires back.

"Not too keen on geography but you'd be better off in L.A. Can't be more than a few hours drive from central Arkansas to southeast Missouri."

Rollie is right about the logistics.

"Can't catch a break," Jim bemoans.

"Don't get down on me," Rollie demands. "Say, is there anything you can think of to help Franklin when he gets to Missouri?"

"Tell him to talk to the neighbors, see if anyone noticed uniform policemen around before he was killed. This will sound bizarre...but have Franklin check on Wallace in the morgue." Jim asks.

"What's he looking for?" Rollie questions.

"To see if the body is still there," Jim answers.

"I don't think the good doctor can get up and walk away," Rollie asserts.

"Hold on, getting a text from Conrad." Rollie reads the text. "Jim's Grandfather called today looking for him...says he has great news about his cancer."

"Thanks for the info about my Grandfather, it makes a grey day bright." Jim shuts the cell off.

CHAPTER FORTY-TWO

In Death We Part

DAVID MOVES AN RC Cola bottle down a narrow metal chute after feeding the soda machine two quarters. The bottle is plucked from the end of the maze and the cap popped off on the side of the metal box falling into a tray. David sips a drink of the prize and bites a soft peppermint stick retrieved from a jar sitting on a counter that is located in a small grocery store, a store with rarely changing prices or products since it was built in 1957.

He comes out of the store, walks over to Jim talking with Rollie on the special cell phone. Carrying a large bag of candy, David patiently waits for the call to finish. He silently offers a peppermint stick to Jim and is taken up on the offer. Jim shuts the cell off and places the peppermint stick in his mouth.

"If I didn't walk these hills twice a day, I'd be busting out of my pants…not much to do but eat." David's prediction happens, he takes another stick of candy from the bag chewing on it.

Jim finishes the candy glancing over at the grocery store. "It's hard to believe places like that still exist...the store has completely ignored the passage of time."

"Yeah, I keep expecting to see Wally and the Beaver to walk out of the door any minute." David reminisces.

"Who?" Jim looks puzzled.

"You know, 'Leave It to Beaver'." David tries to explain.

"Those cartoon characters?" Jim questions.

"No, that's Beavis and Butthead," David laughs. "Way before your time."

The car heads for the cabin. Jim turns to David doing the driving. "It happened, my Grandfather is cancer free."

"That's incredible on so many levels... Gayle Kidd is the real deal. We must celebrate over a drink." David says excitedly.

"It's wonderful but the drink can wait; if they went after Dr. Wallace, she is next." Jim relays.

"Makes sense, what can we do?" David asks.

"It's up to you and me, my friend. I'm going back to visit Cindy Benders...she'll see the light. You go to Baton Rouge to watch over Gayle... we have to protect her."

"I'm with you, it's about this wonderful gift given to mankind; we must protect her regardless of the costs. I'll drive to Denver to fly out...you are the one I'm worried about. Cops will be looking for you." David tells the truth.

"I'll stop to get bleach for my hair, always wanted to be blond anyway." Jim is half serious, half joking.

"My mother left a wig in the cabin, maybe you could pull it back into a ponytail to disguise your appearance?" David offers.

Once at the cabin, David offers the wig and Jim tries it on in the mirror. He ties it back tight and shows David the results.

"That's good on you, someone my age couldn't pull it off but you make it work."

David encourages Jim to use the wig.

Jim looks in the mirror one more time and makes a couple of minor adjustments. It does change his look from afar and decides it's a go. They shake hands and leave the cabin to see what awaits their travels.

The drive back to L.A. has moments of angst; state troopers are pulling cars over in a speed trap inside the California line, but Jim maintains accelerator discipline. Soon he closes the distance to the city without drawing attention.

The long distance tires his body, but the closer he gets to Malibu and Cindy Benders, the more wide awake he becomes. Twenty minutes from her estate, the phone rings and Rollie is on the line.

"Some crazy things going on in this neck of the woods." Rollie offers a big tease.

"Hopefully you've got me out of this mess," Jim responds.

"Steve Hopkins has been murdered...his wife found him gunned down in the garage," Rollie states with a cutting edge.

"Why would someone from the Institute be murdered... that makes no sense?" Jim questions.

"It does if you're cleaning up the loose ends." Rollie clarifies the circumstances. "Look, I'll have your transportation lined up in the next couple of days...be ready to roll at a moment's notice.

"Thanks, Rollie." Jim pulls the car into a small strip shopping center and grabs a Starbucks coffee and a Subway sandwich. It's a little after 11:30 p.m. and Jim wants to make sure Cindy Benders is asleep before approaching her high-end neighborhood.

At midnight he drives by the Benders' compound and sees no lights. A slight ping of panic in Jim's stomach stirs thinking Cindy may be out of town. The Corvette is parked at The Oyster House, a small restaurant on the water more than a mile away. Jim can't take the chance of parking on the street and a passing cop getting too curious, so he jogs the beach approaching the Benders' house from oceanside.

After scaling the compound wall he moves over to the corner of the house and finds the door on the second floor open. He assumes Cindy must be sleeping predicted by David. Up the tree and onto the balcony gets Jim within a few feet of the bedroom. A look inside reveals no one in bed, Jim enters the bedroom and hears classical music coming from the first floor. Jim's heart is pounding making his way down the hallway, pistol in hand. At the top of the stairwell he hesitates, peeks into the room spotting Cindy oblivious to anything but the music in the background. Jim eases along the steps, Cindy reaches for a drink setting on the table but drops it when Jim starts walking across the room in view.

"What the hell are you doing here?" Cindy asks. "Thought you would be deep under a rock by now."

"Crawled out to visit a fellow scorpion," Jim fires back.

Cindy starts to clean up the spilled drink as if Jim isn't standing in front of her pointing a gun.

"If you leave now, I'll wait thirty minutes before calling the cops." Cindy states, an air about the offer.

Jim walks to Cindy and shoves her backwards onto the couch. "Not before some answers."

"Don't threaten me, I have your life in the palm of my hand... get out." Cindy continues to threaten.

"That I have a hard time disputing, but tonight it's just you and me...you're looking at a man connected to three murders, what's one more?" Jim keeps it simple.

Jim waves the gun in Cindy's direction. "Why are you killing the people in the Dr. Benders' experiment? How do they threaten you?"

"Fuck you... get out of my house." A belligerent Cindy snaps back.

Jim grabs Cindy by the throat and starts to choke her. "I will not let you kill Gayle Kidd...call off your dogs now." He backs off, seeing fear in her eyes.

"Couldn't stop it if I wanted to," Cindy states.

"Bullshit." Jim waves the gun in an upward motion. "Nothing but lies... get up."

Cindy complies and Jim leads her to the kitchen placing her in a chair. He starts rifling through drawers, finds a roll of duct tape and tapes Cindy to the chair.

"Is this about money...it always comes back to money, power or both?" Jim asks.

"Money, why would it be about money? I have all the money I'll ever need. If you hear the truth, will you leave me alone?" Cindy is negotiating with Jim at this juncture.

"A good starting point...the truth." Jim agrees.

"For a man clearing a 160 IQ, my husband could be dangerously dumb. He had the talent and science to pull off the DNA infusion, but artificially inseminating a woman to recreate the birth of Christ is blasphemous...totally against God's principles. It's not in the natural order of things...purely evil. Without God's will, there is no Second Coming, Mr. Cirmah." Cindy is steadfast in her beliefs.

"I'll be damned," Jim laments.

"Thought killing people is against God's principles, how crazy of me."

"There are many human sacrifices in the Bible to protect the longterm sacred values. Royce wouldn't listen to reason, hellbent on bringing Jesus to Earth in his lifetime."

Cindy paused. She wanted Jim to fully understand her next statement. "It was all so wrong, only God can anoint us with that privilege," Cindy explains.

"Did you ever consider this is the way God might send his son or daughter back to mankind?" Jim inquires.

"That's ridiculous…no amount of talking by you or anyone else will convince me of that. We have to rid the world of these evil people… and Jim, you helped us do it."

Jim gets down in Cindy's face.

"So righteously indignant… you're the one that's stupid. I have witnessed with my own eyes the healing power of Gayle Kidd. Don't give a damn if she's from hell or heaven, she can heal cancer from a man's body."

Cindy laughs loudly. "So the little lady living in a nuthouse incapable of uttering a word cures cancer? Is that your story?"

"She cured my Grandfather… he had a few months to live." Jim counters.

"Do you think you can cure cancer, Jim?" Cindy asks.

"What does that have to do with anything?" Jim inquires about what he thinks is a stupid question.

"Go in my study down the hallway…look in the bottom drawer on the right. Bring back the stack of files." Cindy gives directions once more.

Jim hesitates. "What am I looking for?"

"Just do it…I'm not going anywhere." Cindy lets it remain a mystery.

A look in the desk produces a series of files and he brings them to the kitchen.

"Dig down, Mr. Cirmah," Cindy says. "A file has your name on it."

Jim finds the file and thumbs through it.

"Let you keep as a souvenir," Cindy's sarcasm reeks through. "Your mother was inseminated with the same Shroud DNA as Gayle's mother. You're one of the 'so called' chosen one's."

Jim digs deeper into the file. No matter how outrageous Cindy's contention is, the reality his mother being in the Benders Institution is clearly defined by the documents.

"How did she pay for it, my parents were broke back then?" Jim asks meekly.

"Grandfather Denzel paid for it...seems your father didn't have enough money or swimming sperm to get anyone pregnant. Ever wonder why your father suddenly left the family when your mother got pregnant with baby sister?" Cindy knows Jim didn't have a clue about the innermost secrets of his family and uses it as a tool.

The picture is starting to get brutally clear for Jim, but he needs to know the truth no matter how much it hurts. "Why did my father leave?"

"Because she got pregnant by someone other than your sterile dad. It seems I know more about your family tree than you do." Cindy keeps pounding Jim's senses, shot after shot of harsh reality.

"It doesn't matter about me or my family, it only matters about Gayle Kidd...this is the last time I'm asking, stay away from this gift to the world." Jim starts regaining strength to fight for what is right.

"No sense of logic is coming from you." Cindy keeps up the mental barrage. "Jim Cirmah, you're a Shroud descendant that blows away his stepfather with a shotgun, dates strippers and fights his way through more bars than the town drunk and has the same amount of miracle gifts as Gayle Kidd. Zero. Have you cured any cancer lately?" Cindy questions.

"I'm nobody... stop talking about me. You're the one going to die soon; did you know Steve was murdered a few hours ago?" Jim fires back at Cindy. "Looks like whoever you hired to do the dirty work is cleaning up all the details...you and Steve are part of those details. I can stop the carnage but you have to give me some names."

Jim pulls off a strip of the duct tape and moves it close to Cindy's face. "Names now or this conversation is over."

"Fuck you, I'm dead either way…at least I stopped these blasphemous acts from occurring." Cindy is defiant to the end.

Jim places the tape over her mouth and leaves the house, no sense of accomplishment followed him.

Cindy struggles to free herself from the duct tape bindings but only succeeds in turning the chair over. She is remorseful for nothing when it came to the death of her husband or anyone else connected with the trail of sin the Shroud had plowed.

All Cindy has to do is make it through the night and the housekeeper will let herself in around 8:00 and release her from these bindings. She'll go to her second home in Italy, hire private security and let this whole nightmare drift away. Steve Hopkins was an idiot in her eyes, helpless in death and unable to control his own fate unlike her.

This kind of internal justification went on for several hours before the side door Jim left unlocked opens to the predawn night. It's way too early for the housekeeper to be arriving. The last thirty seconds of Cindy Benders' life is terrorizing; fate is a cruel mistress. Lying in a heap of helplessness she watches the pistol fired point-blank into the duct tape on her face.

CHAPTER FORTY-THREE

Up In Smoke

ZAK FRANKLIN HAS been a P.I. for Slick Rollie six years and the one Rollie calls to get things done others won't do. He grew up in a second generation Italian home speaking English, Italian, and French. Ties to the mob are rumored, but the subject is never broached by Slick. Fluency in multiple languages goes a long way getting things done socially and legally abroad. Franklin is tall, thin, sporting short cropped hair and good looks to charm most people into believing he's law enforcement of many varieties depending on the circumstantial need. Today that need is a FBI agent investigating the death of Dr. Sam Wallace.

The Cape Girardeau Central Memorial Hospital where Sam practiced also serves as the city morgue. Franklin goes in flashing fake FBI credentials Rollie provided at an extreme expense. It could gain access to the FBI headquarters in D.C. The petite, older lady behind the glass window examines the badge but never questions its authenticity nor the handsome guy presenting it.

"FBI Special Agent Franklin," Zak says with belief. "I'm here investigating the death of Dr. Sam Wallace… is the mortician in, I need to see the body?"

The lady smiles, never meeting a FBI agent except on TV. Franklin is better looking than his TV counterparts, fake nonetheless. She buzzes him in the locked door, he could gain access on looks alone. The agent and nurse walk a hallway to the mortician's office. Dr. Rubio Poke falls for the fake I.D.

"I'm from the FBI office in St Louis, need to see Dr. Wallace's body and your autopsy report," Franklin demands displaying a typical FBI agent attitude.

"The autopsy part is easy," Sanders reaches into a filing cabinet, retrieves the report he hands to Nurse Collier. "Please make a copy for Agent Franklin." He looks back at Franklin. "I'm afraid his body was cremated sometime last night."

"What kind of police work is that?" Franklin asks. "You cremate a murder victim a few days after the event. Who the hell authorized this insanity?"

"His mother insisted… it was in his will, specifically stated to harvest his organs then cremate him. Dr. Wallace is a legend around here, and his wishes are carried out to the Nth degree." Dr. Sanders explains.

Agent Franklin takes the autopsy copy and goes back to the car pulling out his cell and calling Rollie with the news.

CHAPTER FORTY-FOUR

Only The Young Die Good

DAVID REACHES OVER to the bag of candy canes setting on the seat of the rental car and is disappointed in the emptiness. He's normally not a sweet eater, but since his retreat to the mountains boredom leads him down a path of love handles if the eating habits don't change.

Like Jim, he's never been to the State of Louisiana and finds the food and people much nicer than the L.A. crowd over the last couple of days. Baton Rouge is small compared to the big city, but after a few weeks in the mountains it seems overflowing with life.

It feels like old detective times for David, parked outside the asylum several hours a day watching people come and go but no action in sight. All this, familiar to the law profession. A murder attempt inside the complex seems remote, but if it goes down David can't prevent it. All he can do is survey the individuals visiting and use his deductive skills to guess their intent.

Through Jim Cirmah's previous encounter, David is guessing Friday night Gayle will go out into the dark to tent healing in a neighboring city. He's hoping to see miracles to reaffirm his faith. Logic dictates the attempt to harm her will occur then.

Thursday afternoon a car pulls up to the asylum, but David walked to a convenience store for a bottle of water. Coming back he sees two well-dressed men in their mid-thirties exit the building, return to the car and pull away. An uneasy feeling sweeps into David's mind he can't shake.

The night is sleepless for David, he didn't want to make a second mistake. Dr. Benders' death laid its gentile head next to his pillow. He feels a need for strategy confirmation, wanting to communicate with Jim. But the only way to contact Jim is through Rollie and that silver bullet is for emergencies. Perhaps his paranoia is not justified, perhaps.

Friday morning he buys a cooler and packs ice, sandwiches, water, and chips. He'll remain steadfast at his post.

The day is long and tedious. David's punched every channel on the radio numerous times, finding more country music than rock.

Late afternoon a car pulls behind him and the men approach his vehicle from either side. He's been worried about nothing, it's obvious they're local cops.

David rolls his window down as the detectives get parallel on either side of the car. The cop to his left leans over glancing into the interior flashing his badge.

"Sir, please step out of the car. Bring your license and registration with you," Detective Hanes requests.

David complies and the second detective, Dillard Tebeau, goes back to the car to run the information.

"So what's a L.A. man doing in Baton Rouge sitting on this street day after day?" Hanes asks.

David pulls his P.I. license out and hands it to Hanes. "Working a case in your fair city."

"Do you have a weapon?" Hanes requests.

"Yes." David lifts his jacket up, reveals his holstered revolver.

"You know what's coming next... I need to reach for your weapon... then we can all straighten this out. Put your hands behind your head." Hanes demands.

David follows instruction; he would do the same in Denver if the shoe was on the other foot.

Hanes takes the pistol. "Need to see your permit to carry."

After taking his arms down, David points to the car. "The permit is in the briefcase." He starts to open the door.

Hanes stops him. "Hold on, I'll retrieve the permit." The cop pulls the briefcase out and looks inside.

"Top right pocket," David instructs.

Hanes gets the permit and reads it. "You can carry a gun, but your P.I. license is for California... you can't work a case here."

"I'm helping an investigation for the L.A. Police Department." David relays thinking this would end it for most local cops.

Tebeau returns and hands the driver's license and registration back to David. "It's clean."

"As nice as I can put this, don't like individuals coming into my town messing with the citizens. Who you working for in the police department?" Hanes doesn't mix words in a Cajun accent.

"Reaching for my wallet to get a card," David explains. He pulls out Detective Fox's business card and hands it to Hanes.

Hanes turns it over to Tebeau. "Check out his story." Tebeau returns to the police car.

David is agitated. This small-town cop did his job but this is nothing more than a power play. Someone inside the asylum must have pull in this hick town or he's dealing with a real-life Barney Fife.

Tebeau returns shortly. "No answer... left Fox a message to call me back."

"Okay," Hanes summarizes. "Follow me to the station until we can clear this up."

"Hold on," David's had enough. "I was a cop for twenty-two years in Denver... this is bullshit. I've done nothing wrong but park on this street."

Hanes gets close to David's face. "This ain't Denver... you can follow me to the station or I'll follow you to the airport for a plane ride... up to you."

The drive to the police station has David fuming, but nothing can be done but follow directions. The station is bigger than he imagined and a new facility; taxpayers must be doing better in Baton Rouge than other places.

David passes a wall clock telling him it's twenty of six on his way to a large boardroom. Not a problem, plenty of time before the road show begins after 8:00 p.m. He sits in the room for thirty minutes, finally Hanes and Tebeau reappear.

"So, what's the content of your investigation in Baton Rouge?" Hanes asks.

David hesitates for a few seconds, there's no legal ramification for not being upfront but in less than two hours he can't be here. He decides a little bit of truth may help.

"Are you familiar with Dr. Royce Benders?" David questions.

Hanes shakes his head negatively. "Nope."

Tebeau counters. "Yeah, Nobel Peace Prize doctor killed a couple months ago...saw it on Fox News."

"Correct," David is excited someone's I.Q. is above room temperature. "I handled security for Dr. Benders. We believe a person connected to him in Baton Rouge could be next."

"Who is that person?" Hanes questions.

"Gayle Kidd," David responds.

"Kidd, an employee at the asylum?" Hanes asks.

"No," David qualifies. "She's a patient."

Tebeau's cell phone goes off and is answered. He walks out of the room to complete the call.

"How would someone get to a patient?" Hanes innocently asks.

David is not giving out anymore information; the hick cop already got more than deserved. Before he could make up an answer, Tebeau sticks his head into the door and motions for Hanes to join him. Several minutes go by before Hanes reappears.

"We need to register your weapon. Please turn it over." Hanes sticks his hand forward anticipating it being handed to him.

"There's no police protocol for this. I owe you nothing but my permit... you're not getting it." David's had enough.

"Up to you, but we do things differently here...can lock you up for the weekend then take your weapon." Hanes drew a line in the sand and David is swimming upstream losing ground.

"I want to talk with your police captain," David demands.

"On vacation until Tuesday, got a cell where you can wait." Hanes just closed the last door on David's foot.

David hands his pistol over to Hanes and the detective leaves. It's approaching eight. David has made his mind up to leave with or without his weapon or permission shortly. He starts to pace the floor, his mental state pushed to the limit over the loss of control. The call Tebeau received earlier must have been Detective Fox thought David. Whatever was said didn't make a positive impression on Barney Fife or he would still have his weapon.

The blinds are lifted on the window and David looks into the early evening darkness closing fast. Gun or not, he's going back to the hospital to protect Gayle Kidd.

The boardroom door opens slightly and David sees the hallway is clear. His steps are deliberate, not too fast forsaking attention. The front door is made before Hanes notices his escape and the chase begins.

David has a horrible sense of failure building in his stomach. The styrofoam box of ice and drinks is thrown side-to-side in the backseat of the car spilling the contents randomly. David pays little attention to flying sandwiches and even less to the flashing lights gaining on his speeding vehicle.

The asylum comes into view and David drives on the front lawn, jumps out and runs to the rear. Two squad cars climb the curb behind him, and Hanes, along with two other officers, wrestle David to the ground halfway round the building. A struggle ensues before David is finally pinned, cuffed and taken back to the front sidewalk.

A screaming hospital attendant runs out of the front door toward the police cars.

"They took her... God help us all, they took her." He starts to cry and falls to the ground.

CHAPTER FORTY-FIVE

Mad At God

ROLLIE DIDN'T LET his closeness to Jim stymie the blast of truth during their conversation. Jim sits in the parked Corvette this summer evening pounded into submission. It came rapidly over the phone, unforgiving and ugly. Justice and fairness left town, never to raise heads again in any conversation Jim's name has the slightest connection to.

Numbness forms in his mind, a self-defense from childhood to block things hurting too much. And what a litany of evil things to stare down this is. Gayle Kidd's body is found in an abandoned barn. Jim Cirmah is a serial killer in the eyes of the law and making the FBI's Most Wanted list.

Even Rollie lost his slickness, there's no talk of clearing Jim's name, only helping to facilitate his escape to Colombia, South America in a private plane using a small airstrip east of San Diego. A farewell gift to Jim includes a forged passport and new name. Goodbye and don't take Rollie down for aiding and abetting. Farewell to everything and everyone known from this point forward. Erased in the blink of an eye.

Jim sits stunned for a few minutes trying to regain a sense of composure. A brief thought of going to see Janey and getting one last embrace before being cuffed and dragged away like that fateful day in Dallas. The thinking passes, the reality of spending a long life sitting in a tiny cell isolated from fellow prisoners and all the world unbearable.

The 'Vette starts and circles the random lot he pulled into answering Rollie's call. A small light mounted over a wooden door catches his attention and below in the shadow reads 'Grace Faith Church.' Jim gets out of the car and walks to the wooden door wanting to strike something; preferably the so-called God Dr. Benders tried to bring back to Earth.

The door is opened and the scent of old carpet hits his face mixed with burning candles and unwashed bodies. Several people are scattered throughout the pews randomly, no organization seemingly to their placements. An older man dressed in an off-white robe appears from the left and bows before a large cross adorned by the dying Jesus. Jim walks to the front of the dimly lit church. The cross grows larger to his senses and he sees the painted wood is cracked needing repair. In a moment of self-pity, he identifies with the wooden figure's decaying existence.

To Jim's eyes there isn't an agenda to the church's activities until the robed man starts talking about the death of a homeless man seeking shelter from time-to-time. Jim sits on one of the many empty seats and listens to the words describing the man's nomad street life ways. When the old man gestures toward a plain wooden coffin situated off in the corner, Jim's witness to a funeral begins. The few people attending the thirty-one year-old's demise are street people noted by dirty dress and rarely washed skin.

Jim came in mad at God, being personally singled out for transgressions but realizes many suffer in life's walk. In years past Jim didn't have emotion for God, so being mad is one large leap forward to faith.

Rollie gave him $25,000 and of that, $10,000 is to be paid to the pilot flying him to Colombia. When the service is over he gives the startled minister $14,000 plus and drives away to his destiny in South America.

CHAPTER FORTY-SIX

The Unforgiven

THE FIRST COUPLE of months in Colombia, Jim lives on a small family farm twenty miles from Bogota. It's the final gift from Rollie, paying for his living arrangements to get a fresh start. All these arrangements involve a trusted but dubious contact in a country having low standards for the terms trusted or dubious. Getting up before daylight, Jim works his hands tending horses and irrigating a series of crop ditches walking a donkey in an endless circle. Surprisingly it cleanses his thoughts, giving an odd sense of accomplishment doing simple tasks.

The language barrier is less an issue each passing week, Jim has a basic understanding of Spanish from his street work in L.A. Dialect changes the meaning to a certain degree, but the challenge is welcome. The family's eight children vary in ages from four to sixteen. The two youngest sons are soon following Jim's every step. He makes baseballs and gloves from goat hide and teaches them how to play the game. The kids kick around a battered soccer ball following the national sport, but Jim wants a taste of baseball. A field is cleared of rocks except for four used as bases. Jim never mentions the fine art of sliding into a base. Bats are made from broom handles in the beginning, but get more sophisticated when two elders carve a wooden version utilizing various sizes for different age boys. The games are a diversion from the endless work and the villages start their own teams gaining a sense of competitiveness and pride.

Jim travels to Bogota with several farmers to sell coffee one weekend and helps the negotiation for the final exchange of money. His skills prove to be a big hit. The celebration for the sale begins and ends over drinking, the national Colombian diversion.

Showing no interest in the drunken sport and knowing the results are a short way up and a long way down, Jim takes the two youngsters on a walk. He stumbles across an old theater showing a Clint Eastwood movie, *Unforgiven*.

The movie has a special meaning to Jim, his Grandfather Denzel loves anything Eastwood appears in. When the movie came out in the nineties, the two saw the movie three times in one weekend.

Jim didn't mind the Spanish over-dubbing, he knew every word before falling off the lips of Morgan Freeman, Clint, or Gene Hackman. The youngsters have never seen any form of screen activity and sit transfixed by Jim's side. Toward the movie's end, a scene is played where Clint shoots Hackman's character in a saloon gunfight. As Clint takes a drink of whisky, Hackman comes back to life and tries to shoot Clint but quickly disarmed by Eastwood. As Clint aims a Spencer Rifle at Gene's head to kill him, a simple exchange of words occur.

"I was building a house, I don't deserve to die like this," Hackman says staring up at the barrel of death.

Clint in his usual 'less said the better' voice comes back at Gene. "Deserving ain't got nothing to do with it."

Hackman gets one more sentence in before getting shot. "See you in hell, William Munny."

Eastwood ends the exchange with a simple "yeah" and then fires the rifle point-blank into Hackman's face.

When the rifle is fired, Jim feels the floor beneath his feet start to move from side-to-side. The screen goes blank and the building shakes violently in the dark, walls start to fall in a major earthquake. Jim manages to get one of the boys in his arms but loses his brother in the chaos. He pulls, shoves and lifts his way through the rubble to daylight, the four year old in tow. A glance around this section of town shows complete devastation, most of the building walls have fallen and spitting dust and frightened survivors out into the street.

Soon the tide of flight turns to a wave of rescue; hands touch hands exchanging mounds of clay bricks to new piles not filled with crumpled bodies. The bodies are laid in the streets, wives and mothers simply identify the names by wailing over and over.

Hours go by searching for the six year old and others caught in the fall of the theater. The tiny body is finally exhumed and his father cries carrying the lifeless figure back to the village along with three others meeting death in different buildings. As the people of the small hamlet mourn their losses, Jim picks the small boy up from a church bench and kisses the child on his cheek. Before the shocked and soon wildly happy family, the child starts to breathe again and is held close to his mother's breast in awe of the miracle.

CHAPTER FORTY-SEVEN

Lord Of The Rings

DAVID STAYS IN the mountain cabin for several months before moving back to Denver. The isolation outweighed having a strategic advantage if someone came after him. Since Jim's disappearance and the murders of Cindy Benders and Gayle Kidd, things have calmed down to the point where the boredom and candy had to go.

Many changes are occurring in David's mental outlook on life, things witnessed bordering on holy and the occult have twisted and pulled him in several directions. Bishop Pressey met him for dinner one evening and David told him of things seen and the story behind Dr. Benders' experiment. The Bishop's awe of Dr. Benders' talents and his reverence for the Shroud make him believe the unbelievable.

David's at a moment in time needing a sense of stability in his life. He's been living at someone else's home for the last ten years and wants to reestablish a root system. The thought of getting a new home and going out to meet someone is appealing and he sets his sight on both.

The real estate agent is running late, but David sits in his car listening to a lunchtime hour of the greatest hits by the Beatles. The agent shows up apologetic, together visiting a bungalow in Red Rock for a second time. The house has a million dollar mountain view and David has decided to make an offer. The paperwork is signed and the agent leaves to do a selling job on his counterpart.

Lost in a far-away valley gaze on the back deck of his soon to be new home, David picks up the ringing cell, surprised to hear Slick Rollie on the other end.

"David, got a question for you."

Rollie is evasive for a reason.

"Rollie," David responds. "Was talking about you the other night with Bishop Pressey, your ears ringing?"

"Along those lines, can you come to L.A...can't say anymore?" Rollie keeps tight about the purpose.

"Be on a plane tomorrow if you think it's important?" David reads between the lines.

"It will be worth your while...text me your flight info, I'll pick you up," Rollie relays.

David's imagination tops out at 37,000 feet on the flight to L.A., Rollie is hinting major news about Jim without saying anything. It had to be positive if he wanted him to come along.

The GTO is parked in front of the airport and David jumps in. "Packed light, didn't know how long I'm staying," David relays.

"Didn't happen to bring your passport by chance?" Rollie asks hitting the freeway heading south.

"Sorry, didn't know we're going international," David answers.

"Didn't think so," Rollie rightly anticipates. "Made one for you...look in that folder on the backseat."

David opens the folder and a passport showing a better picture than his real one greets the eyes.

"Where are we going?" David asks. "This is about....

Before David can finish the sentence Rollie places his finger on his lips. "Don't say anymore until we get on the plane."

The men head to the same airstrip Jim used seven months earlier and get on the same plane heading to Colombia. In route Rollie reveals his contacts in country told him Jim is roaming the remote areas and performing miracles.

The drive to the small village takes hours. An overturned pickup truck on the narrow road creates the mess. The three getting together will not be confused with a high school reunion. The trail of blood and deceit so precisely paved in the past, a distance is rising within the group.

Rollie notices several changes in Jim, he's much thinner and needs a haircut Slick tries to joke about. Jim shrugs it off, saying barber shops are rare in this part of the world. David is not sure how to approach Jim, a different demeanor toward David is obvious to all.

Rollie asks Jim if the reports are true concerning the miracles being performed. A slight smile erupts. Jim says a conversation over breakfast will clear up the villager's exaggeration in the morning. The three men retire for the evening.

A rooster crows loudly next to the window, introducing the cock of the walk to David and Rollie. One of the teenage girls leads the men to an outdoor brick oven where eggs and bacon are piled high on both plates. Looking around expecting Jim to join them any minute, Rollie asks in fluent Spanish, "Where is Jim?"

The older woman cooking the breakfast ignores his inquiry and continues her duties. Rollie gets up and goes back to the house, David his shadow.

"What's going on?" David asks not understanding a word of Spanish.

"Looking for Jim," Rollie answers.

The two men open the door and head for a room Jim retired to the previous night. The bed is empty.

An elderly man sees their panic and approaches.

Rollie asks the same question in English. "Where is Jim?"

The man points out the window to the distant mountains and in a thick Spanish accent says, "He's gone to the jungle."

CHAPTER FORTY-EIGHT

Like To Get To Know You

SHELBY PRYOR HAS the pedigree to play the game on Wall St. among the big boys. Jennifer's parents struggled financially to pay for a Masters degree from Stanford in spite of the Fulbright Scholarship for the 4.0 grade point average. That was fourteen years ago, now an established bond trader working at Morgan Stanley, she's paid for the education thirty times over.

Shelby's life is sailing along, so much good and bad coming her way. The good is really good, she marries and has twin girls recently turning six. An apartment on the upper East Side and a social life filled with good friends building memories.

The bad is really bad, she divorces two years ago and scales back on the highend living being a single mother. Her ex-husband takes a job on the West Coast and is virtually a non-factor as a co-parent for the twins. The bad gets worse, Shelby is diagnosed with a brain tumor two days from her 36th birthday and has it removed at M.D. Anderson in Houston. It's been five months since the surgery and a CAT Scan reveals the tumor has already grown to seventy percent its original size, a death sentence from a medical standpoint.

Maria Santiago is a fellow bond trader at Morgan and the two women have become best of friends. Maria is a first generation Colombian and fought her way to the top against all the odds. She's never lost touch with family roots and goes back to Colombia twice a year to spend time. On her last visit, the countryside is buzzing around the healing powers of an American known as the 'Regalo de Dios' or 'God's Gift.'

Maria didn't have to sell Shelby too hard on flying to Colombia, the latest medical reality staring her and the twins in the face. Maria's father meets them in Bogota and a Jeep is rented. The social media world is alive and well in Colombia locating Jim Cirmah south of Bogota in the city of Pasto. Nine hours of hard driving gets them to the outskirts of Pasto and a sudden stop. Traffic around the city is stagnant and backed up by thousands flocking to Pasto and hopefully getting touched by the 'Regalo de Dios'.

The city is completely booked for rooms, restaurants, and other facilities. Tents and street venders are springing up and a rock concert atmosphere is spreading. Shelby, Maria, and Mr. Santiago park the Jeep and hike into the city following the crowd. Laughter and optimism is everywhere, a fact not lost on Shelby.

Photos and video are being taken by media outlets beyond the Colombian Press, and multi-languages spoken everywhere. Shelby is amazed at the attention this man is getting far beyond the Colombian boarders from around the world. Her hopes rise in unison surrounding all the attention 'Regalo de Dios' is getting. She grasps a locket hanging from her neck containing a picture of the twins.

Something substantial is happening for the word to spread so quickly on an international level and people from every continent tracking him down for their introduction to hope. Maria grabs Shelby's hand and smiles, both feeling electricity in the air.

The lines feed into a park near the center of town and a small lake. Everyone is civil and patient in spite of the hours it takes getting close to the 'Regalo de Dios'.

Mr. Santiago leaves, finding water and sandwiches after two hours of searching for the girls. Jim Cirmah is sighted in the distance, taking individuals and dunking them in the lake.

Shelby watches the activities anxiously, not sure what the requisite is for the miracle she desperately seeks. She's never been a church goer, more spiritual in belief and hopes it doesn't negate her ability to receive his blessing.

As her turn approaches, Jim's features come into view. He's so young, her preconceived idea shattered concerning what a man of God should look like. He would surely have to be ancient and full of life's experience to be so blessed. A strikingly handsome man, lean and gentle to people getting close, many passing out in his presence. Emotions build like a volcano, and she's not sure if the legs can deliver her body into the water for his embrace. Arms on both sides lift her shoulders up and she stares intently into the most beautiful and energized eyes she has ever witnessed.

Only a whisper falls to her ears, his arms wrapped around her waist. "God is with you." She senses the light and sounds go silent embraced by the water around her head for a few seconds. Jim pulls her back from the shallow depth and smiles inches from her face. Joy and relief pound her heart. Fear and cancer are gone.

The crowd grows into a larger mass over the next four days longing to be touched by Jim's gift. He stands in the water never losing his energy and greets all that touch him with grace and humility.

Jim's path of healing is interrupted on the fifth day when U.S. Marshall's and Colombian officials take him into custody for extradition back to the United States to stand trial for multiple murders.

CHAPTER FORTY-NINE

Connecting The Rot

CAPTAIN CYRIL AND Detective Fox drive Sunset Boulevard early evening in an unmarked car.

"Where's this character at?" Cyril asks.

"Was told he'll be here around eight-ish, going to that nightclub 'Rebel Nights' on fifth," Fox answers.

"Where did your tip come from?" Cyril demands.

"Reed in narcotics… says he'll be on time, the junk hidden under his spare tire." Fox responds.

The car moves up and down the Strip for another twenty minutes before the limo of Danny Draino comes into view and is spotted by Fox.

"That's our boy, Danny Draino, only a couple minutes late." Fox relays positioning his car behind the limo.

"What kind of name is Draino?" Cyril questions.

"An acquired one," Fox relays. "His real name is Danny Webin, picked up the name Draino after forcing a bottle of Draino down a prostitute's throat a few years back…all his whores stay in line since."

"Success through leadership… going to like Danny, let's get to know him a little better…pull him over." Cyril proclaims.

Fox turns the lights on and the limo pulls over. The driver gets out license in hand but Fox ignores him. He reaches for the handle on the backdoor but it's locked.

"Open this up, rock head." Fox demands.

The back window is opened and Danny looks up at Fox. "What the fuck do you want, cracker?"

"A little conversation...private like," Fox answers.

"Take a walk, Smith." Danny opens the door as the driver moves down the sidewalk.

"Need a favor," Fox sits on the seat. "Need you to take care of someone in the county jail."

"What the fuck are you smoking...get out of my car spouting shit like that? I can smell a set up ten miles away. Go get a crackhead to do a job for you. Fuck off." Danny says in terms not to be misunderstood.

"Open your trunk." Fox directs.

"You open it... I don't know a damn thing about this car other than the pussy I get in the backseat." Danny confesses.

Fox goes to the driver's door, opens it up and pops the trunk. He and Danny walk to the back and Fox removes the spare tire, underneath is three kilos of cocaine.

"What do we have here, Danny?" Fox asks. "Looks about three kilos to me."

"You motherfucker...this ain't nothing but a plant. Calling my attorney right now," Danny screams as he flips his phone out.

"That won't be necessary," Fox assures. "You need to talk to someone a lot more important than your attorney."

Fox walks Danny back and puts him in the backseat of the squad car. "Meet Captain Cyril... he runs the law in Orange County." Fox introduces Cyril.

"What the fuck you want man... got no time for this?" Danny spouts off.

"Shut the hell up for one minute...start using your ears instead of your tongue...this isn't anything but a business deal. You'll be at the club in fifteen minutes if you play it right. If not, you'll get five to seven years for dealing coke." The Captain now has control of the conversation.

Danny throws his hands up. "All ears, big man."

"Do you know who Jim Cirmah is?"

"Yeah, U.S. Marshals got his ass down in Colombia...serial killer dude." Danny reads the police reports on-line every night to see if any of his girls get caught.

"He's locked up in county... needs to go bye-bye in the next few days. No federal trial for Cirmah." The Captain explains.

"I got it...man gets dead we never had this cocaine stop." Danny decided to play the game.

"Correct...now Danny, you keep the three kilos as a gesture of goodwill, but if you fuck me over, there will be an even bigger problem for you next month, maybe next week." The Captain's case is stated for Danny to note.

Danny gets out of the car, shuts the trunk on the limo and waves his driver back.

The Captain turns to Fox. "Can he get this done for us, Cirmah knows way too much to let this drag out?"

Fox starts the car. "Hell yeah, Draino owns the county jail. Half the staff gets laid by his ladies for free.

CHAPTER FIFTY

Truth and Consequences

A LOT OF things make Rollie a highly successful entrepreneur. A man of focus, determination and willingness to skirt the law would certainly be in his bio if someone else penned it. If Rollie wrote it himself, he'd describe it as obsessive compulsive, always running away from his childhood and trying to find the things never had in his youth. In that regard, he and Jim Cirmah have much in common.

When Jim left for Colombia, Rollie was well on his way to selling much of his rental property and downsizing. His intent is to turn over the Pawnshop and Bonding business to the management of Conrad and a longtime CPA friend quitting his own practice to work full-time for Slick Rollie's financial empire.

As a result of this day-to-day shifting of personal management responsibilities, Rollie found a new subject for his obsessive compulsive nature: Jim Cirmah. There's always a trigger point for people blessed or cursed with obsessive personalities when it comes to the target of that obsession.

When David and Rollie met Jim in the small Colombian village, Slick could never understand why Jim left the next morning without a word exchanged. It ate on him for weeks and he's determined to find out why Jim turned his back on Rollie after all that transpired in their relationship over the years.

The publicity surrounding Jim Cirmah and his connection to the murders of so many high profile individuals across multiple states intrigues the public's attention worldwide. Rollie and the Pawnshop have become a constant destination point for reporters and the public alike.

Business for the Pawnshop has gone through the roof, but so have the constant requests for interviews and photo sessions. Rollie eventually hired a PR firm to handle them. In the beginning of all this public speculation and curiosity, Rollie enjoyed the ride giving several interviews to the media. That's how he met Jason Huckabee, a seasoned reporter at the *L.A. Times* matching Rollie pound for pound surrounding obsessive tendencies and a tenacious focus on a subject.

Huckabee made an impression on Rollie during the initial interview. He told Rollie he was writing a book about the so called 'Jesus Killer', and wherever the fact finding process led him, he'd expose the truth about Jim good or bad. Rollie found the honesty refreshing, doing two more interviews with Huckabee to help reveal those facts.

The moment Jim's extradition from Colombia cleared and he was brought back to L.A., Rollie, Huckabee, and a high profile attorney named Stephen Summers arranged a meeting with Jim in the county jail. The three meet at a coffee shop close to the jail to discuss strategies. A parallel set of agendas need to be covered, one centering on Jim's defense and the other to clear up facts about what happened to the Dr. Royce Benders' experiment. The three agree on the agenda and go to the jail to meet Jim.

Jim sits at a table shackled in chains connected to his waist, bound to his hands and feet. Rollie isn't sure who he's going to see during the meeting. Jim seemed distant during the Colombia event. Much to his surprise Jim greets him, a smile on his face like he just walked into the Pawnshop without a worry in the world.

Rollie wants to hug him, but two guards are in the room and no contact is allowed. Jim sits four feet away across a scarred desk witnessing this process before. Rollie makes the introductions and tells Jim what needs to be accomplished.

Jim leans forward on the desk. "No need for an attorney, although I do appreciate you getting one, Rollie. My fate's been decided."

"Mr. Cirmah," Summers jumps in. "Your situation is dire with legal counsel… impossible without one."

"I'll arrange a meeting in two days, Mr. Summers… we can discuss legal tactics at that point."

Jim turns his attention to Huckabee. "You can get things out to the public's eye needing to be told, Mr. Huckabee. Are you writing a column for the *Times* or a book?"

"Actually both," Huckabee responds. "I have so many questions, do you mind if I record this?"

"Not at all," Jim encourages strongly. "But I will convey what answers you get, no more no less. No other questions please. There's a reason for my direction not to be disclosed…we all face our destinies."

"I defer to your request…I'm thankful for the opportunity," Huckabee responds.

"One last thing before we get started, Mr. Huckabee," Jim relays.

"A copy of this recording must be delivered to Mr. Summers' office this afternoon. Not tomorrow, today."

"Understood." Huckabee agrees.

"Dr. Benders, a fair place to start for all." Jim acknowledges. "I never had a chance to meet the man unfortunately, but his brilliance is unquestioned. I owe him a lot, his heart was filled with courage and success he didn't get to see. A manuscript Dr. Benders wrote is on my computer describing why and what he did, if the police haven't destroyed it. If you can't recover there, you can find one on Wayne Davis' computer."

"Why would the police destroy evidence?" Summers asks.

Jim moves his fingers to his lips to silence the request.

"Sorry," Summers replies.

"The Benders' experiment is a success. Dr. Sam Wallace and Gayle Kidd have a gift to relieve the pain and suffering so many face. So much more could have been done, but when good rises so does evil."

Huckabee reaches into his briefcase pulling out a photo showing thousands of people gathered in Posta, Colombia and places it in the middle of the table.

"This was taken by a Colombian journalist five weeks ago. Thousands of people came to the deepest reaches of the jungle to be with you. Jim, you have the same gift to heal," Huckabee explains.

"This conversation is not about me, please honor that," Jim says.

Rollie leans on the table toward his long-time friend. "You didn't mention Joe Tramazzo, wasn't he the first person you went after?"

"Tramazzo is a killer... sent to protect evil." Jim answers.

"David Sanders said that Tramazzo died, then resurrected," Rollie adds.

"Evil can be resurrected like the holy." Jim throws the answer out and it settles on the table top.

One of the guards comes over to the meeting. "Time is up, gentlemen."

Jim rises to his feet and the guard starts to escort him back to the cell.

Rollie stands quickly. "Jim, I have to know why you ignored me in Colombia after all our history?"

"The answer is in this book." Jim holds up a Bible. "We'll discuss it the next time we meet." He tosses the Bible to Rollie and leaves, guards on either side.

CHAPTER FIFTY-ONE

Bow to Your Destiny

BLANE TERRY IS nicknamed 'Rat Pack' by his fellow inmates in the county jail because he procures a wide range of items the prisoners want delivered to their cell door. Always a price attached determined by the illegal status and scarcity of said product.

Today he's delivering a special package to a serial killer in cellblock D that's enraged and fascinated everyone watching a TV set or reading a single line of newspaper print in the last month. What's even more annoying about the killer, he carries a Bible and refuses to proclaim his innocence because his stepfather beat him and molested his sister as a child. Jim Cirmah is despised and revered outside and inside these prison walls.

The county jail is not a typical prison facility, for most of the inmates it's a stopover on their way to trial or getting out after serving a short sentence. No courtyard exists like a Federal or State pen where the prisoners workout and socialize together. Jim is here going through the arraignment process, but tried in Federal Court and sent to a different facility, a Federal facility Captain Cyril has no control over.

A loud buzzer goes off mid-morning in cellblock D alerting inmates the coffee wagon is making its rounds. When approaching Jim's cell, Rat Pack discreetly drops a cyanide tablet in a cup and pours in hot coffee rapidly dissolving the poison. The cart has bottled water as an alternative to the coffee.

Jim listens for the familiar squeaking wheels of the cart in its approach. He sets the Bible down on his bunk and moves to the front of the cell waiting on Rat Pack to open a small hinged gate in the door to slide the drink through. The metal hinges clank, yelling at the small door lowered in place and Rat Pack stands eye-to-eye with the man he's about to murder.

The last sentence uttered by Jim Cirmah is a simple one. "Mr. Rat Pack, what should I drink today...water or coffee?"

Rat Pack looks into the cell opening realizing the man standing in front of him knows exactly what is going to transpire.

Rat's lip starts quivering and his throat is dry like a desert breeze, but he finally pronounces the death sentence. "Coffee."

The poisoned coffee is set on the door's ledge and Jim reaches in taking it back to his bunk. The squeaky wheels roll to the next cell, Rat Pack's insanity is already starting to affect his rationale.

Jim takes a large drink of the coffee and a second sip. He lies on the bunk and places the Bible on his chest firmly gripped in his hands. A sudden heave in his upper torso throws the Bible to the floor. Soon following the Bible's discard, convulsions and a foamy substance generated by the stomach in a last second attempt to expel the poison spews from his lips. His features turn to a ruby purple color and the body finally stops the muscle reflex spasms and remains still. Jim Cirmah is dead.

CHAPTER FIFTY-TWO

Wake Me Up

ROLLIE PULLS UP in front of the Pawnshop when he gets the call from Stephen Summers telling him of Jim's death. Early indication is Jim somehow got cyanide into the jail and committed suicide. Rollie literally starts laughing on the phone at Summers' naive acceptance of the county jail's storyline.

"If you believe Jim Cirmah took his own life, you need to take the pink panties off and get outside more often." Rollie is angry and thinks Summers doesn't have one ounce of street smarts or balls.

"Rollie," Summers counters. "I admit you're much closer to the street than me, but you have to concede Cirmah said incriminating things during our meeting about his destiny."

"Jim knew he was going to die at that meeting, but not by his own hand. Send me a bill, don't send a Christmas Card." Rollie hangs up the cell and walks into the shop.

Drug Lord meets Rollie's entrance, the usual "hands up," but Rollie is not in the mood. He heads straight to Conrad's new office next to the boardroom and sits in front of Conrad's desk.

"What's wrong, Uncle Rollie?" Conrad quickly reads the body language.

"Jim's dead," Rollie rubs his neck and leans back in the chair flush emotionally. "Someone had him killed in that shithole county jail."

"I'm so sorry...he always treated me nice, never looked down on me because of my age. Uncle Rollie, he never killed anyone...never," Conrad adds.

"You and I know that, but the rest of the world thinks he's Jeffrey Dahmer. I will get to the bottom of this sooner or later...heaven help the bastards when I do."

Rollie pulls his briefcase up and sets it on the desk. He reaches in retrieving the Bible Jim tossed him in the jail meeting.

"You're a smart guy, Conrad," Rollie employs. "Jim left me a few hours after I arrived in Colombia without so much as a goodbye. Bugged the hell out of me for months... just thought we had so much between us. I asked him why at the jail, said the answer is in this Bible... what could the answer be?"

Conrad picks the Bible up and thumbs through a few pages looking at the headings. "Wow, a lot of content to narrow down the answer. Must be something that marks the reason."

A slow and methodical moving of the pages is made by Conrad's fingers. Rollie stands up. "Going to make me a damn strong drink...would you like one?"

"Yeah," Conrad answers, "like to salute my friend, Jim."

Rollie leaves, goes to his office and opens a desk drawer pulling out two shot glasses and a bottle of Wild Turkey. A return trip to Conrad's office and the bourbon is poured into the two glasses. The men click the glasses together. "To my man, Jim... best damn P.I. I ever knew." Rollie salutes.

"Here, here," Conrad adds; both throw the glasses back.

Conrad returns to his page thumbing.

"What exactly are you looking for?" Rollie inquires.

"Not sure, but maybe a passage underscored...a note made someplace?" Conrad answers.

Rollie pours another drink for himself, intent on feeling numb at this point. "Want another drink?" Rollie points the bottle in Conrad's direction.

"Not now," Conrad says politely.

"Be in my office if you find something," Slick says, taking the bottle and leaving. He turns back to Conrad. "Conrad," Rollie states, "thanks for your help."

"No problem," Conrad answers. "Love to find something for you."

Rollie goes to his office, turns classical music on and closes his eyes sipping on the Turkey. He drifts off into a haze when Conrad opens the door twenty minutes later.

"Uncle Rollie, found this tiny ribbon bookmarker...may have something." Conrad brags.

"What did it mark?" Rollie is wide awake at this moment.

"It's the night before Jesus is arrested, put on trial. He tells his disciples before the rooster crows in the morning he will be betrayed." Conrad relays with excitement.

"Son-of-a-bitch, it's been under my nose from the beginning...David Sanders is behind all of this. Jim didn't want to be around the bastard, it wasn't me he ran from but that devil. Thanks Conrad...got some things to do." Rollie has picked up the tempo.

"What are you going to do?" Conrad asks.

"Better you don't know." Rollie pours another drink.

CHAPTER FIFTY-THREE

Rathole

THE OCEAN ROLLS on the beach behind Rollie's house but he pays little attention to the view. Wood stakes are pounded into the ground, string tied from stake to stake, and the dirt is leveled in preparation for a concrete pour in two days to create an extended deck. A walk around the side of the house provides privacy from the workers and he makes a call to David Sanders.

"David, my friend, I have some great news...wanted to share with you." Rollie looks around to make sure no one from the construction crew is near. "Had several meetings with Jim before he committed suicide, spilled his heart out to me about this whole Benders' experiment...got everything on tape. I've contacted Jason Huckabee at the *L.A. Times* on an exclusive, we're having a meeting 9:00 tomorrow night at my house to put it all together....thought you would like to come over, add your two cents worth."

"Love to hear all the details...make me part of the true story concerning Jim, help clean up his reputation. Great guy that died too young." David's voice came across in complete sincerity.

"If you want," Rollie adds. "Spend the night at the house, we'll throw down a couple to salute Jim's life."

"Thanks, see you tomorrow night." David's voice fades off the phone.

Rollie hits an auto-dial on the phone. Zak Franklin, the P.I. Rollie sent to Missouri, answers the other end.

"Rollie, you have a job lined up for me?" Franklin doesn't know what kind of job he's about to walk into.

"You alone?" Rollie asks.

"Yep, something wrong?" Franklin feels Rollie is amiss.

"Everything is great," Rollie answers. "My only problem is a rat I need taken care of...pays $10,000. You in?"

"Must be a big rat." Franklin counters.

"Murdered Jim Cirmah." Rollie is confident what the answer will be at this point.

"Hell yeah, I'm in... be a pleasure," Franklin responds.

"Be at my house tomorrow night around 6:00, we have a big rathole to dig," Rollie reports.

"I can do better than that, my brother's a general contractor... has a backhoe. Wouldn't be the first time I've dug a rathole." Franklin recommends.

"Perfect," Rollie adds. "Bring the backhoe over tomorrow afternoon."

While Rollie and Zak Franklin are discussing landscaping, David walks out on his back deck. He looks off into the distant valley and dials his cell phone, on the other end of the line answers Captain Cyril.

The Captain answers in less than a happy mood.

"I told you never to call me on this phone," the Captain snarls.

"We have a big problem; it couldn't wait," David relays.

"Hold on," The Captain goes to his office door and shuts it. "This better be important."

"It is important, Slick Willie brought in a reporter from the *L.A. Times*...seems they had a number of meetings recorded with Cirmah before his accident. Lots of things being told. Been invited to Rollie's house tomorrow night to add anything I know; thought you might want to attend shortly after I arrive at nine." David informs.

"I can work that out...need to wrap up the loose ends," the Captain assures.

CHAPTER FIFTY-FOUR

Birds Of A Feather Die Together

DAVID LOOKS AT his watch a few blocks from Rollie's house in his parked car and it reads 8:20. A reach into his briefcase retrieves his pistol and he does a weapon's check. Locked and loaded, he places it back into the briefcase, takes a small bottle of vodka bought on the plane ride, removes the cap and downs the contents. It burns for a few seconds but steadies his nerves.

He enjoys the killing part of his business, but anytime you kill a man, there's a chance things can go wrong and you end up on the wrong side of the dirt. Drinking always countered getting too high on the rush of the confrontation.

The car is started at 8:45, he didn't want to arrive too early before backup came on the scene to make sure all ended the right way. He pulls into Rollie's driveway, suffering an envy bout admiring Rollie's empire built over the years.

Slick answers the door, a contrived smile on his face and drink in hand.

"Come into my humble abode," Rollie encourages. "Have a drink."

The two walk to the bar situated around Rollie's swimming pool and below is a backhoe, a pile of dirt situated next to a deep and wide hole. David notices the construction and hole.

"You expanding this small place of yours, Rollie?" David jokes.

"Yes, made the decision to add another deck with an adobe kitchen sitting on it. What do you think?" Rollie asks.

"I think you're too rich and too bored, but I'm sure it'll be beautiful." David answers.

"What are you drinking?" Rollie questions.

"Vodka on the rocks, a lime please," David requests.

"You got it," Rollie assures.

As Rollie goes to the bar, Zak Franklin walks through the kitchen to the pool area.

"David," Rollie says making the drink. "Like you to meet, Jason Huckabee with the *L.A. Times*. Jason, this is David Sanders."

Franklin pretends to be a reporter and David pretends to be a real human being. They shake hands intending to kill the pretense shortly.

Franklin takes a beer from Rollie, and the three men salute Jim Cirmah as the Pacific Ocean swallows the setting sun.

"Speaking of our friend Jim, he mentioned Tramazzo came back from the grave. Hell of a thing, huh?" Rollie states.

"Not sure about this resurrection stuff, but some crazy things did happen over the course of the Benders' experiment," David adds.

"Like to show you guys something, just in case there's an ounce of truth to the resurrection," Rollie mentions.

Rollie leads the two men down the hallway to his art vault and opens the door. In the middle of the room is an ambulance gurney, a sheet draped over it. Rollie walks to the gurney, pulls the sheet back and Jim Cirmah's body is revealed.

A glass of vodka hits the floor shattering behind Rollie. Franklin and Rollie turn to see David staring at the body, the shattered glass dances around his feet.

David appears in shock for a few seconds, but recovers his composure.

"Sorry," David explains. "Wasn't expecting to see Jim like this."

"I claimed his body, going to give him the burial he deserves. Thought I'd wait a couple days to see if a miracle occurs."

David leans over to pickup the glass, but Rollie stops him. "Don't worry about that, we've got more important things to do. I'll leave the door open tonight, the cleaning crew will pick it up tomorrow. Will move Jim into the vault closet to prevent a freakout."

The three go back to the swimming pool deck, and Franklin pulls out his weapon completely surprising David.

"What the hell is this all about?" David receives the second shock to his senses.

"Let's go look at my new adobe kitchen foundation," Rollie orders.

David glances at his briefcase setting next to the bar, rushes over and grabs it. Franklin catches up, pounds his head using the pistol grip putting him on the floor bleeding.

Rollie walks over to David and kicks him in the side.

"Damn you David, bleeding all over my floor...can't let the cleaning crew see that."

He kicks him a second time. "Can't stand a mess.

Franklin pulls David to his feet and moves down the terrace. The hole awaits his arrival. When David rounds the corner of the house, Fox and Cyril have guns drawn shooting Franklin in the head.

"Man, I'm glad to see you." David was two minutes from the bottom of his grave.

"So this is the crew pulling all the strings," Rollie says, venom spewing from his tongue. "Sorry motherfuckers."

"That we are," Captain Cyril directs. "Shoot him."

Fox turns and guns down Rollie taking directions like always.

Cyril takes a close look at Franklin. "Who the hell is this guy?"

"A writer for the *L.A. Times*," David relays. "Huckabee, I believe."

"Jason Huckabee?" Cyril questions.

"Yeah, that's it...Rollie said he's doing a book on Jim Cirmah." David answers.

"That's not Jason Huckabee," Cyril notes. "I know him well, done several interviews." The Captain pulls Franklin's P.I. license out. "He's one of Rollie's boys." Cyril empties the wallet of cash and stands back counting it.

David grabs Franklin's feet and gives Fox more directions. "Grab his arms, throw both in the hole."

Again Fox bends over taking directions, but Cyril stops him. "Either one of you geniuses run a backhoe?"

Silence meets Cyril's ears. "Didn't think so, not sitting out here half the night throwing dirt in that hole only to have them dug up tomorrow when Rollie is missing. Too much evidence lying around. Take them to the house, we'll burn away the traces."

"Get rid of Cirmah, too," David adds.

"What does that mean, get rid of Cirmah?" Cyril demands.

"Rollie brought him from the county morgue, he's up in the house," David answers.

"Rollie, that crazy bastard...was he going to mount him on the wall?" Cyril counters.

"Hoping he would come back to life," David offers.

"That's a lot of optimism…I'll meet you in the house to clean this mess up."

The Captain walks toward the pool and goes inside the house discovering Jim's body.

Blankets and sheets are pulled off several beds and brought to the art gallery and scattered about. Soon the room is filled with the bodies of Rollie, Franklin, Jim, and piles of wooden furniture stacked around.

The Captain turns to Fox. "I have five gallons of gas in the trunk, go get it." He tosses the keys to Fox leaving David and Cyril alone.

"What do you attribute your charmed life to, David? We run two minutes late, you're dead. Sniper gets shot coming after you. What kind of lucky charm do you have tattooed on your ass?" Cyril asks.

"Got a guardian angel looking over me," David answers.

Fox rounds the corner carrying the gas can and Cyril shoots David in the chest, walks over and pumps a second bullet in his head.

"Why did you do that?" Fox demands.

"Shut the fuck up, let me do the thinking…you do the pouring." Cyril directs once again and Fox follows.

After covering the wood and bodies with gas, Fox looks over at the Captain. "Got a match?"

"You annoy me," the Captain asserts.

He shoots Fox and fires a second bullet at close range in his chest. He wipes the fingerprints off a cheap Bic lighter, lights a handkerchief and throws it on the gas. Flames leap in all directions and the Captain barely escapes without getting burned.

He drives off before the flames spread to other parts of Rollie's once gorgeous home burning for three hours before being controlled by the fire department.

CHAPTER FIFTY-FIVE

The Short and Winding Road Continued

Part Two

DAVID SANDERS IS nervous waiting on the police to arrive on top of Mulholland Drive. That anxiousness is compounded by the stranger appearing out of the dark. David is all out of trust. Someone planned an elaborate scheme to run him off the road, lite breathing and conversation is not coming easy.

"What do you mean, the cops can't help me?" David asks after the stranger makes the bold prediction.

"Cops staged this little scene for you, really high ranking cops." The stranger greets his question with terror, he'll never be safe anywhere.

"How do you know this?" David humbly requests.

"At the loss of humility, I know all." The stranger enlightens.

David backs up slowly from the stranger, convinced he's a washed-up actor walking a make-believe dog and dangerous. He points the gun at the hoodie.

"Why don't you keep moving along, somebody is probably looking for you now." David directs ever so meekly.

A thunderous laugh slides up and down the canyon walls from the hoodie.

"A frightened man keeps his sense of humor." The stranger predicts. "I like that. Some of the best lines in history came from men standing on the gallows. Mr. Sanders, you are one of those men."

"Stay away from me, I won't hesitate to fire." David's voice is stronger.

"You'll have better results turning the gun on yourself than me, but shoot if it will make you feel better," the stranger predicts.

"You are insane." David made his mind up, if the man takes one step he'll shoot.

"Insane, love that word. Let me show you insanity, look over the side into the canyon. You'll see your BMW burning," the stranger offers.

David looks over his shoulder at where the BMW came to rest a few minutes earlier, it's gone. Further examination of the road shows the two sawhorses in tact and shinning brightly. Skid marks lead him to the edge of the hillside and a look downward proves the stranger's prediction true, the BMW is on the canyon floor engulfed in flames.

"With a flick of these fingertips, you'll be burning in that BMW, Mr. Sanders," The stranger states.

David's shoulders feel heavy, he steps away from the edge afraid he'll pass out falling off the cliff. The stranger, in a blink of an eye, is by his side holding his limp body up. The man helps him walk back a few paces and leans him against the reappearing BMW no longer burning at the bottom of the canyon.

David Sanders has nothing left to fight. He feels insane, looking at death in the face is ugly and frightening. "What do you want?" He asks, ready to give.

"More importantly, it's what you want that counts." The man is gentle and comforting in his touch and speech. "We'll start with death, I'm assuming you like cheating the closed casket… I'll give you a guardian angel; if that fails, resurrection, the ability to spit death in the face."

"What do I give you, my soul?" David offers.

"You've watched too many cheap movies, I only want the trust you get from others… a slight of hand deception to make sure your Dr. Benders fails miserably at this stupid experiment. Simple to pull off, a small price to pay… immortality is such fun, really no need for a soul, but you can keep yours if it makes you feel better." The stranger offers his hand and David takes it.

A police car rounds the hillside lights flashing. The stranger is gone.

CHAPTER FIFTY-SIX

Dog Eat Dog

NO MATTER WHAT you do in life, virtually everyone dreams about making a living doing something else. Sometimes it's about the money, sometimes it's about the ego and fame, but regardless of the reason it occupies the conscientious and drives many to do good and far more to do bad.

Captain Ronald Cyril has always seen himself the next Stephen King or James Patterson, an author writing best sellers and turning those books into blockbuster movies. A touch of writing success came when he blackmailed a publisher through drug charges, but other than getting published it sold virtually nothing. He blamed that on the lack of marketing dollars spent on the book by the publisher, not the less than stellar writing style. This satisfied his entry level ego, talking about his new found status on the party bound social scene, however, that high soon wore off and his body craved more.

Ronald Cyril is a lot of miserable things, dumb is not one of them. It's a real craft to negotiate all the politics, backstabbing, and of course his murder-for-hire empire and still have enough time to run a fairly cohesive police department. He'd trade all his cash in six bank boxes for a book putting him on the Best-Seller List.

Finally realizing his writing may not facilitate his end-goal, Cyril convinces Jason Huckabee to co-author a book about Jim Cirmah titled, *Jesus Kills*. It wasn't a hard sell to convince Huckabee to partner up. Cyril has a lot to offer including access to evidence files, an insider on so many levels and cooperation from the FBI on Cirmah's activities in Colombia and his final capture.

Huckabee did the writing and Cyril provided every research source spitting out data at his beckoning. The last piece solidifying the union are the evidence photos; in Huckabee's wildest dreams he couldn't imagine bringing murder to the public on such a personal level.

Jesus Kills rushes to number one on the New York Times' Best-Seller List, and the largest agencies in show business make offers to negotiate the movie rights handing out large cash advances. Life is good for Misters Cyril and Huckabee, so many decisions are on the horizon their regular jobs are getting in the way; so Huckabee resigns from the *Times* and Cyril takes an early retirement.

The ex-captain is beside himself with joy taking in all the sights and sounds of fame. Not wanting to miss his connection by an adoring public, he embarks on an ambitious book signing tour, his second stop north of San Francisco in Napa Valley.

The reason he arranged a book signing in such a small population center is love. His newly acquired girlfriend wants to spend a few days in the Valley before he flies off to New York and beyond in a fourteen city signing tour. His wife of twenty-eight years didn't fit his sleek new Hollywood image nor his future plans.

The Barnes & Noble parking lot is overflowing with cars and the adjoining mall lot catches the spillover. It's the perfect storm of public interest, a story containing religious overtones gone bad and a mad scientist playing God manipulating DNA. Throw in the whispers of miracles and you have what appears on the surface of 'Jurassic Park' meets 'The Passion of Christ.'

All this adds up to the extension of a three-hour signing session to six hours. The girlfriend cuts the line off at 5:30, disappointing another forty or so patrons, books in hand. Cyril is exhausted and full of excitement, there's no end in sight for the future as he exits the store, new girlfriend hand-in-hand. A woman he intends to marry after the divorce papers are served this afternoon and buys his way out of the marriage.

Joe Tramazzo lies on top of the mall's parking deck, the highest building point in town. The view is clear to the back entrance of the Barnes & Noble. Joe doesn't want to repeat the same mistake made in L.A. when he anticipated Cyril would come out the front entrance of a bookstore and vanished through the back.

The .50 caliber rifle rests against a mounted tripod, a steady foundation for the proper calculations on distance and loss of elevation for the shot. Tramazzo's training gives him unlimited patience waiting on the target to appear. An extra three hours is nothing in his profession.

The three-hundred and sixty yard shot is a relatively short one. The tricky part is taking the shot before Cyril gets to a series of steps, his chest losing eight inches on each step-down complicating the hitting zone. At the bottom of those steps a limo is waiting and will interfere with the line of sight.

The scope and Tramazzo's eye focuses on the backdoor, Cyril opens the door and walks out into the sunlight. Four steps along the flat surface, and one step removed from going down the stairway, Tramazzo fires and the bullet hits perfectly square in Cyril's sternum and exits out his back.

The guardian devil brakes down his weapon calmly, the evil voice in his head idles back to neutral, happy for the results.

David Sanders walks the sidewalk to the fallen Captain and glances up at the building top where Tramazzo fired the rifle. Tramazzo and Sanders make eye contact for a couple of seconds, and Tramazzo disappears. Sanders climbs the steps, looks at the gapping wound in Cyril's chest and coolly enters the backdoor of the Barnes & Noble. The crowd starts to gather around Cyril's body, a suddenly famous dead man that really didn't have a clue what evil he tried to walkover.

EPILOGUE

SHELBY PRIOR CUTS an article from the *Wall Street Journal* concerning Jim Cirmah and neatly mounts it in an album. The pile of articles taken from magazines and papers is overflowing in a cardboard box used to collect the Cirmah story over the last few months since his death. She's obsessed over the man's life since he saved hers. No matter what the authorities said about his transgressions, she knows the truth after looking into his eyes in Colombia. Shelby will go to her grave viewing his perfect smile and chiseled features, a man so rare his touch erased the tumor from her body.

Three books have already hit the newsstands surrounding the Cirmah story and Shelby has read two. The third book, *Killer Jesus*, is packed in her briefcase to read on the trip she and Maria are taking to Italy this afternoon. It's a trip to celebrate her new lease on life.

Shelby and Maria act like college kids in Venice the first two nights; chasing pizza, flirting with the locals in a bar, and drinking too much wine. The next morning, headaches intact, they board a train for Rome and Shelby gets into the book after napping the first couple of hours. It's surprising to learn of Jim's childhood, it must have been tough living under the rule of his stepfather.

The train pulls into the Rome station, and the girls grab their carryon's stepping out into the vast system of rails heading to directions all over Europe and beyond. The crowd funnels toward the station, Shelby rolling a suitcase with one arm and briefcase hanging from the other. Tucked under one arm is the book.

It's wall-to-wall foot traffic and Maria is reading directions, her Italian sketchy but functional. Shelby starts to lose grip of the book and slows to reposition it. She bumps into an oncoming stranger and the book falls from her grasp, sliding off the platform under an outbound train a few feet away. Shelby yells "holdup" to Maria and goes to the side of the passenger train hoping to retrieve *Killer Jesus*.

Setting her luggage down, she gets on her knees to see the book perched precariously on the edge of the rail three feet below. Shelby stands up, resolved the book can't be picked up until the train moves away from the station.

Not sure if she wants to wait for the book or not, the train starts to move slowly away from the station. Maria comes closer to help her friend in the decision making process. Shelby is eye level to the passenger car no more than three feet away.

An unconscious glance into the train window reveals Jim Cirmah leaning against the window inside the car and staring into her face. He smiles and she returns the kind gesture by doing the same.

The train gathers speed and Shelby moves a few steps matching the pace. There is no time for her emotions to digest the moment and explode with happiness, that will come in a couple of minutes.

Maria watches Shelby walking after the train and sees what has generated her fixation. Jim places his fingertips against the glass remembering the American woman he held closely in Colombia. Both are alive and well.

The train hits a higher speed and Shelby can't keep up with Jim Cirmah and his destiny.

About The Author

Fowler's writing background started in the screenplay industry twenty plus years ago having sold or optioned properties to production companies like MGM, Prelude Pictures, Studio 54, IO Productions and Lions Gate. He has been commissioned to rewrite and polish many other individual's screenplays along the way.

Crisscross, a book about a railroad serial killer hunted by railroad bull (cop) across five states, was published in 2013 by Venture Galleries. It is available on Venture Galleries, Amazon, or Barnes & Noble. A third book, *Like Hell,* will be released in the spring of 2015.

Fowler resides in South Florida with his wife, Maria and has three children, Seleck, Calaine, and Sutton. He can be contacted at dalefowler@bellsouth.net.

www.ingramcontent.com/pod-product-compliance
Lightning Source LLC
Chambersburg PA
CBHW020910200626
46814CB00001BA/273